Praise for Susan Mallery
and her *New York Times* bestselling
Fool's

"Romance novels don't get much better than Mallery's expert blend of emotional nuance, humor and superb storytelling."

—*Booklist*

"[A] classic blend of lighthearted humor, intense emotional conflict, and a setting so real and appealing readers will want to start scoping out real estate."

—*Library Journal* on *Until We Touch*

"Susan Mallery is one of my favorites."
—#1 *New York Times* bestselling author
Debbie Macomber

"Heartwarming... Deft characterization and an absorbing story line will keep readers coming back."
—*Publishers Weekly* on *When We Met*

"Mallery delivers another engaging romance in magical Fool's Gold."
—*Kirkus Reviews* on *Just One Kiss*

"Both smile and tear inducing. Mallery is one of a kind."
—*RT Book Reviews* on *Two of a Kind*, Top Pick!

"The wildly popular and prolific Mallery can always be counted on to tell an engaging story of modern romance."

—*Booklist*

"Mallery infuses her story with eccentricity, gentle humor, and small-town shenanigans, and readers... will enjoy the connection between Heidi and Rafe."
—*Publishers Weekly* on *Summer Days*

To see the complete list of titles available from Susan Mallery, please visit SusanMallery.com.

SUSAN MALLERY

thrill me

HQN™

ISBN-13: 978-0-373-78898-9

Thrill Me

Recycling programs for this product may not exist in your area.

This edition published by arrangement with Harlequin Books S.A.

For questions and comments about the quality of this book, please contact us at CustomerService@Harlequin.com.

® and TM are trademarks of Harlequin Enterprises Limited or its corporate affiliates. Trademarks indicated with ® are registered in the United States Patent and Trademark Office, the Canadian Intellectual Property Office and in other countries.

www.HQNBooks.com

Printed in U.S.A.

Being the "mom" of an adorable, spoiled little dog, I know the joy that pets can bring to our lives. Animal welfare is a cause I have long supported. For me that means giving to Seattle Humane. At their 2014 Tuxes and Tails fund-raiser, I once again offered "Your Pet in a Romance Novel" as a prize.

In this book you will meet a wonderful beagle named Sophie. Her parents gave generously at the auction to have their adorable, inventive, sweet girl in this book.

One of the things that makes writing special is interacting in different ways with people. Some I talk to for research. Some are readers who want to talk characters and story lines, and some are fabulous pet parents. Sophie's mom was so generous with her time. She told me stories about her girl, sent me a hysterically funny DVD and made her Sophie come alive. I hope I've done her justice in this book.

My thanks to Sophie and her parents and to the amazing people at Seattle Humane (SeattleHumane.org). Because every pet deserves a loving family.

* * *

A special thank-you to Dani Warner from Pixel Dust Productions for her technical help. Any mistakes on the "movie making front" are mine.

CHAPTER ONE

MAYA FARLOW TOLD herself there was a perfectly good explanation for the mayor of Fool's Gold to have a picture of a man's naked butt on her computer screen. At least she really hoped there was. She'd always liked Mayor Marsha and didn't want to find out something more than a little icky about the woman who was now her boss.

Mayor Marsha sighed heavily and pointed to the screen. "You're not going to believe this," she said, and tapped a key. The picture moved as the video played and the audio started up.

"The contest closes on Friday at noon. Text your guess to this number."

Maya stared at the computer. When the picture stopped again, she studied the phone number on-screen, the seventy-something female host frozen midgesture and the picture of the naked butt behind her. The naked, *male* butt, Maya corrected mentally, not sure the gender mattered as much as the nakedness.

"Okay," Maya said slowly, knowing that she would

be expected to say something else. Possibly something, you know, intelligent. But honestly, she couldn't think of what that could be. How on earth was she supposed to make an old lady in a tracksuit talking about a naked butt contest make sense? Of course, that was a much happier concern than finding out Mayor Marsha watched porn.

Mayor Marsha pushed a couple of buttons on her computer and the image disappeared. "You can see the problem we're having with Eddie and Gladys's cable access show."

"Too many naked butts?" Maya asked before she could help herself. Stating the obvious was never helpful, but what on earth else was there to say?

Mayor Marsha Tilson was California's longest serving mayor. She looked exactly as she had twelve years ago when Maya had been a nervous sixteen-year-old, moving to a strange little town and hoping to fit in. The mayor still wore classically tailored suits and elegant pearls. Her white hair had been swept up in a tidy chignon. As a teenager, Maya hadn't known what to make of the mayor. Today, she thought the other woman was someone to be admired. Mayor Marsha ran her town with a firm but fair hand. Even more important to Maya, the mayor had offered her a job right when Maya had known she had to make a change in her life.

So here she was, the shiny new communications director for Fool's Gold, California. And the old lady with the naked butt contest was apparently now her problem.

"Eddie and Gladys have always been colorful," Mayor Marsha said with a sigh. "I admire their zest for life."

"And interest in younger men," Maya murmured.

"You have no idea. Their cable access show is extremely popular with locals and tourists alike, but we've been getting some emails and phone calls about some of the content."

"You need me to rein them in."

"I'm not sure if that's possible, but yes. We don't want to have to deal with the FCC. I know two of the commissioners and I don't want to be fielding calls from friends in high places, so to speak." The older woman shuddered. "Or explain what on earth is going on in this town."

After seeing a clip of the show, Maya would have guessed there was nothing anyone could say for the rest of the day that would surprise her more than a woman pushing eighty showing a naked butt on television and inviting viewers to text in their guess on which famous local celebrity it might be. Maya would have been wrong. Mayor Marsha personally knowing an FCC commissioner or two beat naked butts hands down.

So to speak.

She made a few more notes on her tablet. "Okay. I'll talk to Eddie and Gladys and explain about the indecency restrictions for broadcast shows."

She had a good idea what the requirements were but would have to look up the specifics. She had a feeling the TV duo were not the types to be intimidated by vague rumblings of FCC rules. She would have to go into the discussion armed.

"You are getting thrown in the deep end, aren't you?" Mayor Marsha smiled at her. "This is only your second day. I hope you're not regretting your decision to take the job."

"I'm not," Maya assured her. "I love a good challenge."

"Then consider yourself blessed." The mayor glanced at her notepad. "Next up we need to discuss our new video campaign. The city council wants a two-pronged approach. The first set of videos will be about our town slogan. Fool's Gold: A destination for romance. The second set will be in support of general tourism."

They'd discussed the new campaign at Maya's interview. "I have a lot of ideas for both," she said eagerly.

"Good. We're still coming up with more ways to use the videos. They'll be put on the town's website, of course. But we'll also want them to be used for commercials. Both on the internet and television."

Maya nodded as she typed on her tablet. "So thirty-second spots for sure, with additional cuts of the material in one- and two-minute lengths? The message varying, depending on the target audience?"

"I'll leave the technical aspects of it to you, Maya. Also, any ideas you have for increasing viewership of the videos would be appreciated. The city council is a dynamic group, but we're not tech savvy. You're going to have to lead the way on that."

"Happy to."

She had some contacts, she thought. Not anyone at the FCC, but friends in advertising who would be happy to brainstorm ideas. It would be easy to edit material so that it appealed to different interests. Focus on the outdoor activities the town had to offer on ESPN and sports websites. Show family-friendly things to do on cable channels more traditionally watched by women, with links on websites that appealed to women with children.

While this kind of work was different from what she was used to, she was excited by the possibilities. Her previous job, at a local TV station in Los Angeles, had become too comfortable. And her attempts to get hired by the network had failed, leaving her at loose ends. The job offer in Fool's Gold had come along at exactly the right time.

"You're going to need some help," Mayor Marsha told her. "There's simply too much work for one person. Especially if we want the videos done by the end of summer."

Maya nodded in agreement. "I'd prefer to do the editing myself. There's an art to it." And trusting someone else with her content would be difficult. "But I could use someone to help preproduction and during the shoots."

"Yes. Plus an on-air talent person. Is that what it's called? Or is *host* a better word?"

Maya felt a minor twinge. After all, in a perfect world, she would be hosting the videos. But the truth was, the camera didn't love her. It liked her well enough, but not so much with the love. And in the business that was any kind of recorded media, passion was required. Which meant they needed someone who dazzled on-screen.

"Someone local?" she asked, thinking of all the sports celebrities in the area. Plus, she knew that action movie superstar Jonny Blaze had just bought a ranch outside of town. If she could get him, that would be a coup.

"I had someone else in mind," Mayor Marsha said.

As if on cue, the mayor's assistant knocked on the door and then stepped into the room. "He's here. Should I send him in?"

"Please do, Bailey," Mayor Marsha told her.

Maya glanced up, curious as to whom the mayor would consider for such an important job. There was a lot on the line for the town and Mayor Marsha always put Fool's Gold first. If he—

Maybe it was a trick of the light, Maya thought frantically as her eyes focused. Or a mistake. Because the tall, broad-shouldered, slightly scruffy guy walking toward them looked alarmingly familiar.

She took in the too-long curly hair, the three-day beard and the oversize, well-worn backpack slung over one shoulder. As if he'd just stepped off a pontoon plane direct from the Amazon forest. Or out of one of her dreams.

Delany Mitchell. Del.

The same Del who had stolen her virginity and her eighteen-year-old heart and had promised to love her forever. The Del who had wanted to marry her.

The Del she'd walked out on because she'd been too young and too scared to take a chance on believing that she was the least bit lovable.

His jeans were so worn they looked as soft as a baby's blanket. His white shirt hung loose, the long sleeves rolled up to his elbows. He was that irresistible combination of disheveled and confident. The ultimate in sex appeal.

How could he be back in town? Why hadn't she known? And was it too late to bolt from the room?

Mayor Marsha smiled with pleasure, then rose. She crossed to the man and held out her arms. Del stepped into her embrace, hugged her, then kissed her cheek.

"You haven't changed at all," he said by way of greeting.

"And you've changed quite a bit. You're successful and famous now, Delany. It's good to have you back."

Maya stood, not sure what she was supposed to do or say. Back as in *back*? No way, no how. She would have heard. Elaine would have warned her. *All living, breathing, handsome proof to the contrary*, she thought.

Ten years later, Del still looked good. Better than good.

She found herself fighting old feelings—both emotional and physical. She felt breathless and foolish and was grateful neither of them was looking at her. She had a second to get herself under control.

She'd been so young back then, she thought wistfully. So in love and so afraid. Sadly, fear had won out and she'd ended things with Del in a horrible way. Maybe now she would finally get the chance to explain and apologize. Assuming he was interested in either.

The mayor stepped back and motioned to her. "I think you remember Maya Farlow. Didn't the two of you used to see each other?"

Del turned to glance at her. His expression was an ode to mild curiosity and nothing else. "We dated," he said, dismissing their intense, passionate relationship with casual disregard. "Hello, Maya. It's been a long time."

"Del. Nice to see you."

The words sounded normal enough, she told herself. He wouldn't guess that her heart was pounding and her stomach had flopped over so many times she feared it would never be right again.

Was it that he didn't remember the past, or had he truly put it all behind him? Was she just an old girlfriend he barely recalled? She would have thought that was impossible, and she would have been wrong.

He looked good, she thought, taking in what was new and what was exactly as it had been. His features were sharper, more honed. His body bigger. He'd filled out. Grown up. There was a confidence to his gaze. She'd fallen in love with a twenty-year-old, but before her was the adult male version.

The puzzle pieces fell into place. Her meeting and discussion with the mayor. What was expected of her as far as promoting the town. The need for a well-known person to host the videos.

Her lips formed the word *No* even as her brain held in the sound. She turned to Mayor Marsha.

"You want us to work together?"

The older woman smiled and took her seat at the conference table, then motioned for Del to sit, as well.

"Yes. Del's back in town for a couple of months."

"Just for the rest of the summer." He settled in a chair that seemed too small for him. His grin was as easy as his posture. "You guilted me into helping."

Mayor Marsha's blue eyes twinkled with amusement. "I might have done what needed doing to get you to agree," she admitted. She turned to Maya. "Del has experience with filming. He's made some videos himself."

He shrugged. "Nothing that special, but I do know my way around a camera."

"As does Maya. I would like the two of you to collaborate on the project."

Maya told herself to keep breathing. That later, when she was alone, she would scream or keen or throw something. Right now, she had to remain calm and act like a professional. She had a brand-new job she very much wanted to keep. She loved Fool's Gold, and since moving back to town, she'd felt more content than she could remember ever feeling before. She didn't want that to change.

She could handle Del being back. Obviously he was 100 percent over her. Which was a good thing. She was over him, too. Way over. So over as to almost not remembering him. Del who?

"Sounds like fun," she said with a smile. "Let's set up a meeting to brainstorm what has to be done."

She was smooth, Del thought, watching Maya from across the small conference table. Professional. She'd stayed friends with his mother, so he heard about her every now and then. How she'd been promoted to senior producer at the local news station in Los Angeles, and how she wanted to get to a network position. Showing up in Fool's Gold was an unexpected left turn in her career path.

Just as unanticipated had been the call from Mayor Marsha, inviting him to be a part of the town's new publicity project. She'd phoned about fifteen minutes after he'd already decided he was coming home for the summer. The woman had mad skills.

"How about tomorrow?" Maya asked. "Why don't you call me in the morning and we'll set up a day and time?"

"Works for me."

She gave him her cell number.

Mayor Marsha's desk phone beeped.

"Excuse me," the mayor said. "I need to take this call. I'll leave you two to work out the details."

They all rose. Del and Maya walked into the hallway. Once there, he half expected her to bolt, but she surprised him by pausing.

"When was the last time you were back?" she asked.

"It's been a couple of years. You?"

"I came home to visit Zane and Chase a couple of months ago and never left."

Her brothers, he thought. Technically her stepbrothers, but he knew they were the only family she had. While he'd grown up in a loud, close-knit, crazy family, Maya hadn't had anyone but an indifferent mother. She'd made her own way in the world. Something he'd respected about her, until that trait had turned around and bit him on the ass.

"You're a long way from Hollywood," he said.

"You're a long way from the Himalayas."

"So neither of us belongs here."

"Yet here we are." She smiled. "It's good to see you, Del."

You, too.

He thought the words, but didn't say them. Because it was good, damn her. And he didn't want it to be. Maya was born trouble. At least she had been for him. Not that he would make that mistake again. He'd trusted her with everything he had and she'd thrown it back in his face. Lesson learned.

He nodded at her, then swung his backpack over his shoulder. "I'll talk to you tomorrow."

Her smile faltered for a second before returning. "Yes, you will."

He watched her go. When she was out of sight, he thought about going after her. Not that there was anything to say. Their last conversation, a decade ago, had made everything clear.

He told himself the past was the past. That he'd moved on and was long over her. He'd gone his way and she'd gone hers. Everything had worked out for the best.

He walked out of City Hall and toward the lakefront. There was a continuity to the town, he thought as he looked around and saw tourists and residents coexisting. City workers were changing the banners, taking down those celebrating the Dog Days of Summer Festival and hanging the ones proclaiming the Máa-zib Festival. This time last year, they'd been doing the same thing. And the year before and a year from now. While there were a handful of recent businesses opening, truth was the heart of the town never changed.

Brew-haha might be a new place to get coffee, but he knew that when he walked inside he would be greeted, very possibly by name. There would be a bulletin board advertising everything from dog-walking services to upcoming civic meetings. That while some of the friends he'd had in high school had moved on, most of them had stayed. Nearly all the girls he'd kissed as a kid were still around. Most of them married. This was their home and where they felt they belonged. Their kids would grow up to go to the same elementary school, middle and high school. Their kids would play in Pyrite Park and go to the same festivals. Here, life had a rhythm.

Once Del had thought he would be a part of it. That he would stick around and run the family business. Find the right girl, fall in love and—

Talk about a long time ago, he told himself. Talk about being a child himself. He could barely remember what it had been like back then. Before he'd left. When his dreams had been simple and he'd known that he was going to spend the rest of his life with Maya.

For a second he allowed himself to think of her. Of how in love he'd been. Back then he would have said *they'd* been in love, but she'd proved him wrong. At the time he'd been devastated, but now he was grateful. Because of her, he'd left Fool's Gold. Because of her, he'd been free to leave and could return home the conquering hero.

He waited for the flush of pride. There wasn't any. Maybe because in the past couple of months, he'd started to realize he had to figure out a new direction. Since selling his company, he'd been restless. Sure there were offers, but none that interested him. So he'd come back to where it all started. To see his family. To celebrate his dad's sixtieth birthday. To figure out where he went from here.

For the second time in as many minutes, he thought about Maya. How nothing had ever been as beautiful as her green eyes when she smiled up at him. How—

Del hesitated for a nanosecond before crossing the street, then he brushed the memory away, as if it had never been. Maya was his past. He was moving forward. Mayor Marsha wanted them to work together, which was fine by him. He would enjoy the challenge, and then move on. That's what he did these days. He moved on. Just as Maya had taught him.

WHILE THE MITCHELLS couldn't claim to be one of the founding families of Fool's Gold, they'd only missed that distinction by a single generation. They'd been around longer than most and had the interesting family history to prove it.

Maya had first met Elaine Mitchell over ten years before when she'd applied for a part-time job with Mitchell Fool's Gold Tours. The friendly, outgoing woman had promised fair pay and flexible shifts. As Maya had been saving every penny for college, she'd been thrilled with the offer. There wasn't going to be any help from her family, so it was up to her to get scholarships, grants and loans, then supplement the rest with whatever she could save.

Two unexpected things had happened that fateful summer. Maya had met and fallen in love with Del—Elaine's oldest son. But she'd also made a friend in the Mitchell matriarch. Elaine was married to famous glass artist Ceallach Mitchell and was the mother of five boys. She'd been born and raised in Fool's Gold. Her life was the best kind of chaos—one defined by a growing, happy family.

Maya had been the only child of an exotic dancer who had married for money and suffered the consequences. While Maya had felt badly for her mother, she had loved moving to Fool's Gold and being a relatively normal teen for the first time ever.

On the surface the two women had little in common, Maya thought as she hurried out of City Hall and headed for her car. They were worlds and lifetimes apart. Yet they'd always seemed to have something to talk about and, despite how Maya's relationship with Del had ended, she and Elaine had stayed in touch.

Now she got in her car and drove the six miles out of town toward the Mitchell family house. It stood on acres of land, separate from the town. Ceallach needed quiet for his creativity and space for his huge glass installations.

So the family lived outside of town and the five brothers had grown up on the side of a mountain, running through the rugged terrain, doing whatever it was young boys did when outdoors and unsupervised.

Maya thought back to all the stories Del had told her, when they'd been together. And what Elaine shared in their frequent emails. She knew her friend missed having all five of her sons at home. Del and the twins had moved away, and while Nick and Aidan were still in town, neither lived at the family house anymore.

Maya turned left and headed up the long driveway. When she finally reached the house, she was relieved to see Elaine's SUV parked in front.

She'd barely made it up the front porch stairs when the door opened and Elaine smiled at her.

"You're an unexpected surprise. What's up?"

Del had his mother's eyes. The rest of him— his size, his build—came from his father, but those brown eyes were pure Elaine.

"You didn't know?" Maya asked, climbing the porch stairs. "Del's back."

Elaine's openmouthed surprise confirmed what Maya had expected. Her friend *hadn't* known. Which was so like a guy. Why tell your mom you were coming home?

"Since when?" Elaine asked, hugging her, then motioning her inside. "He could have called. I swear, he's the worst of them." Her mouth twisted as she led the way to the kitchen, her athletic shoes making no sound on the hardwood floors. "And the twins. I should disown all three of them."

"Or post their embarrassing baby pictures on the internet," Maya offered, stepping into the huge kitchen.

"That would be a better solution," Elaine said as she crossed to the refrigerator and pulled out a pitcher of iced tea. "Then I'd hear from them for sure. So what happened? Where did you see him? What did he say?"

"Not much. I was too surprised to ask many questions."

Maya took her usual seat at the big kitchen table. The overhead light fixture was made up of five pendant lights—each a rainbow of colors that swirled and seemed to move, even as they were perfectly still. She'd earned decent money as a senior producer back in Los Angeles, but there was no way she would have been able to afford those pendant lights. Or the stunning piece in the corner of the family room. Ceallach's work was scattered throughout the house. *One of the advantages of being married to a famous artist*, she thought, accepting the glass of tea Elaine passed her.

Her friend already knew about Maya's new job as the Fool's Gold communications director. Now Maya told her about the meeting with Mayor Marsha and the plans for the various videos.

"We agreed there should be a host," Maya continued. "Someone good on-screen."

"I know where this is going." Elaine gave her a sympathetic glance. "What about you?"

"You're sweet to pretend I had a chance, but being in front of the camera…" Maya wrinkled her nose. "Anyway, I thought about some of the athletes who live in town. I mean why not? Or maybe Jonny Blaze."

"Too young for me, but still sexy."

Maya grinned. "I agree on the latter, if not the former."

Elaine laughed. "And that's why we're friends. So not Mr. Blaze?"

"No. As if he'd been listening in the other room, in walked Del. I couldn't believe it."

Elaine pulled her cell phone from her jeans pocket and glanced at the screen. "Me, either. I wonder how long he'll be in town. He's not texting me about staying here at the house, which means he's bunking somewhere else." Her mouth twisted. "Apparently I did a bad job with my boys."

"Don't say that. You were a great mom."

Maya would know. Her own mother had been on the dark side of awful, so she had a frame of reference. While her mother had been busy making sure Maya understood that she was the reason for her every disappointment, Elaine had been raising happy, loved children.

"Besides, isn't the point of raising children to get

them to where they're contributing members of society?" Maya asked gently. "You did that times five."

Before her friend could answer, the doggie door moved a little. Maya caught sight of a brown nose, followed by a happy blur of colors as Sophie, Elaine's beagle, raced into the kitchen.

Sophie was a bright-eyed sweetheart. Her traditional white with brown-and-black splotches was very beagle-like but her personality was pure Sophie. She lived with gusto, pouring all her energy into whatever had captured her attention. Right now it was giving her mom a couple of quick kisses before moving to greet Maya. In a few minutes she would probably be figuring out a way to open the refrigerator and devour whatever was planned for dinner.

"Hey, pretty girl," Maya said, lowering herself to the hardwood floor and holding out her arms.

Sophie raced toward her, her soft puppy mouth forming a perfect O as she bayed out her greeting. She then climbed onto Maya's lap for a proper snuggle. Big paws scrambled as Sophie gave her best kisses and shimmied even closer for hugs.

"You have the prettiest eyes," Maya said, admiring the rim of dark brown, then rubbing the dog's ears. "It must be nice to be a natural beauty."

"Unlike the rest of us," Elaine murmured. "There are mornings when I swear, it takes a village."

"Tell me about it."

Maya gave Sophie one last pat, then returned to her chair. Sophie circled the kitchen, sniffing the floor, before settling into her bed by the fireplace.

Maya looked at her friend. She noticed dark circles under her eyes and an air of something—maybe weariness.

"Are you okay?"

Elaine stiffened. "What? I'm fine. I'm upset about Del not telling me he was coming home. He mentioned in an email that he might, but there were no firm plans."

"Maybe he wanted to surprise you."

"I'm sure that's it."

Maya decided a change of subject would probably be a good thing. "How are the plans for Ceallach's big party going?"

"Ceallach won't make a decision whether or not he wants a big blowout or a small family get-together for his birthday. At this rate, I'm going to have to lock him in a closet until he makes up his mind."

Maya smiled. Elaine's words were tough, but there was a lot of love and time behind them. Del's parents had been together over thirty-five years. Theirs had been a love match, when both Elaine and Ceallach had still been in their early twenties. The ride had been bumpy. Maya knew about Ceallach's drinking and artistic temperament. But Elaine was devoted and they'd raised five kids.

For a second she wondered what that must be like. To be married so long, it was hard to remember any other life. To know your place in the long line of family members who had come before and would come after. To be one of the many.

She'd never had that. When she'd been little, it had

just been her and her mom. And Maya's mother had made it clear that having a child around had been nothing but a pain in her ass.

CHAPTER TWO

MAYA HAD HOPED that hanging out with her friend would be enough to chase all the Del from her mind. But she'd been wrong. The night had been an uncomfortable experience of being awake more than asleep. And when she finally did doze, it was only to dream of Del. Not current, sexy, stubbly Del, but the twenty-year-old who had stolen her heart.

She woke exhausted and with memory hangover. Funny how, until she'd seen him, she'd been able to forget him. But now that he was back, she was trapped in a past-present rip in the space-time continuum.

Or she was simply dealing with some unfinished business, she thought as she stepped into the shower. Because as much as she might like to think the universe revolved around her, truth was, it didn't.

Thirty minutes later she was reasonably presentable. She knew the only thing that would make her day livable was lots and lots of coffee. So she left her tiny rental house, pausing to give her newly planted flowers a quick watering before heading to Brewhaha.

Fool's Gold had grown in the ten years she'd been away. Giving walking tours of the city as a part-time

job in high school meant she was familiar with the
history and layout. She had a feeling the schedule of
festivals she'd once memorized still existed in her
brain. Probably stored next to all the words to Kelly
Clarkson's "Since U Been Gone."

The thought made her smile and, humming the
song, she walked into Brew-haha.

The coffee place had been decorated simply, with
bright colors and lots of places to sit. There was a long
counter up front, a display of tempting, high-calorie
pastries and a tall, broad-shouldered man at the front
of a six-person line.

Maya froze, half in, half out of the store. Now
what? She was going to have to face Del at some
point. Thanks to Mayor Marsha, they would be working together. But she hadn't thought she would have
to deal with him precoffee.

*The downside to an otherwise perfectly lovely
town*, she thought, sucking up her doubts and joining the line.

As Del finished placing his order, whatever he'd
said had the cashier laughing. He moved over to wait
for his order and immediately started talking to the
barista.

Had he always been so friendly? Maya wondered,
watching him, while trying to appear as if she *wasn't*
paying attention at all. A trick that had her still-
slightly sleepy self struggling to keep up.

The line moved forward. Several other customers
stopped to talk to Del, greeting him and then paus-

ing to chat. *No doubt catching up,* she thought. Del had grown up here. He would know a lot of people.

A few words of the conversations drifted to her. She caught bits about his skysurfing and the business he'd sold. Because when Del had left town, he'd not only gotten involved in a new and highly risky sport, he'd designed a board, founded a company and then sold it for a lot of money. Which was impressive. And the tiniest bit annoying.

It wasn't that she didn't want him to have done great. But maybe he didn't have to be so good-looking at the same time as being so successful. Was a disfiguring scar too much to ask for? Something to level the playing field?

But no. With his three days' worth of beard and easy smile, he was still movie-star handsome. She would know. She'd seen plenty of him on video and he was impressive. The camera loved him and that meant the audience did, too.

She reached the front of the line and placed her order for the largest latte they had. She thought about ordering an extra shot of espresso, then acknowledged she would be most likely returning later. Better to spread out the caffeine.

She stepped to the side to wait for her drink. Del was still talking with a couple of people. She expected him to finish his conversation and leave. Instead, he headed for her.

"Morning," she said as he approached. Her lingering sleepiness faded as odd tingles began in her toes and raced up to the top of her head. Horror replaced trepidation.

No, no, no! There couldn't be tingles or awareness or any of that. Uh-uh. No way. Not her. She refused to be attracted to Delany Mitchell. Not after ten years and thousands of miles. The miles being metaphorical for her and literal for him. They were done. They'd moved on. Okay, technically she'd dumped him in a cruel and immature way, but regardless of her failings, it was so over as to be a relationship fossil.

Exhaustion, she told herself desperately. The tingles were the result of exhaustion. And maybe hunger. She would probably faint next and then everything would be fine.

"Morning," he said as he stopped in front of her. "You ratted me out to my mother."

The words were so at odds with what she'd been thinking that she had trouble understanding their meaning. When the mental smoke cleared, she was able to breathe again.

"You mean I told her you were in town?"

"Yeah. You could have given me fifteen minutes to get in touch with her."

She smiled. "You never said it was a secret. I stopped by to see a friend and told her you were back. She was surprised."

"That's one way to put it. She gave me an earful."

The barista handed Maya her latte. Maya took it and started for the door. "If you're expecting me to feel guilty about that, it's so not happening. How could you not bother telling your mother you were coming home? I'm not the bad guy here."

Del fell into step with her. "I wanted it to be a surprise."

"Is that what we're calling it these days?"

He held open the door of Brew-haha. When they got to the sidewalk, he pointed to the left and she walked along with him. Because, well—why not?

"You're saying I should have let her know I was home for the rest of the summer?"

"Speaking as your mom's friend, yes, you should have told her you were coming. Or that you'd arrived. And if you didn't want me to tell her, you should have said something. If she scolded you, it's your own fault. I accept absolutely no guilt or blame on the topic."

He surprised her by laughing. "You always did have attitude."

Back then it had been bravado. She liked to think she now had a little experience or even substance to back it up.

They reached the lake. Del turned toward the path that led to the rental cabins on the far side. Maya went with him. The day was sunny and promised to be plenty warm. August was often the hottest part of summer in Fool's Gold. Up in the mountains fall came early, but not in the town itself.

Along the shores of Lake Ciara, just south of the Golden Bear Inn, was a cluster of summer cabins. They ranged from small studios to large three-bedroom structures. Each cabin had a big porch with plenty of room for sitting out and watching the lake.

There was a play area for the kids, a communal fire pit and easy walking access to Fool's Gold.

Del led the way to one of the smaller cabins. There was plenty of seating on a surprisingly large porch.

"Not a suite at Ronan's Lodge?" she asked, taking the chair he offered.

He settled next to her. "I spend enough time in hotels when I travel. This is better."

"But there's no room service."

He glanced at her, one brow raised. "You think I can't cook?"

It had been ten years, she thought. "I guess I don't know that much about you." *Anymore.* She didn't say the last word, but she thought it. Because there had been a time when she'd known everything about Del. Not just his hopes and dreams, but how he laughed and kissed and tasted.

First love was usually intense. For her it had been that and more. With Del, for the first time in her life she'd allowed herself to hope she might not have to go it alone. That maybe, just maybe she could believe that someone else would be there for her. To look out for her. To give a damn.

"To start with, I can cook," he said, drawing her back to the present. "There was a last-minute cancellation so I got the cabin."

A couple of little boys played down by the water. Their mother watched from a blanket on the grass. Their shrieks and laughter carried over to them.

"It's going to be noisy," she said.

"That's okay. I like being around kids. They don't know who I am, and if they do, they don't care."

Some people would care, she thought, wondering how difficult his version of fame had become.

He'd made a name for himself on the extreme sports circuit. Crazy downhill snowboarding stunts had morphed into skysurfing. He'd become the face of a growing sport with the press clamoring to know why anyone would jump out of a plane with a board attached to their feet and deliberately spin and turn the whole way down.

After a few years of being a media darling, he'd made yet another change, designing a better board, and then starting the company that built them. That move had made him more mainstream—at least for the business crowd—and he'd become a popular guest on business shows. When he'd sold the company— walking away with cash and not announcing what he would do—he'd become the stuff of legends. A dare- devil willing to take life on his own terms.

She'd wanted that once. Not the danger, but the being famous part. It would have been one of the perks of being in front of the camera instead of be- hind it. For her it hadn't been about money or getting a reservation at a popular restaurant. It had been about belonging. That if others cared about her, she must have value. Be worthy, in some small way.

Time and maturity had helped her see the fallacy of that argument, but the hollowness of needing it had never completely gone away. With that dream over, she would have to find another way to make peace with her past.

"What are you thinking?" he asked.

She shook her head. "Nothing. I'm getting way too philosophical for this early in the morning." She sipped her coffee. "So you're back for the rest of summer and you're going to be helping me with the promo videos. I appreciate that."

He gave her a look that implied he wasn't buying that.

"I do," she repeated. "You'll be a great host."

"If you say so."

"I do."

He studied her. "I'm back because my dad's turning sixty and I haven't seen my family in a while. What are you doing here?"

A direct question. She decided on a direct answer. "I was tired of what I was doing. I'd made my third and what will be my final attempt at a network job." She drew in a breath. "The truth is I don't translate well on camera. On paper, I should be exactly right. I'm attractive enough and intelligent enough and warm enough, and yet it simply doesn't work. Going back to producing hard news was an option, but I couldn't get excited about it. I was visiting my stepbrothers and while I was here, Mayor Marsha approached me about the job. I said yes."

The offer had been unexpected, but she hadn't taken long to accept. Getting out of LA had been appealing and being close to family had felt right. She'd never considered that Del would be coming back.

She glanced at him from under her lashes. Would that have made a difference? She told herself it wouldn't have. He was only home for a few weeks. She could manage to hold it together for that long. Besides, the tingling was probably a onetime thing. A knee-jerk reaction to an unexpected visit from her past.

Del had been her first love. Of course there would be residual emotions. Knowing him, caring about him, had changed her forever.

"About the videos," she said.

"You have lots of ideas."

"How did you know?"

He looked at her, his dark eyes bright with amusement. "You always did and you were forceful with your opinions."

"That's not a bad thing."

"I agree. You told me what they were, then explained why I was an idiot if I didn't listen to you."

She sipped her coffee. "I doubt I said *idiot*," she murmured.

"You were thinking it."

She laughed. "Maybe."

She had been forceful and determined. Instead of finding her annoying, Del had encouraged her to explain herself. He'd wanted to know what she was thinking.

"You had some good ideas to improve the tours," he said. "I'm sure you'll have good ideas about the videos. Of course, I have some experience with the medium myself."

He could have acted like a bastard, she thought, remembering how things had ended. Of course, if he'd still been angry, he would have refused to work with her.

"Challenging my authority?" she asked lightly.

"We'll see."

She glanced at her watch. "I need to get to work." She suggested a day and time for their first official meeting, then stood and walked back toward town.

Partway down the path, she had the urge to turn back. To see if Del was watching her. When she glanced over her shoulder, she saw he wasn't. He'd gone inside.

Foolishness, she told herself. Just like the tingles. If she ignored it, it would go away. At least that was the plan.

DEL FINISHED HIS COFFEE, then accepted the inevitable and drove to his parents' house. As he pulled into the long driveway, he braced himself for the inescapable drama. Because this was his family and nothing was ever easy.

He parked and walked toward the front door. The huge rambler looked as it always had—sprawling with a large garden front and back. Beyond the rear yard was the workshop his father used. Two stories of windows in a steel frame, because of the light. Ceallach also had a studio on the far side of town for when he needed to get away.

His father was a famous glass artist. World famous. When he was good, he was the best. But when he drank...

Del tried to shake off the memories, but they were persistent. His father had been sober several years now. He no longer destroyed a year's worth of work in a single afternoon's drunken tantrum and left the family desperate and destitute. It was better now. But for Ceallach's five sons, better had come too late.

A happy bark drew him back to the present. A brown, black and white beagle raced around the side of the house and headed for him. Sophie bayed her pleasure as she rushed at him.

"Hey, pretty girl," he said, scooping her up and standing. She wriggled in his arms, trying to get closer and give kisses at the same time.

"You probably don't remember me," he told the dog. "You'd be this happy to greet a serial killer."

Sophie gave a doggie grin in agreement. He put her on the ground and followed her to the front door. His mother opened it before he could knock and shook her head.

"You couldn't shave?"

He chuckled, then hugged her. "Hey, Mom."

She held on tight, then drew back and shook her head. "Seriously. Would it kill you to use a razor?"

He rubbed his jaw. "Most mothers want to talk grandchildren."

"That would work for me, too. Come on." She held open the door.

He stepped into the house and back into the past. Very little had changed. The living room had different sofas, but in the same spot. His father's glasswork was everywhere, all carefully mounted or secured so Sophie or her wagging tail didn't do any damage.

Del turned his attention back to his mother. Elaine had met Ceallach Mitchell when she'd been twenty. According to her, it had been love at first sight. His father had never told his side of the story. They'd married four months later and Del had been born a year after that. Four more sons had followed, each about a year apart until the twins.

His mom looked as she always had, with dark, shoulder-length hair and an easy smile. But as he studied her, he saw that there were a few differences. She was older, but it was more than that. She seemed tired, maybe.

"You okay, Mom?"

"I'm fine. I don't sleep as well as I used to." She shrugged. "The change."

He wasn't sure exactly which change she was referring to, but he wasn't going there. Rather than take a safe step back and escape, he moved to the sofa. Sophie jumped up next to him and immediately settled in for a nap.

His mother sat across from him. "How long are you in town?"

"The rest of the summer. You said to be home for Dad's birthday. I came back early."

"Your father will be pleased."

Del was less sure about that. Ceallach might be brilliant, but he was also temperamental. In his mind what mattered was art. Everything else was a far second. A lesser kind of living. He had no patience for or interest in mere mortal lives or pursuits.

"You're here by yourself?" his mother asked.

Del nodded. Last time he'd been home he'd brought Hyacinth. He'd been so sure they were going to make it. But they hadn't. She'd been unable to promise herself to a single man and he'd been unable to accept the string of what she swore were insignificant lovers that moved in and out of her bed. While he'd loathed the cheating, the dishonesty had been just as bad.

"Traveling light," he told his mother.

"Del, you need to settle down."

"I've never wanted to settle."

"You know what I mean. Don't you want a family?"

"Finally playing the grandkid card?"

She smiled. "Yes. It's time. Your father and I have been married thirty-five years and yet none of my boys has ever gotten married. Why is that?"

He couldn't speak for his brothers. He'd been in love twice in his life, first with Maya and then with Hyacinth. Both relationships had ended badly. And the common denominator? Him.

His father strolled into the living room. Ceallach Mitchell was tall and broad-shouldered. Despite being weeks away from turning sixty, he was still strong, with the muscles required to wrestle large pieces of molten glass into submission. Del acknowledged his father's genius—there was no denying brilliance. But he also knew it came at a price.

"Del's home," Elaine said, motioning to the sofa.

Ceallach stared at his son. For a second Del wondered if his father was trying to figure out which of his offspring he was.

"He came back for your birthday," his mother added.

"Good to know. What are you doing these days? Surfing?"

Del thought about the board he'd created, the company he'd started, how much he'd sold it for and the impressive amount sitting in his bank account.

"Most days," he said, dropping his hand to rub Sophie's tummy. The beagle shifted onto her back and sighed.

"You seen Nick?" his father asked. "He's still working in that bar, wasting his talent. No one can get through to him. I'm done trying."

With that, Ceallach walked out of the room.

Del stared after him. "Good to see you, too, Dad."

His mother pressed her lips together. "Don't be like that," she said. "You know how he gets. It's just his way. He's glad you're back."

Del was less sure about that, but didn't want to start a fight. Nothing had changed. Ceallach only cared about his art and other people with the potential to create art, and Elaine still stood between him and the world, acting as both buffer and defender.

"What *are* you up to these days?" she asked. "I know you sold your company. Congratulations."

"Thanks. I'm still deciding what's next. I've been offered some design work."

"Are you going to take it?"

"No. I came up with my board on my own. I'm not a designer. There are a couple of venture capitalists who want to fund my next big idea." Which would be great if he had one. What he most wanted to do— Well, that wasn't going the way he'd hoped.

"You have time to decide what's important."

The right words, but again he had the sense she was hiding something. Not that he was going to ask again. Secrets were an ongoing part of life in the Mitchell family. He'd learned early to wait until they were shared.

"You could go to work for your brother," she said.

"Aidan?" Del laughed. "At the family business? No thanks. And I doubt he'd appreciate you offering my help."

"He's busy all the time. Especially in summer."

He couldn't imagine what his brother would have to say about his advice. These days they barely kept in touch. Del remembered when they'd been close and wondered what had happened. Sure he'd been gone, but he emailed and texted.

Another problem for another day, he told himself and rose.

"Good to see you, Mom," he said as he crossed to her and kissed her on the cheek.

"You, too. I expect to see a lot of you while you're in town."

"You will."

"And shave."

CHAPTER THREE

MAYA'S OFFICE WAS in the same building as the Fool's Gold cable access studio. The local news had its own location on the other side of town. Until this minute she'd enjoyed the separation. Having to see "real" reporters on a daily basis would have been depressing. It wasn't that she wanted to be one anymore. It was just having to look into the eyes of her abandoned dream, as it were, could have been difficult. Although at this second, facing down a wild, hungry bear would have been preferable to what she was doing.

"I don't understand," Eddie Carberry said stubbornly. "People *like* our show. Did one of the Gionni sisters say something to you? Because I know they're pissed that we're getting better ratings than they are. Who wants to watch a TV show about hair when there are naked butts to be seen? Plus, they each have a show because of their feud, so it's twice as much of the same."

"The shows are about styling hair," her friend Gladys pointed out. "Not that watching someone work a curling iron is all that interesting."

Eddie and Gladys had to be in their seventies. They were spry enough and certainly determined, Maya thought grimly. Had Mayor Marsha realized the impossibility of the task when she'd hired Maya? Because Maya had always thought she and the mayor were friends. Maybe she'd been imagining the connection.

"Styling or talking, hair is hair. What we do is more interesting and Bella and Julia can't stand that." Eddie put her hands on her hips. As she was wearing a bright yellow velour tracksuit, she looked a bit more comical than intimidating, but there was a gleam in her eye that had Maya keeping a safe distance.

She continued to hold out the piece of paper. "I've cut and pasted the exact language from the government website," she said firmly. "It's very clear. The FCC has defined broadcast indecency as 'language or material that, in context, depicts or describes, in terms patently offensive as measured by contemporary community standards for the broadcast medium, sexual or excretory organs or activities.'"

"What's *excretory*?" Gladys asked.

"What does it sound like?" Eddie gave her a pointed look.

Gladys wrinkled her nose. "Yuck. We'd never do that. What about free speech? We claim the First Amendment."

"What she said," Eddie added. "We have the right to free speech."

Maya looked at her notes. "The court says that you can't show naked butts when children might be watching."

Gladys and Eddie exchanged a look.

"So not on our five o'clock broadcast but we can show them at eleven?" Eddie asked.

Maya held in a groan. "I'd rather you didn't show them at all."

"But you're not the boss of us," Eddie pointed out. "And what about all those TV dramas that show butts?"

"They're on at ten," Gladys added. "So we'll show butts at eleven. It's an excellent compromise."

One Maya hoped Mayor Marsha could live with.

"But not at five," she clarified. "You don't want the FCC shutting you down or fining the station. If we had to pay a fine, we'd lose our budget and then you wouldn't have a show at all."

"Your job is to make sure that doesn't happen," Eddie told her.

"No, my job is to manage the cable access shows. *Your* job is to follow the rules."

Eddie gave her a smile. "You have backbone. I like that. I remember when you were a teenager, waiting to go off to college. Look at you now—all grown-up."

"Ladies."

The male voice had them all turning. Maya caught sight of Del and nearly threw herself in his arms. Not that she wasn't thrilled to see him, but the distraction was even better.

"Del!" Gladys hurried toward him. "You're back."

"You know it."

He caught the old lady in his arms and hugged her, then turned to Eddie. After kissing them both on the cheek, he winked.

"Are you two making trouble?"

"Always," Eddie said proudly.

Maya shook her head. "No more trouble. They both just agreed not to show naked butts before eleven. It's a victory for decency standards."

Eddie sniffed. "But after eleven, we're all butts, all the time. Del, give us a picture of yours. We hold a contest for people to guess whose butt belongs to whom. No one's seen yours in ages. It would be fun."

He laughed and hugged them. "I've missed you two. There's no one like you anywhere I've traveled."

"If you think we're all that," Gladys said, "why don't you come back and sleep with us? Seventy is the new thirty-five."

Del's amusement didn't waver. "Let's not ruin the promise of what can never be," he told them.

"He's turning us down," Eddie said with a sigh. "Men are idiots."

Gladys patted his cheek. "She's right, but you can't help it."

The old ladies waved and walked out of Maya's office. She sank into her chair and wondered if she'd actually escaped so easily or if there were more early-afternoon butt issues in her future.

Del took the empty chair across from hers. "They're really doing a butt contest?"

"Yes, and I'd rather not talk about it. Mayor Marsha is worried about the FCC getting involved. I had to look up the definitions and everything. Not my favorite part of the job."

He glanced toward the door. "I missed them a lot. They're one of the best parts of this town."

"Seriously? They frighten a lot of guys."

"No way. They're fun."

"I wonder if we should redefine our terms," she murmured.

He leaned back in his chair. "Relax. They like you. They'll listen."

"I hope you're right. What brings you here?" Their appointment wasn't for a couple of days.

He shrugged. "I was in the neighborhood."

Easy enough to be, she thought. Fool's Gold was hardly a big place. But still. "Everything okay?"

He hesitated just long enough for her to wonder what wasn't going well before saying, "It's great. I saw my mom. You can't hold that over me anymore."

"Because you were so worried I would. Do you want to talk business while you're here?"

"Sure."

She pulled out the two folders she'd started on their projects.

"Mayor Marsha and the City Council want a two-part campaign. Part one will support local tourism efforts. I'm working with several city officials on that. The goal is pretty simple. Make videos that entice people to visit the area."

She thought about the format discussed. "You'll be hosting and starring in those."

He raised an eyebrow. "You're saying I'm the talent?"

"You wish."

He was dressed much as he had been the past two times she'd seen him. In jeans and a casual shirt. He looked at ease, as if comfortable in any environment. The beard was a little thicker, the hair a tad longer. The word *scruffy* came to mind, as it had before. But the sexy version.

She forced her attention back to the conversation. "The second part is a campaign celebrating the town's new slogan. *A destination for romance.*"

"Interviewing people in love?" he asked.

"Easy enough," she agreed. "I have a list of potential couples, including one that has been together for over seventy years."

"Impressive. On the tourism videos, what do you want to do? Go film different locations with me talking about them?"

"Yes, but I'm hoping we can do something more inspired. If the clips are interesting, we can use them in advertising."

"Or get them picked up by local news."

"I'm less sure about that. Local news stories average forty-one seconds. National news stories average two minutes and twenty-three seconds. I'd rather get *Good Morning America* interested."

"There are a lot of people trying to get noticed on GMA," he said. "We'll have to be innovative."

She liked that he hadn't dismissed her idea outright. How strange that they were working together like this, she thought. Until moving back to Fool's Gold a few weeks ago, she hadn't thought of Del much at all. Since returning, he'd been on her mind, but that had been a proximity thing. Hard to ignore the only man she'd ever loved when she was returning to the scene of the heartbreak. Then, out of the blue—thanks to Mayor Marsha—he was back in her life.

She wondered if he ever thought about the past. Before meeting him, she would have guessed they had to clear the air. But he didn't seem to be upset about what had happened between them. Nor could she figure out a good way to broach the subject.

"Hey, Del, sorry I was such a bitch when I broke up with you." No, that wasn't going to happen. Maybe she would wait and see if there was a more organic way to have the conversation.

"Any celebrity contacts you can use?" he asked.

"I did the studio work in LA," she told him. "The celebrities don't know me."

"Sorry you didn't get to meet Ryan Gosling?"

"The pain keeps me up at night, but I'm dealing."

He chuckled, then the humor faded. "How'd you get away from news?"

A question she'd asked herself a thousand times. "I was tempted by the devil and gave in," she admitted, knowing it was true. "I'd been working my way up in local news, producing more and more segments. The gossip show gave me a chance to be in front of the camera." Sadly, her lack of chemistry had made that a short-lived solution. "When that didn't work, they offered me a promotion working behind the scenes. With the wisdom of hindsight, I'm pretty sure that was their plan all along. But they knew I would never have left the job I had to take the producer job."

"Hard feelings?"

"No. I made the choices. I get to live with the consequences."

"And now you're here."

She smiled. "So far, so good."

"Except for Eddie and Gladys," he teased.

"I'll figure out how to get them to toe the line. Just in a way that doesn't break their spirit. I like that they push boundaries."

"You're taking their side?"

"I'm saying creativity should always be encouraged."

His shirt pocket beeped. He pulled out his phone and glanced at the screen. "Mayor Marsha. She said to ask you about the videos you did of me." Both eyebrows rose. "Did I make it onto your celebrity show?"

"No," she said, lying before she could stop herself. "Strange. I have no idea what she's talking about."

His dark eyes gave nothing away. "She must have you confused with someone else."

"I'm sure that's it." She glanced down at her open folder. "I thought we could do a segment on Priscilla, the elephant, and her pony, Reno."

"Who and who?"

She wasn't sure if the distraction worked, but if he was willing to pretend, then she was, as well. Before she showed Del any videos she'd done, she needed to have someone else look at them. Someone she could trust to have her back. The last thing she wanted was for her ex-boyfriend/fiancé to think she'd spent the past ten years unable to get over him.

DEL HEADED ACROSS TOWN. He and Maya had plans to work on the videos starting in a few days. She still had preproduction schedules to work out, including renting equipment. While the camera was important, the right lenses could make or break a shoot. She would be renting the ones they needed.

Until then, he was on his own. As he'd already started down memory lane with his family, he might as well continue. He crossed the street and headed into The Man Cave.

While the sign out front said the sports bar was closed, the door was propped open. He stepped inside and looked around.

The overhead lights were on, illuminating the big, open space. The ceilings were high with a second-story balcony wrapping around like a catwalk. Tables and chairs had been pushed out of the way for cleaning. There were dartboards, pool tables and a big stage at one end. The long bar dominated the room at the other end.

Sports memorabilia covered the walls. There were sports posters, along with a Tour de France jersey, and signed footballs and helmets.

His brother walked out from a back room and grinned.

"I heard you were dead," Nick said cheerfully.

"You wish."

"Naw. I like being the middle brother. It adds symmetry."

They hugged briefly. Del studied his sibling. Nick looked good. Older and comfortable in his surroundings. Whatever Ceallach had going on about Nick's chosen profession, Nick wasn't equally troubled.

"Have a seat," Nick said, pulling a table out from the cluster by the wall, then grabbing two chairs. "Want a beer?"

"Sure."

Nick went behind the bar and pulled a bottle out of a refrigerator. He poured himself a soda. Del was about to ask why, then told himself Nick worked in a bar. Probably best if he wasn't sampling product in the middle of the afternoon.

Nick returned with the drinks and they sat across from each other.

His brother was about his size. All the Mitchell sons were within an inch or so of their father's height. Nick was more muscled than Aidan or Del. Some of that was genetic and some of it came from the heavy materials he worked with. *Or it had*, Del thought, wondering when his brother had stopped working with glass and started managing a bar.

"How's business?" he asked.

"Good." Nick grinned. "We had a bit of a rough start, but we're busy now. We get a good crowd. A nice mix of tourists and locals. The karaoke is popular." He nodded at the stage. "You should come sing sometime."

Del laughed. "That's not gonna happen." He glanced around. "How long have you been working here?"

"Since it opened." Nick's humor faded. "Don't you

get on me, too. I have to take that crap from Dad. You don't get to talk about it."

The "it" being his brother's talent, Del thought. Because while he and Aidan lacked Ceallach's phenomenal ability, Nick and the twins were nearly as gifted.

Del held up both hands. "Fine. I won't say a word."

Nick glared at him for a second before sighing. "You saw him, didn't you?"

"Yesterday."

"That's the same tone of voice Aidan uses when he talks about Dad."

"We're not chosen," Del said lightly, thinking about how Ceallach always dismissed their mother's small tour company as unimportant, despite how many times it had put food on the table. From what he'd seen so far, their brother Aidan had grown the company even more. But none of that would matter to Ceallach.

"You're still doing well," Nick said. "Congratulations on selling the company."

Del sipped his beer. "How'd you know?"

"I read the business section of the paper every now and then. You got a big write-up here. Local boy makes good. What are you going to do next?"

"I have no idea."

"Part of the reason you came home?"

"That and Dad's birthday."

"Which isn't for a few weeks. That's a long time to contemplate your navel."

Del chuckled. "Not my style. I'm helping Maya Farlow with some promotional videos for the town. To support tourism and the new slogan."

Nick's brows rose. "Seriously?"

"It's no big deal."

"You were going to marry her, and when she dumped you, you left town. Mom was hysterical for weeks. That Maya?"

"Yes, and thanks for the recap."

"You're welcome." Nick studied him. "You're really going to work with her?"

"So it seems."

Del thought about seeing Maya. She had become an interesting combination of the girl he remembered and someone completely different. Still gorgeous, but beautiful women were easy to find. She was smart, and he liked that. Conversation was as important as sex, in his world.

"We were friends," he told his brother. "There's no reason for that to have changed. Besides, I'm grateful for what happened."

"That's an interesting way to look at it."

Del thought about the life he'd had planned. Before Maya, he'd been ready to take over the family business and live out his days in Fool's Gold.

"Because of her I got to travel and see the world. There's a whole lot of interesting stuff going on out there. If I'd stayed, I would have been miserable."

"Even with Maya?"

A question he couldn't answer. Nor did he want to try. If Maya had married him...

For a second he allowed himself to picture a house with a yard and a couple of kids. Maya pregnant with a third. Could he have been happy with her? With them?

Ten years ago, he would have sworn the answer was yes. Now, while he wanted the wife and kids, he wasn't sure he could handle the settling down in one place part.

"I'm happy," he said firmly. Lonely, maybe, but still happy. "What she and I had was over years ago. I can work with her, no problem."

Nick picked up his soda. "I find it hard to believe you're that forgiving, but okay. I applaud your mature, if slightly puzzling, response to her being back in town." He brightened. "Hey, make her fall in love with you again, then dump her."

"When did you get vindictive?"

A muscle tightened in Nick's jaw. "Shit happens."

Del thought about asking what, but figured Nick would tell him when he was ready. "Thanks for the suggestion of revenge, but no thanks. Wanting to punish her means I'm not over her, and I am. Completely."

He was a one-woman man, still looking for the right woman. He'd thought he'd found her twice. First with Maya and then with Hyacinth. One of the things both women had taught him was the importance of being honest. With the other person and with yourself. Hyacinth and Maya had lied to him. In different ways, but they'd still withheld the truth. If a woman couldn't be direct and open, he wasn't interested.

Nick raised his glass. "To getting over her."

Del raised his bottle. He knew who his "her" was, but wondered about Nick's. Not that he would find out. Theirs was a family that flourished on secrets.

THE NICHOLSON RANCH had been in the Nicholson family for something impossible like five generations. Maya wasn't sure of the exact number. What she knew for sure was how impressed she'd been when she'd first seen it twelve years ago. She'd been a scared sixteen-year-old who'd only ever lived in Las Vegas. Going from barren desert that grew neon rather than actual trees to the ranch had been like something out of a PBS miniseries.

The two-story house had seemed impossibly huge. There had been acres of grass and trees, horses and cattle, along with cashmere goats.

Her mother had hit the jackpot when she'd met Rick Nicholson. They'd dated for two weeks, then had married in a drive-through church. Less than a month later, Maya and her mother were leaving everything behind and moving to California. Maya hadn't known what to expect, but every hope and dream had been fulfilled when she'd first seen the ranch.

It didn't matter that Rick wasn't especially friendly. Being ignored by her mother's new husband was far preferable to the attention from some of the woman's previous boyfriends. She'd had her own room, with a bathroom! Three meals a day and two stepbrothers. While the older brother, Zane, had glared at her with contempt, little Chase had been adorable.

Even more incredible, had been the town. Fool's Gold had been clean, friendly and welcoming. She'd made friends, she'd had teachers who not only knew her name but cared about how she was doing. For the first time in her life, Maya had allowed herself to hope she could have a future. She'd dared to whisper the possibility of going to college.

Now she drove onto the ranch property and headed for the main house. After her mother and Rick had divorced, Maya had stayed in touch with both Zane and Chase. While her relationship with Zane had been more adversarial than familial, she hadn't given up on him. The previous month, they'd reconciled, helped by Zane falling totally and completely in love with Maya's best friend, Phoebe.

Maya parked and grabbed her oversize bag before heading toward the house. She knocked once on the front door, then stepped inside.

"It's me," she called.

Phoebe, a petite, curvy brunette, stepped out of the kitchen and smiled. "Yay. I love it being you."

They hugged, then walked into the kitchen, where Phoebe poured them glasses of iced tea.

Maya sat at the old, battered table and watched her friend collect a salad from the refrigerator, along with tiny sandwiches.

"You didn't have to feed me," Maya said, knowing Phoebe couldn't help herself. She was born to take care of the world.

"I thought you might be hungry."

Phoebe set the food on the table, then collected napkins and flatware.

She moved easily—as if she'd always lived in the old house. Even better, Phoebe looked content. Happiness radiated out of her brown eyes. She was relaxed. Every now and then, she glanced at the diamond ring sparkling on her left ring finger. The beautiful solitaire would soon be joined by a wedding band.

Phoebe sat across from her and grinned. "The ranch closed. I got my commission check."

It took Maya a second to make the transition.

Recently, Phoebe had sold a nearby ranch to action movie superstar Jonny Blaze. It had been Phoebe's last real estate deal before moving in with Zane and probably the only one where she'd made any money. Until the unexpected deal with Jonny Blaze, Phoebe had specialized in starter homes—a challenge in the expensive LA real estate market.

"You're rich," Maya teased gently.

"I am for me." Phoebe sounded thrilled. "I have no idea what to do with the money. Zane told me to keep it in a separate account. That I earned it before the wedding, so it's mine rather than ours."

Because Zane would always take care of her, Maya thought, still amazed at how falling in love had mellowed her usually tight-ass brother.

"Are you going to listen to him?" Maya asked.

Phoebe nibbled on her bottom lip. "I think it should be ours."

"Zane has the ranch. Keep the money. You'll feel better having a nest egg."

"Maybe."

"You're going to buy him something, aren't you?"

Phoebe laughed. "I haven't decided. So what's going on with you?"

Maya told her about the videos planned for the town. "I'll be working with Del."

Phoebe's brown eyes widened. "Del, the guy you knew after high school? The one who wanted to marry you?"

Maya shifted on her seat. If only it was that simple. "He's the one," she said, hoping her tone sounded light rather than guilty.

"What's that like?"

"I don't know. I thought it would be awkward, but he seems fine with us handling the project together."

"How do you feel?"

"Confused." Maya pulled the tablet out of her bag. "I told you that Del and I fell crazy in love that summer."

"Uh-huh. It was after high school, right?"

Phoebe knew enough about her past that Maya didn't have to explain about her mother or how difficult times had been before the move to Fool's Gold.

"I loved him," Maya said, feeling the guilt forming a knot in her stomach. "But I was so scared. Scared of what getting married would mean. Scared of getting stuck."

"Scared you'd turn into your mom."

Maya nodded. "I always knew that there wasn't going to be a white knight on a horse riding in to rescue me. I knew I'd have to rescue myself. But with Del, I started to believe."

"Loving him wasn't enough," Phoebe said quietly.

"It wasn't. The closer we got to the date when we were going to run off, the more I started to freak. I finally had an opportunity to break free. To make something of myself. Was I really going to give that up for a guy?"

Phoebe leaned toward her. "Did you ask him about that? About going to college with you or finding some kind of compromise? Did you tell him you were scared?"

"No." Maya swallowed. "I dumped him. I told him he was boring and this town was boring and that I didn't want anything to do with him. Then I left."

The truth was, she'd run. Away from Del, away from Fool's Gold. Part of her wondered if she was still running. Fear was a powerful motivator.

"Ouch. You never talked to him again?" Phoebe asked.

"Not until a few days ago, when he walked into Mayor Marsha's office."

"How was he?"

"Fine. Friendly. Charming. He didn't say a word."

"How do you feel?"

"Guilty," Maya admitted. "Like I have to apologize. But the timing is tricky. We're working together. I don't want it to be weird, but I owe him an apology and an explanation. Even if he has completely moved on, I need to do it for myself."

"Then you have a plan."

"I do. I also need you to look at a video I did. It's a story about him. I have no idea how Mayor Marsha ever saw it, but she did and mentioned it to Del. So I'm going to have to show it to him. Can you watch it and tell me if it's okay?"

What she really meant was, were there signs of

unrequited love or anything else remotely humiliating? But she wouldn't have to say that to Phoebe. Her friend would understand what she meant.

"I love watching your work," Phoebe told her. "Let's see what brilliance you've created."

Maya set her tablet on the table, then cued up the video. While Phoebe watched it, she crossed to the family room and took in the changes her friend had made.

The chintz chairs and dark red sofa had been replaced with large couches covered in warm, family-friendly fabric. The walls had been painted and the artwork moved around. Fresh flowers in pretty vases had been scattered around the room.

Phoebe couldn't help improving everything she touched, Maya thought, a little envious of the skill. Phoebe had never cared about ambition. Her dreams had been about belonging.

They'd met in college. Phoebe always told the story as if Maya had rescued her from loneliness and obscurity, but Maya knew it was the other way around. Her friend had been a rock—one of the few stable relationships she'd been able to count on.

Zane had been there, too, Maya thought. In his own curmudgeonly way. And Chase. But Chase was a kid, and Zane and she had had some difficult times. Being friends with Phoebe had always been so very easy.

Phoebe looked up from the tablet. "You're so talented. I love this. You bring Del alive. I've never met him and I already like him. I love how you take us on the journey as he goes from extreme sport media darling to supercool businessman." She looked at her watch. "In what? A three-minute segment? There's nothing to worry about. This is an impressive story told by a news professional."

Maya returned to the table and took the tablet. "Thank you. I don't deserve the compliments, but I'll accept them because I'm needy." She paused. "So there's nothing..."

Phoebe shook her head. "No unrequited like, let alone love. Don't worry."

"Thank you." Maya dropped the tablet into her bag. "Enough about me. Tell me what's going on with the wedding. Are you freaking out yet?"

"No, but it's in my eight-day plan." Phoebe grinned. "Actually I don't think I have to freak out. Dellina Ridge is planning everything and she's so into the details. Oh, that reminds me. We're going to have a fitting for our dresses soon. I'll let you know the second they come into the store."

Phoebe had only wanted one attendant, and that was Maya. Chase would stand up with his brother. *A family affair*, Maya thought, still touched by the decision.

"I can't wait," Maya told her, and meant the words. She wanted to be there when Phoebe married Zane. She wanted to be a part of things. She might not have gotten the network job she'd wanted, but coming back to Fool's Gold was going to be a good thing.

An hour later Maya hugged Phoebe goodbye. Before heading to her car, she detoured by the barn. Zane kept his office there. She found her ex-stepbrother working on his computer. When he saw her, he smiled.

"Phoebe said you were stopping by. Did she mention the dresses will be in soon?"

Maya stared at the man who had always seemed so disapproving and stern. "Seriously? You want to talk wedding fashions?"

"If it's important to Phoebe, it's important to me."

She grinned and took the visitor's chair. "Is that a chill I feel from the depths of hell?"

"Just taking care of what matters."

Maya couldn't believe how mean old Zane had changed. Although the truth was, he'd never been old or mean. He'd been the one trying to hold the family together after his father died, and neither she nor Chase had made that job easy. His younger brother had been more than a handful and she'd enjoyed pushing Zane's buttons.

She studied him now, taking in the handsome lines of his face. In truth, they weren't blood relatives and they'd only lived in the same house for two years. A case could be made that they could have fallen for each other. Only from the second she'd met him, she'd seen him as a brother. An annoying brother with a stick firmly planted up his ass, but family all the same. From what she could tell, he'd thought the same about her. Minus the stick.

Which meant he'd been available to fall for Phoebe. A fact that still made Maya very, very happy.

"She does want to discuss what color the Jordan almonds will be. Lilac, light blue or mauve."

He made a note on a pad of paper. "I'll talk to her about it later."

She blinked. "Really? Just like that."

"Sure."

Maya shook her head. "You really are crazy about her. There's no Jordan almond question. I was just messing with you."

His mouth curved into a smile. "I'm happy to help her decide. After I look up what they are."

"Thank God for Google."

"Absolutely." He studied her. "It's nice to have you around, Maya."

"It's nice to be around." She thought about her earlier conversation with Phoebe. How she'd felt safe for the first time when she'd moved to Fool's Gold. How her teachers had cared and she'd gotten a scholarship for college.

"Was it you?" she asked. "Who funded my college scholarship?"

Zane shook his head. "Sorry, no. I should have offered to help pay for it, but I didn't think of it. Money was tight back then, so I don't think my dad would have agreed."

She remembered. But their brand of money being tight had been a whole lot nicer than her mother's.

"I just wondered. Somebody put up the money. Mayor Marsha would never tell me who."

"Maybe they wanted to be anonymous. You should let it be."

She laughed. "Because I'm going to start taking your advice now?"

"Stranger things have happened."

"Maybe, but that's not one of them." She stood and circled the desk, then gave him a hug. "You're going to research Jordan almonds, aren't you?"

"Of course."

Which only made her love him more.

CHAPTER FOUR

DEL SAT ON the front porch stairs of his cabin. It was late in the afternoon but still a long way from sunset. The temperature was warm and the kids in the area were out playing. He could hear shrieks of laughter, along with friendly taunts.

Being lazy felt good, he thought, reminding himself he should enjoy the moment. Because soon enough he would get restless and want to be doing something. The question was what. He wasn't an entrepreneur by blood. He'd stumbled into his sky board company in an attempt to please himself. Despite the many offers to collaborate, he wasn't interested in trying to duplicate the success.

A sleek gray convertible pulled up next to his battered truck. The visitor's car screamed LA and he knew who it was before she got out.

In the past ten years Maya had changed, the way women did when they grew up. Like the car, she was sleek, with great lines and plenty of power. The analogy made him chuckle. He doubted she would see the compliment.

She wore jeans and boots. A simple loose T-shirt had been tucked into her jeans. She slung a tote bag over her shoulder as she walked toward him. She looked confident and sexy. A nearly unbeatable combination.

For a second, as he watched her, he remembered what it had been like before. When Maya hadn't been quite so in charge. When she'd stared at him wide-eyed, her mouth trembling right before he'd kissed her.

Their first meeting had been a lightning strike—at least for him. He'd seen her and wanted her. Later, when he'd gotten to know her, he'd found himself as attracted to every part of her. Hearing her laugh had made his day brighter. He'd fallen hard, and for that entire summer, he'd known she was the one.

When she'd accepted his proposal, he'd expected they would spend the rest of their lives together. He'd imagined kids and a yard and everything that went with happily ever after. When she'd dumped him...

"Hey," she said as she approached.

He wrenched his mind from the past and focused on the present. Maya stopped at the porch stairs and held out her tablet.

"I brought over a copy of that video Mayor Marsha mentioned. I thought it would give you an idea of how I work."

The video she'd claimed to know nothing about? *Curious*, he thought as he stood. Why had she pretended to be confused and why the change of heart? He thought about asking, then decided it was probably a chick thing and he was better off not knowing.

"Let's take a look," he said, and headed inside.

The cabin was simply furnished with an open floor plan. The kitchen and living room were up front with a half wall dividing the sleeping area from the rest of the cabin. The only separate area was the small three-quarter bath.

Del walked to the square dining table by the window and sat down. Maya handed him the tablet, but instead of sitting next to him, she hovered just behind his right shoulder.

"Just push the button," she told him.

"Nervous?" he asked without turning to look at her.

"A little. It's my work."

Which implied it had significance to her. He got that but, "It's not like my opinion is going to make a difference."

"You're the subject. Of course I care what you think."

Good to know, he thought as he glanced at the screen.

The frozen picture showed him just after he'd jumped from an airplane. He pushed Play and the piece started.

It was about two or three minutes long with Maya providing the voice-over. The footage was all stock stuff, easily available on the internet. There were clips from other interviews he'd done while he'd still been involved in the sport and later, when he'd transitioned to entrepreneur.

When the video ended, he turned to look at her. "This wasn't for your TV show."

She gave him a nervous smile. "No. You were famous, but not that famous." One shoulder rose and fell. "Unless we were talking about your love life. Then you made the show."

"At the end," he said absently, thinking that his relationship with Hyacinth—a world champion figure skater—had captured the media's attention, if only on the periphery.

"I did some freelance work," she added. "Pieces like this that could be used on local morning shows."

He turned back to the tablet and tapped the screen to watch it again. This time he turned off the sound and studied the pictures. She'd taken ordinary shots and woven them together into something greater than the individual clips.

She was a good editor—better than good. He'd taken some video himself and tried to edit it, and the results had been dismal.

"Nice," he said, pointing at the screen. "I like what you did here. You cropped the shot differently. Or something."

She pulled up a chair and settled next to him. "You're right. The action was great, but you weren't at the center of the frame. I moved you as best I could. The line of sight is better, too."

She kept talking and motioning to the action playing on the tablet, but he wasn't paying attention. Not anymore. Not when he could inhale the scent of what he guessed was her shampoo, or maybe her lotion. Maya had never been one to wear perfume. Although he guessed that could be different now.

She'd changed just enough to be intriguing, he thought. The line of her jaw was tighter. Her walk a bit more determined. He didn't know what she'd been through over the past ten years, but whatever it was had honed her.

She probably saw differences in him, too, but he found those less interesting. He knew what had happened to him. None of it was especially compelling.

He turned and looked into her green eyes. Ten years ago he would have sworn that he would never forgive her for what she'd said. For how she'd rejected him. For lying. Now he searched for residual anger or resentment and there wasn't any. They'd both been gone too long for any of that to matter.

She was a beautiful woman. Under other circumstances, he might have been tempted. But while he could forgive and move on, he wasn't going to give her a second chance. Not when he knew she hadn't told him the truth. She had said that she loved him and wanted to marry him, but it had all been a lie. Still, they were going to work together. It made sense to be friends.

"Want to have dinner?" he asked.

She blinked. "There's a shift in topic. Now?"

"Sure. We can go to the store and grab a couple of steaks. Barbecue them here. There's a communal grill by the lake. You in?"

She gave him a slow, sexy smile that hit him like a fist to the gut.

"I'm in."

They rose and walked toward the front door.

"Wait," she said, and ran back for her tablet, then tucked it in her tote. "I can't let my technology out of my sight."

He nodded, because it was still too difficult to breathe, let alone speak.

He knew what that fist to the gut meant and he planned on completely ignoring the message. He was willing to forget the past, to work with Maya and even to be her friend. But he was never going to allow himself to be tempted by her. Not now, not ever.

Been there, done that and bought the T-shirt. He was a guy who looked forward. To something new. And that didn't include her. Once his mind was made up, Del refused to be swayed. There was no way he was going to let Maya get to him.

MAYA PUT THE green salad on the table Del had carried from the kitchen to the grassy area on the side of the cabin. From there they had a clear view of the lake. Because of how the other cabins were spaced, that side of his place was relatively private. They could hear the other families, but not see them or be seen.

Under other circumstances, she would have thought the setting romantic, but she knew better. She and Del were collaborating together. This was a working relationship, which she appreciated. They were both professionals. They respected each other's abilities. If she found him handsome and appealing, well, that was nice, but not helpful. Or useful. Friendship was much better. Or at the very least, safer.

She returned to the kitchen for the bottle of red

wine they'd purchased, along with the deli potato salad. She collected two glasses and went back out just as Del called that the steaks were done.

They met at the table and each took a chair. He used the jumbo tongs to put her steak on her plate while she poured wine. Music drifted out from one of the cabins, and down by the water, several children shrieked and laughed.

"There's a lot of humanity around here," she said as she passed him the green salad.

"I like it. Being around kids is fun. They always have the most interesting questions and so much curiosity about what life is like everywhere. That's what I got asked the most when I traveled. Is America really like the movies?" He grinned. "That and if Wolverine was real."

"What did you say?"

"That he was one of the good guys."

She laughed. "I didn't know the two of you were close."

"I don't like to talk about it."

"Fool's Gold must seem so small," she murmured, and cut into her steak. "How do you stand being away from your bromance?"

"He texts me all the time. Sometimes it gets annoying."

She nodded. "I can imagine. Speaking of famous people, have you seen your dad?"

"Killjoy."

"Should I take that as a yes?"

Del leaned back in his chair. "I stopped by the

house and saw both my parents. My father wanted to talk about Nick wasting his talent."

Maya remembered how Ceallach had always preferred the three younger sons. The ones who took after him. "I suppose there's some comfort in consistency."

"That's the optimist in you. I prefer to think of my father as..." He reached for his glass. "No reason to go there." He sipped. "Yes, I saw my father and he seems well." He glanced at her. "Are you going to be helping my mom with the plans for my dad's party?"

"I've offered. Why?"

"Because it's a lot for her to do on her own."

"You could take care of some of it."

"I'll do my best, but you know halfway through, she'll take it all away from me and explain how she can do it better."

Maya sighed. "Yes, she will. Elaine does like to maintain control over every situation."

"So do you."

"I wish. I gave up control a long time ago. A hazard of the job. There are a million things that can go wrong on any given story and I've had to deal with them all."

"Is that why you left television?"

"Partly. I left because I was tired of beating my head against a wall that was never going to give way." She frowned. "Is that what's supposed to happen? The wall gives way? You break through. Man, I hate it when I don't think through a cliché."

He grinned at her. "Good to know you're not perfect."

"I'm far from that."

Miles, she thought. *Miles and miles.* Although being with Del was nice. More comfortable than she would have thought. He'd always been easy on the eyes, but she'd thought there might be some tension between them. Because of how things had ended.

Apparently not. Here they were, having dinner as if they were old friends. She took a bite of steak. Maybe they were. Maybe they'd both moved on enough that the past didn't matter.

"There's no Mr. Farlow?" he asked, the question unexpected.

"Uh, no. What about you?"

"No Mr. Mitchell," he said, his eyes bright with amusement.

She groaned. "You know what I mean."

"Hey, my romantic life was public knowledge."

It had been, she thought. "That kind of comes with being semifamous and then dating a beautiful figure skater," she said gently.

"Semifamous." He pressed a hand to his chest. "Way to go for the kill shot."

She rolled her eyes. "Oh, please. You know what I mean. You were known, but not a tabloid regular. Plus, you're not interested in fame."

"You sure about that?"

She studied him for a second, then nodded. "Absolutely."

He picked up his wine. "You're right. I never liked

that part of dating Hyacinth. There were choices made to put us more in the public eye. I didn't love those, either." He shrugged. "Relationships are all about compromise."

There was something in his tone. "You say that like it's not a good thing."

"Oh, it can be. Until one person needs the other to go too far."

Interesting, she thought. Not that she had a clue what it meant. She'd heard that Del and Hyacinth had broken up, then gotten back together for a short period of time before ending things a year or so back. What she didn't know was why.

There had been speculation that one or the other had cheated. She would put her money on Del staying faithful. Despite his traveling lifestyle, he was a traditionalist at heart. A one-man, one-woman kind of guy. She couldn't say for sure how she knew that, but believed it down to her bones.

"What about you?" he asked. "You had the luxury of a private life. Who do you want to trash over dinner?"

"No one," she said with a smile. "There were relationships and they didn't work out."

"Or there'd be a Mr. Farlow?"

"Exactly."

She'd dated, but had never gotten serious with anyone. Not since Del. She'd figured out the reason. She'd learned early that she couldn't trust anyone to rescue her. She was going to have to take care of herself. While that wasn't inherently a bad thing, it had kept her at an emotional distance from the men in her life. The ones who had wanted more had been frustrated by her reluctance to risk getting more involved.

Unfortunately, knowing the problem didn't seem to make it easier to solve. As long as she wasn't willing to take the chance, she would never have that elusive happily ever after ending. A part of her genuinely didn't think she had it in her to love anyone, so why try? But without trying, she would never get there. An emotional paradox.

"So what festival are you looking forward to the most, now that you're back?" Del asked.

"A tidy change of subject? Is this to ensure I don't pry into your reasons for not being married?"

"Something like that."

She laughed. "An honest man."

"I try."

She thought for a second. "I think the Book Fair is my favorite."

"An unexpected choice. I would have thought something at the holidays."

"No. The Book Fair."

Because that summer they'd spent together, Del had first told her he loved her during the Book Fair. They'd made love in her bedroom. She'd been a virgin and he couldn't have been more considerate and careful. Not to mention quiet, what with everyone else in her family sleeping on the same floor.

They'd been so young, she thought wistfully. So confident in their feelings for each other. So sure of their future. Even though she knew exactly what had happened and why, she couldn't help wishing it had been different. That *she* had been different.

Not that she regretted going to college. That had been the right choice, and Del had obviously needed to leave Fool's Gold. She'd unexpectedly provided the catalyst. But if she could take back the words, she would.

"I like the Tulip Festival best," he said.

She stared at him. "Seriously?"

"Sure. They're pretty. It's a sign of spring coming. The changing of the season."

"Tulips?"

"What? You're saying a real man doesn't like flowers?"

"I'm saying you surprise me."

"That's me. A constant mystery. Chicks dig mystery guys."

"If only you had a cool scar."

"I know. I kept hoping for some scar-inducing injury, but it never happened. I'm just that good."

She laughed, and the opportunity to discuss the past and maybe apologize was over. But she could get there, she told herself. This new version of Del might not need to hear the words, but they needed to be said.

"ACTION!"

Del looked at the camera, knowing that while he might be uncomfortable staring directly at the lens, looking somewhere else didn't translate well. His job was to engage with the viewer and that meant making eye contact.

"In Fool's Gold, you can taste wine," he said, then raised a glass of local merlot. Despite the fact that it was only a few minutes after sunrise, he pretended to take a sip. When this was done, he was so getting more coffee.

Day one of shooting had started at an ungodly hour and would go until sunset. They were starting with the tourist videos—showing all sides of the town. He and Maya had an aggressive filming schedule that would take them over much of Fool's Gold. This morning they were focused on the wineries, followed by a couple of shots in town. The afternoon, with the harshest light of the day, would be spent by the wind turbines outside of town. If the sunset was cooperative, they would end with a view of the sun setting behind the town.

"Again," Maya said. "Wait a second."

She moved from behind the camera and got one of the equipment boxes, then dragged it toward him. When he started to move to help, she held up a hand.

"Stay where you are. You're framed perfectly. I don't want to have to start over." She pushed the trunk in front of him, then stared at him. "Okay, put your left foot on the trunk, like you're doing a lunge. I want you leaning forward. The wine goes in your right hand."

He did as she asked. "This feels awkward."

"No one cares," she said as she returned to her spot behind the tripod. "It looks great. Really great. The camera loves you. Love it back."

She turned and adjusted one of the lights, then

stepped back to the camera. "Okay, leaning forward. You love the wine. You're going to have sex with Scarlett Johansson later."

He shook his head. "I'm not a big fan of Scarlett."

Maya glared at him. "Del, it's early days yet, but I can be forced into killing you. Just so we're clear."

"You're crabby."

"Yes. It would help to remember that. Wine and sex and action."

She picked up the clapperboard, changed take one to take two, then positioned it in front of the camera and snapped it shut.

"Sound speeding," she said. "And we have action." She pointed at him.

Del hesitated a second, feeling ridiculous, then obligingly thought about wine followed by sex. Only instead of the very pretty Ms. Johansson, he remembered what it had been like to kiss Maya.

Her mouth had been soft. The kind of soft that gentled a man, despite how much he wanted the woman in question. Because a mouth that soft deserved attention. Slow attention and careful nurturing.

Even though he and Maya had become lovers that summer, he'd made sure to spend a lot of time just kissing her. Because that had been its own reward. And if he'd known how rare a mouth like hers was, he would have done it even more.

"Del?"

He swore silently and pushed the memories away. "In Fool's Gold, you can taste wine."

She motioned for him to do it again.

He said the line three more times, using different inflections, sometimes smiling, sometimes not. When they were done, he glanced at the sunrise.

"We should have that over my shoulder," he said. "It would be a great shot."

She glanced to where he pointed, then shook her head. "Too much light. I can't control it with the equipment I have with me. Plus, the way the sun is angled will mean shifting the picture so the eye line will be off."

"It's a great shot," he repeated. "We should try it." When she didn't answer, he added, "I've done some shooting of my own, Maya. I know what I'm talking about."

He waited for her to say something like his amateur shoots were nothing compared to her professional experience. He had a feeling that in her position, that was what he would have been saying.

"Fine," she said at last. "We'll do it my way, then we'll do it your way. Once we're back in the studio and editing, we'll see what's what. Fair enough?"

He nodded.

They shifted the equipment so that the sun was over his shoulder, then he put his foot up on the trunk and raised his glass of wine.

"I'm thinking about coffee this time," he told her as she reached for the clapperboard. "Lots and lots of coffee."

She laughed and called for action.

MAYA WAS STILL tired when she walked into The Fox and Hound to meet Elaine for lunch. The previous day's photo shoot had gone until sunset. They'd gotten some great footage, but today she was wiped out. She was sure Del was equally tired. Posing in front of a camera didn't sound like work, but it required complete focus, not to mention a lot of standing. By the end of the day, her brain was fuzzy and her back hurting and she was sure he felt a lot of the same. Today she was playing catch-up and tomorrow would be all about the editing. She was curious to see how their shooting styles would translate onto the screen.

She wanted to say she knew her stuff would be better, but she'd been in the business long enough to know it wasn't always possible to judge. Sometimes the unexpected jumped out at the viewer. Not often, of course, but sometimes. Del could surprise her.

She smiled when she saw her friend had already been seated at a booth.

"Hi," she said as she sat across from Elaine. "How's it going?"

Before Elaine could answer, their waitress walked over. Maya studied the sixty-something woman and tried to hold in a grin. It seemed that in the past ten years, Wilma hadn't changed a bit.

She still wore her hair short, with glasses perched on her nose. She snapped gum and looked ready to take on the world.

"You're back," she said to Maya, then nodded at Elaine. "We're doing a new roast beef sandwich with a horseradish cream. The bread is from the bakery.

Trust me, order that, or you're an idiot. What would you like to drink?"

They both ordered iced tea.

"I'll give you a minute to look over the menu," Wilma said with a sigh. "Not everyone listens to me."

When she'd walked away, Maya leaned toward her friend. "I think I'm getting the roast beef sandwich."

"Me, too. How was the photo shoot yesterday?"

"Good. Long." Maya shook her head. "Your son can be stubborn. He seems to have forgotten I'm in the business. He had ideas about every location."

"Good ones?"

"We'll see when we start editing."

Elaine smiled. "I can tell by your tone, you're thinking he's made some bad choices."

"They're his to make. As I said, we'll see. Maybe he's secretly brilliant."

"If he is, he wouldn't make a secret of it. Trust me, none of my boys would."

Wilma returned with their iced teas. As Elaine ordered the sandwich, Maya noticed there were shadows under her eyes. She studied the other woman more closely and couldn't help thinking she seemed tired. No, not tired. But there was something off.

Maya waited until their waitress had given them a choice between fruit, chips or fries and then walked away. She picked up her tea, put it down, then decided to simply spit it out.

"Are you okay?" she asked, doing her best to keep her voice from sounding abrupt. "Tell me I'm crazy, but I feel like something isn't right."

Elaine's eyes widened. "Why would you say that?"

"I have no idea. Am I wrong?"

The other woman hesitated just long enough for Maya to realize she'd stumbled on the truth. Even if she didn't know what it was.

"Tell me," she said gently. "Please."

Elaine nodded. "I hadn't planned on saying anything to anyone. You weren't supposed to guess."

Normally Maya would have made a joke about being perceptive, but somehow this didn't seem like the right time.

"I need you to promise not to say a word to anyone," her friend continued. "I mean it, Maya. You have to swear."

Maya was clear on the danger of making a promise without having all the facts. Even so, she didn't hesitate. "I promise I will keep your secret for as long as you tell me to. No matter what it is."

"Thank you." Elaine gave her a shaky smile that faded quickly. "I have breast cancer. The tumor is small and was caught early, but still. Cancer."

Maya's stomach tightened as she did her best not to visibly react. Fear for her friend ripped through her. She reached across the table and grabbed Elaine's hand. "What? No. I'm so sorry. What can I do to help? How can I make this better?"

"By keeping my secret."

Maya drew in a breath. "You're not telling Ceallach?" she asked in a whisper.

"No. Or the boys. I don't want them to know. They won't take it well. You know they won't. The last thing I need right now is to be making them feel better. I just want to get through it."

Maya nodded, even if she didn't agree with the decision. Elaine would need support from more than her. She was dealing with a scary diagnosis and the treatment that would follow.

Elaine explained how her routine mammogram had detected a small mass. It had been biopsied and she'd gotten the diagnosis. She paused as Wilma returned with their lunches.

"Eat up," the older woman instructed before leaving.

Maya stared at her sandwich and knew she would have to take it home.

"We have to eat," Elaine told her. "Not only because Wilma will yell at us if we don't, but because not eating won't help me. We're both going to need our strength."

"Okay." Maya reluctantly took a bite. "So what's the treatment plan?"

"A lumpectomy followed by six weeks of radiation."

"You have to tell them," Maya said quietly. "They need to know."

"They don't. Maya, I appreciate what you're saying, but this is my decision. I'm going to get through this, then I'll deal with my family." Her dark eyes narrowed. "You gave me your word."

"I know, and I'll keep it." Even though she knew her friend was wrong. Ceallach and her sons would want to know. They would want to be there for her.

"I've rented a studio apartment in the same building as Morgan's Bookstore," Elaine told her. "A place to go rest after my radiation. I've heard the treatment can make me tired. I can get myself back and forth to the clinic or whatever it's called for that, but I will need help after the lumpectomy."

Maya forced herself to chew the bite she'd taken, but the sandwich had no flavor and she knew she wouldn't be able to get down much more.

"Of course. What can I do?"

"Drive me there, then bring me back to your place. I'd like to stay the night."

Because she would have had surgery, Maya thought. "Can you schedule for a Friday morning? We can say we're having a girls' weekend. You won't have to go home until Sunday. By then you should be feeling better."

Elaine gave her a grateful smile. "Thank you. They said the lumpectomy shouldn't take long."

"However long it takes, I'll be there."

Maya was more than happy to take care of her friend, but she now regretted the promise to keep the secret. Elaine was making a mistake. But as of now, it didn't seem as if she could be talked out of it.

CHAPTER FIVE

DEL STUDIED THE screen in front of him. "You were right," he said flatly. "The sunrise doesn't work at all."

Maya barely glanced up. "There's too much light and it's in the wrong place. It was impossible to make the shot and keep you in the center. So it feels off."

He saw she had identified the problem. While he hadn't been able to define what was wrong, he'd sensed it. Now he was able to see how he wasn't in the middle of the screen. Although he was supposed to be the focus, he was off to the side, with the sun making a glaring appearance.

He waited a second, then said, "Are you going to say 'I told you so'?"

She continued to stare at the monitor in front of her. "You said it for me." She finally looked at him. "It's okay, Del. I do this for a living. The show I worked on was small enough that I had to handle more than just producing the segments. I edited, I wrote copy and sometimes I worked the camera."

"Meaning I should shut up and keep out of your way?"

"No." She gave him a faint smile. "Meaning there's

more to producing good material than simply pointing a camera and pushing a button. Look at this."

She typed on the keyboard and brought up more
of his footage, then started it running. There wasn't
any sound, but he remembered the shot. It was taken
up by the wind turbines.

He was walking through the frame, pointing and
talking. Everything was in focus, but he knew instinctively something was off.

"It's the eye line," she told him, using her pen to
point at the screen. "As a rule, the screen in divided
into thirds, horizontally. The subject's eye should
be even with this line." She drew an imaginary line
across the screen. "You're too low in the shot. There's
nothing in the eye line. Not you, not the wind turbines."

She typed again and brought up her footage of the
same scene. The camera focused on him and this time
his face was right where she said it should be. As he
watched, the camera panned, bringing the wind turbines into view. Then the center of the blades was in
the eye line.

"Just like that," he said and shook his head.

"There's some other stuff," she told him. "You
changed the camera settings at the same scene. You
shot half your material in SD and half in HD. While
we can bring HD down to SD, there's no way to take
it up. Because some of this material may become a
TV commercial, we have to shoot in HD. It would be
different if we were just going to put it on a website."

High definition instead of standard definition, he

thought, remembering that he'd wanted to confirm the settings, but must have changed them instead.

"Why didn't you say something?" he asked.

She turned to him. They were sitting close. Close enough for him to be aware of the curve of her cheek and the shape of her mouth. Dark lashes framed big, green eyes.

Need started slowly, almost in the background. It was more of a whisper, a hint, one that grew over time. He thought about how her skin would feel against his fingers if he touched her. Of the way her lips fit against his. If he took her in his arms, would she be as he remembered, or were there changes?

He would have thought he would be pissed at her, or disinterested. He was neither. Being around Maya was easy. She challenged him. They got along. The wanting might be a problem, but he was a big boy. He could keep himself under control.

"You were determined," she said, drawing him back to the conversation. "I figured it was easier to let you do what you wanted and see what happened. Maybe you were naturally gifted."

He laughed. "You're saying I'm not?"

"I'm saying what I said before. It's harder than it looks."

She turned back to the screen and pulled up her footage. He watched her edit the few seconds of video. She then played as much of the clip as she had finished.

"Nice," he told her when it was done. "Mayor Marsha is going to be happy."

"I hope so."

He glanced at Maya. "You okay?"

She stiffened, then relaxed. "Sure. Why?"

"I don't know." Something was off. He couldn't figure out what, though. Women were mysterious that way. "You feeling all right?"

She smiled at him. "I'm completely fine. Now let me get back to work. Taking pictures is sometimes the easy part of the job."

"Pretend I'm not here," he said, leaning back in his chair and watching her do her thing.

She was good, he thought. Better than good.

For a second he debated telling her about his project. The one he wanted to be his next act, only he hadn't been able to make it work. Looking at her raw footage, he knew that he'd been the problem. Could what he had be fixed?

He studied Maya's profile, then looked at her rapidly manipulating the mouse. He had a feeling that if his project could be saved, she was the one to do it, then he shook his head. No, he told himself. He liked Maya. He respected her, but there was no way he was willing to trust her with something like that.

After a couple of minutes, she glanced at him. "Are you just going to sit there, staring, watching me work?"

"Pretty much."

She smiled. "I don't think so. I mean this in the nicest possible way, but get out."

"Just like that?"

"Uh-huh."

Del stood and stretched. "You'll miss me when I'm gone."

Something flashed in her eyes. An emotion that was gone so quickly, he wasn't able to read it. Had she missed him? Before? When she'd ended things so abruptly? Had she regretted her decision to end their relationship?

Not that it mattered, he told himself. The past was firmly in the past. He didn't believe in going home, all evidence to the contrary. Because he wasn't back for more than his father's birthday. Over the past ten years he'd learned a lot of things. And one of the most important was that he didn't go back. Not ever.

AFTER MAYA KICKED him out, Del wandered around Fool's Gold. Somehow he found himself heading for the Mitchell Adventure Tour offices. Despite the small size of the town, he hadn't run into Aidan since he'd been back.

As he crossed the street, he wondered when Aidan had changed the name—adding the word *adventure*. And when their mother had left the business. Assuming she had. Del supposed his mom could be handling the behind-the-scenes stuff or the bookkeeping.

As he approached the brightly colored storefront, he saw his brother step onto the street. He was with a tall brunette in cutoffs and a tank top. The woman—pretty, tanned and obviously a tourist—gave Aidan a brief kiss on the mouth, then murmured something in his ear. She waved and walked away.

"Is that how it is?" Del said as he approached. "You're preying on innocent tourists now?"

Aidan turned and saw him. Instead of responding with humor, his brother simply watched him get closer. When Del stopped in front of him, there was an awkward moment of silence. At least Del found it awkward.

"So, uh, how's it going?" he asked.

"Good."

Aidan was his height—just over six feet—with the same dark hair and eyes. Growing up a Mitchell brother had been pretty easy in this town. They were all dark-haired and dark-eyed. All five brothers were good-looking enough and athletic enough to fit in. Sports came easy, schoolwork hadn't been that hard. Del and Aidan didn't have Ceallach's brilliance, but most days Del figured that was more of a blessing than a curse.

"Got time for a coffee?" Del asked his brother.

"Sure."

Aidan turned and they started walking toward Brew-haha.

"Who was the girl?" Del asked.

"Santana."

"That's her name? Santana?"

"Uh-huh. She's in town for a couple of weeks."

Del grinned. "So you *are* dogging the tourists."

"I offer a short-term good time. Guaranteed happy memories and no one gets hurt. What's wrong with that?"

"Sort of a full-service vacation?"

Aidan's mouth twitched. "Something like that."

Del understood the appeal. There would always be someone new on the horizon, there was no commitment and when it was over, geography kept things from getting messy. Funny how it was exactly what Hyacinth had liked in a relationship. Because to be with the same person all the time would be boring, right?

Familiar anger knotted at the base of his spine and started to radiate outward. He breathed through the sensations. Hyacinth was the past. He was never going to have to deal with her again.

"Business looks good," Del said. "I like what you've done with the building. It's eye-catching."

Aidan came to stop on the sidewalk. They were a couple of blocks off the main streets on a weekday and there weren't many people around. Aidan glared at Del.

"You can't help it, right? You always have to crack a comment. What is it with you? You're back for Dad's birthday. Yay, you. But if you're looking for something from me, you can forget it. I'm not going to be lining up to watch your 'hail the conquering hero' parade."

Del couldn't have been more surprised if Sophie, his mother's beloved beagle, had suddenly turned into a vampire.

"What the hell are you talking about?" he demanded. "I said it looks like you're doing well. What are you going on about?"

Aidan's stare darkened as anger and hostility radiated from him. "You don't get to approve. You have no part of the business, of what I've done with it. You gave up that right when you disappeared."

Del didn't know whether to punch his brother or walk away. "I'll say it again, what the hell are you talking about?"

"You. The business. All of it. It's been ten years, Del. Ten damn years since you left. You were up and away, leaving me with everything. There was no warning. One day you were handling things and the next you were gone. I was a kid and you dumped it on me without a word. I was in my first year of college. I had things I wanted, dreams. But when you bugged out, it all fell on me. I had to take care of Mom and the family. I had to make sure there was food on the table when Dad went on one of his benders."

Aidan took a menacing step forward. "That first year, you never called, you selfish SOB. You never bothered to find out if we were okay. You were my big brother. I trusted you. And you turned out to be as much of an asshole as Dad."

Del took the verbal hits without saying anything in return. He didn't bother to point out he'd only been a year older than Aidan, and running the family business hadn't been his choice, either. Because that didn't matter. He'd disappeared without warning—reacting to his breakup with Maya.

"Aidan," he began, then paused.

His brother turned away. "Don't bother," Aidan said. "You go be famous. I have a business to run."

MAYA WAS UP at sunrise, anxiously watching the sky. The forecast called for cloudy skies—perfect for filming. The diffused light was much easier to work with. She'd told Del that on their first overcast day, she wanted to shoot the big opener, with him introducing the town. Since then, she'd been monitoring the weather reports.

Now she looked at the thick clouds and absence of sun. *Perfection*, she thought happily. She texted Del, confirming the time and place of their shoot, then headed for the shower.

Nearly two hours later, she was carting equipment from the parking lot off the edge of the highway to a meadow a couple hundred yards away. She'd scouted out the area the previous week and had hoped to use it for the intro. She had a feeling that handsome Del was going to look good in a field of wildflowers, backed by trees.

She'd told him to wear jeans and a faded light blue shirt. She hoped he was the kind of talent who listened.

She set up two cameras along with her lights. She and Del had already gone over the script, and she'd blocked out the shoot. If all went well, they would be done before the brightest part of the day. If not, they would have to take a break and return later in the afternoon. Unless the sun came out.

But while the complications might have given someone else fits, Maya was perfectly happy with the uncertainty. This was way better than worrying about which star had cheated on his or her significant other. Back in LA her life had been defined by gossip and celebrity sightings. While this wasn't curing a disease, at least it would bring some good to the town.

Thinking of the town had her mind drifting to Elaine. The cancer news was still a bombshell. She'd checked in with her friend a couple of times, and so far the other woman sounded okay. She had a diagnosis and a plan. According to her doctor, the prognosis was good. Maya would take care of her friend as best she could, although she still strongly disagreed with Elaine's decision to keep the information a secret from her family.

A problem for another time, she told herself, and returned to setting up equipment.

Right on time, Del walked into the meadow. He headed for her.

"What the hell?" His gaze was sharp. "Why didn't you tell me to get here earlier? I thought I'd be here to help with the setup. You carted all this yourself? That's ridiculous. I'm not some actor you've hired. Jeez, Maya. Give a guy a break. I could have helped you with unloading."

He was really pissed, she thought, staring at him. He might even have a point. It was kind of hard to know for sure, because she couldn't really think.

He'd shaved. Gone was the three-day growth that looked so good on him. Now his skin was smooth, his features clearly defined. The look suited him, even if it might be hell on the video continuity.

Stubble Del was dangerous and maybe a little wicked. Clean-shaven Del was more like the guy she remembered. He seemed a bit younger and more approachable, but just as sexy.

Her gaze settled on his mouth as she wondered how the two Dels would be different in the kissing department. Would the stubble scratch or just be delightfully abrasive? Would the smoothness be more or less appealing? Was it wrong to want to find out?

Instinctively she glanced at the camera and saw he was perfectly framed. She pushed the button to get a test shot.

"Maya?"

His impatient voice snapped her back to the present.

"What? Oh." She released the camera already sitting on the tripod. "It never crossed my mind."

"Asking me to help? Do you really think I'm that much of a jerk?" He swore. "When did I become the bad guy?"

"No, you're not. I'm just used to handling this sort of thing on my own. It comes with my job." She studied him. "Del, why are you mad about this?"

He waved to the setup. "This says you think I'm showing up to do my part and nothing else."

She crossed to him. He'd dressed as she'd requested, and the faded blue shirt looked as good as she'd hoped. The color was perfect on him, and the camera was going to have a mini meltdown from all the sex appeal. Worse, the camera might not be alone in its reaction.

But first, she had to figure out what was going

on. She stopped directly in front of him and put her hands on her hips.

"I don't think so," she said quietly. "You're not mad at me. You're right. I should have mentioned when I was getting here. I genuinely didn't think about it. Next time I'll offer to let you fetch and carry. I promise. So tell me what happened?"

She knew he hadn't found out about his mother. That would have scared him, not made him furious.

He ran his hand through his hair, rumpling it delightfully. She so was not going to comb it back into place before filming.

Del sighed. "You're right. This is only part of what's wrong."

She lowered her arms to her side and waited for him to continue.

He sucked in a breath. "It's Aidan. He's pissed. Seriously pissed."

"At you?"

He nodded. "For leaving ten years ago. I honest to God never thought about it from his perspective, but he's right. I took off and all of it got dumped on him. The business, the family. There was no warning. He got stuck because I took off."

"And you got stuck before him."

He shook his head. "No, I didn't."

"You did. You grew up knowing you had to take care of everything. You had to be there for your mom and your brothers. No one asked you if that was what you wanted. There wasn't a discussion."

"Why are you taking my side?"

She gave him a slight smile. "You're the Mitchell brother I like best. You know I'm right. You were expected to take care of everything. What if you wanted something different? No one asked."

"And I took off, leaving Aidan to pick up the pieces." He swore again. "I'm a selfish bastard."

Something prickled her skin. While the attraction was still there, she had a feeling that wasn't the cause. It took her a second to recognize what it was. Guilt.

"It's not your fault," she told him, wondering how much he was going to hate her when he realized the truth. "It's mine."

"How do you figure?"

"I'm the reason you left."

His dark gaze settled on her face. "I wondered if we'd get to that."

"We had to," she whispered. "It was inevitable."

One corner of his mouth turned up. "I'd love to dump this on you, but I was a big boy. I made my choices."

"No, you reacted to mine. To me breaking up with you." She reached for him and rested her fingers on his forearm. "Del, I promised to marry you. We were going to run off together."

"Yeah. So either way I was leaving. Why didn't I see that before?"

She shook his arm. "That's not the point. I'm trying to apologize here. If you could listen?"

"No apology required. You changed your mind. You're allowed. I wish you'd been honest with me—

You could have told me you had concerns. But you didn't. It's not like I was the love of your life."

She listened for bitterness and heard only resignation. Which made her feel awful. Why did he have to be so accepting? Anger and resentment would be a lot easier to deal with.

So here it was. Her moment to come clean.

"I'm sorry," she told him. "About what happened. About what I said. I know it's too late and that hearing it now doesn't change anything, but I want you to know, I lied."

His gaze sharpened. "About?"

She glanced down at the wild grass and flowers below, then forced herself to stare directly into his dark eyes. "I didn't have concerns. Not the way you think. It was… I was terrified. I loved you more than I ever thought I could love anyone. You were my entire world. But I couldn't trust you."

He started to pull back, but she held on to his arm. "It's not personal," she told him. "Watching my mom and how she was with men. The things she said. I was so afraid that no one could love me. At the same time I believed you did, and that was more than I could handle. I guess the truth isn't that I didn't trust you, I didn't trust myself."

She dropped his arm and wanted to turn away. But this apology had been ten years in the making. She had to see it through to the end.

"You were my first love and my first time and when you asked me to marry you, I was thrilled. And so frightened. What if it didn't work out? I knew having you leave would destroy me. Plus, I wanted to go to college and have a career. What if I asked for that and you said no? So in my eighteen-year-old logic, I decided I had to end things in such a way that you wouldn't try to talk me into staying."

She swallowed against the emotion tightening her throat. "That's why I said you were too boring. To hurt you and make you hate me. It was never true. I loved you and wanted to be with you. But I didn't know how. I'm sorry. I was cruel and I regretted what I did immediately. I knew the outcome was right, but how I did it was horrible. And I apologize for that."

Del's expression tightened. She braced herself for the well-deserved explosion, only there wasn't one. He reached out and gently stroked her face.

"Well, damn," he said softly. "I wouldn't have thought it would matter to hear that, but it does. I get it. What we had was intense."

"That's one word for it."

He smiled. "You were my first time, too."

Her eyes widened. "What? No way. There were other girls."

"Not like you. Not like that. I was shaking, Maya. Couldn't you tell?"

"I was too nervous. What if I was horrible in bed?"

"Not possible." The smile returned. "I came in eight seconds."

She laughed. "I was a virgin. I didn't know any better. Besides, you made up for it later. Over and over again."

"To be that young again."

Their tones were light, but she was feeling a lot of subtext. Maybe it was just her, but it seemed the cloudy morning had just gotten a little warmer. Del seemed to be standing close. Closer than he had been.

Danger signs flashed, but she ignored them all. Because this was Del, and maybe a girl was always supposed to have a special place in her heart for that first guy.

"I did love you," she told him. "I hope you know that."

"I loved you, too." The sexy smile returned. "Talk about a lot of confessions for a very early-morning shoot."

With that, he stepped in and kissed her.

Maya had about two seconds to brace herself, but instead of retreating, she leaned in. Maybe it was closure, she thought, as his mouth brushed against hers. Maybe it was simply something that had to happen so they could move on. Maybe it was the perfect light of a cloudy morning.

His lips were warm and soft with a hint of firmness. The kiss was exactly right. Not too demanding, not too sweet. There was a dash of heat and plenty of promise.

She put one hand on his shoulder. He rested his fingers on her waist. There was no reaching, no tongue. Just the perfect, wonderful *I used to love you* kiss.

They drew back at the same moment and stared into each other's eyes.

Wanting was there, along with regret, she thought. But also a sense of rightness.

"I take it that means you accept my apology," she said.

He chuckled. "Sure. Because I'm one of the good guys."

"Ready to get back to work?"

He nodded.

She retreated to behind the camera. The red light was on, which meant she'd recorded the whole kiss. Talk about incriminating evidence.

She reached for the delete button, then reset the camera to record what they were here to do. She had enough memory to get through the shoot. She would deal with the wayward clip later.

CHAPTER SIX

THE COUPLE SITTING in front of Del had to be the oldest people he'd ever seen. Albert was ninety-five and his wife, Elizabeth, was ninety-two. They'd been married seventy-six years. Together they looked like those apple dolls, with wrinkled faces and tiny raisin eyes. They were small, bent and walked so slowly, Del wondered how they ever got anywhere. But despite their outward infirmities, they were both still mentally sharp and verbally outspoken.

Del sat on their front porch on the warm afternoon. The overhang provided enough shade for Maya's liking. The C stands for the 3-point lighting she favored barely fit on the porch, but it softened the faces of the older couple.

He and Maya had already discussed the best way to handle the interview. They'd agreed that the technology might be intimidating and distracting. So they'd decided to simply do a two-camera setup and get what they could in a single long shot.

"Tell me what it's like to be married for seventy-six years," Del prompted.

Albert shook his head. "I know what you really

want to know, sonny. Do we do it? You know what? We do. So put that in your pipe and smoke it."

Elizabeth sighed. "Albert, he's our guest. Be polite."

"We do it," Albert repeated. "A little slower because of our bones, but the deed gets done."

Del held in laughter. He remembered he was on camera and kept his attention on the older couple. "Thanks for the inspiration," he replied. "What's the secret to a long, successful marriage?"

Elizabeth looked at him. "What makes you think our marriage is successful?"

"You haven't killed him yet."

She laughed. "You're right. I haven't."

"She's threatened to plenty of times," Albert said. "But I knew she didn't mean it."

They sat next to each other on a padded bench. Their hands were clasped loosely together, fingers laced. Del wondered how many hours of their lives had been spent holding hands. Could it be measured in weeks? Months?

"Don't take love for granted," Elizabeth said. "Don't assume he's annoying you on purpose."

"Talk a walk," Albert added. "Clear your head. And don't always have to be right."

Although they were here to talk about romantic relationships, the last comment made him think about Aidan. Del wasn't trying to be right, but he also wasn't sure he'd been listening. While Aidan's outburst had seemed to come from nowhere, he knew he'd heard the complaints in one form or another over the years.

They wrapped up the interview. Del thanked the couple for letting him speak to them, then he helped Maya load up the equipment. By noon they were heading back to Fool's Gold. He'd driven his truck up the mountain and now she relaxed in the passenger seat.

"They were impressive," she said, leaning back against the headrest, her eyes closed. "Married for seventy-six years. How did they do that?"

"They married young."

"It was probably considered normal, back then. Today everyone wants a career first." She opened her eyes and looked at him. "Female economic success is changing the social structure of our country."

He grinned. "I heard that, and no."

"What?"

"There was a challenge in your voice. As if you expected me to step into your trap. I'm not getting involved in a discussion about equal rights for women with you, Maya. I still have another interview to do, and I'm not showing up bruised and bloodied."

She laughed. "As long as you admit I'd best you."

"You'd hold your own."

She relaxed against the seat again. "I'd win."

She probably would, but he wasn't going to admit that. Maya was tough when she had to be. Meticulous when it came to her work. Although it was the town's win that she hadn't gotten the network job, he thought whoever had made the decision not to hire her had been an idiot. She was obviously brilliant and a hard worker.

There was a lot about her he liked and admired. Which meant even as a kid, he'd had good taste. Because it was all about him.

He smiled as he drove, thinking that while his relationship with his family was totally screwed up, hanging out with Maya was turning into one of the best parts of coming home. They'd cleared the air between them. That was good.

Things could have been awkward after that kiss, but they weren't. They'd said what needed to be said and now they could move on. The fact that he wanted more than a chaste kiss was his problem and not something he would share with her.

But ever since his mouth had touched hers, he'd been unable to forget the heat of her, the sound of her breathing. He wanted to do it again, only this time kiss her deeply. He wanted to taste her, to touch her. He wanted to make love with her until they were both satisfied.

Not going to happen, he reminded himself. Because they were friends now. Nothing more.

MAYA LOOKED THROUGH the camera lens at the couple seated at a bench. Del had suggested the location for their second interview of the day and she had to admit it looked good. From the various props they'd dragged along in the back of his truck they'd pulled out an old chair for Del to sit in. He looked delightfully masculine on the small seat supported by spindly legs.

He was obviously older than the teenagers he was interviewing, but in the best way possible. *Talk about appealing*, she thought, her mind trying to drift back to their brief kiss. She had to remind herself she was here to do a job and not daydream about her close encounter with a yummy man's mouth.

"Okay, let's start," she said. "You two ready?"

Melissa, a pretty redhead, leaned into her boyfriend. "Are you ready?"

"I was born ready."

The young couple looked good together. Percy had medium brown skin and short, dark hair. His broad shoulders contrasted with Melissa's more delicate build. They were obviously comfortable with each other, which was part of their appeal. Sometimes when she looked at a couple she had the feeling there was nothing beyond the sexual tension. But with Percy and Melissa, she had the sense they really got along.

"How did you meet?" Del asked.

"He came up and talked to me at a festival," Melissa said with a laugh. "It was last summer. I was home from college. Here was this skinny boy who thought he was all that."

Percy looked at her. "I wasn't a boy."

"You're younger than me."

"Only in years, babe. Only in years."

They stared at each other for a second. There was a flash of silent communication, of something significant shared. The moment was so personal, Maya felt she should look away, but knew that didn't matter. The camera would capture the glance and turn it into viewing gold.

Two hours later, they completed the interview. The young couple had explained how they met and that they both believed that without the magic that was Fool's Gold, they never would have fallen in love. While Melissa was going away to college, Percy had stayed in Fool's Gold to get his GED. He was now registered in community college. Despite the distance, they'd stayed close.

They were charming, articulate, sensible and completely in love.

"They were perfect," Maya said with a sigh as she and Del packed up after the interview. "I really liked them. They know what they want and they're making it happen. I'm about a decade older and not nearly that together. It's intimidating."

"You're doing just fine," Del told her.

"I wish, but no. Did you see how they looked at each other?"

"Yeah. They're in it for the long haul."

"So in seventy-five years, they'll be Elizabeth and Albert, out in the woods."

He grinned as he closed the truck gate. "I don't see those two living out in the wilderness, but otherwise, they'll be the same."

His gaze lingered on her and she wondered what he was thinking. That if they'd stayed together, they could have been the little old couple?

She wanted to say yes, but she wasn't sure. As a teenager, she hadn't been willing to trust Del. Lessons learned early were difficult to overcome. Maya had grown up with the sense of being in the way. Of never being loved or even vaguely important to anyone. She'd vowed she would never wait to be rescued, that she would take care of herself. A promise that made it difficult to give her heart to a young man she'd known for two months.

"They're going to be a great segment," she said.

"I agree."

He walked around to the passenger side of the truck and held open the door. When she went to step inside, he placed his hand on her arm.

"It's okay that we didn't make it."

The unexpected comment caught her by surprise. She felt a quick jab of pain. Or maybe just loss. "I never gave us a chance. We can't know what would have happened, although I have to admit, I don't think our odds were great."

"Because you didn't love me enough?"

"No. You were never the problem. It was me. Until I moved to Fool's Gold, I'd never seen a successful marriage. Except for the ones on TV and those weren't real."

He shook his head. "I don't understand. What do you mean?"

Of course he would have questions, she thought. Because as a teenager, she'd never told anyone the truth. Being honest came at too high a price. So she'd glossed over the ugly details, mentioning only that her dad was gone and her mother enjoyed having a kid.

"My dad took off before I was born. My mom had

a string of boyfriends, but none of them lasted. She didn't have girlfriends she hung out with." Her mouth twisted. "I had friends at school, but I wasn't exactly the girl you invited home for a sleepover. I think I made the other parents nervous. So I didn't get to see what normal was like until we moved here."

She squared her shoulders as she spoke, prepared to defend herself if necessary. Because you never knew.

Instead of speaking, Del pulled her close for a brief hug. When he released her, he said lightly, "So you're lucky I came along, huh? Learn from the best."

She groaned. "You have such an ego."

He winked. "Is that what we're calling it? And thank you."

As quickly as that, equilibrium was restored. *An impressive gift*, she thought as she climbed into the passenger seat and he shut her door. Just one of many.

Two DAYS LATER Maya sat at a big table at Jo's Bar, enjoying lunch with the girls. She couldn't remember the last time she'd done anything like this. Sure, she and Phoebe ate lunch or dinner together. But that was just the two of them. In her world, Maya hadn't had much in the way of group girlfriend plans.

As she listened to the easy conversation going around the table, she wondered why that was. She supposed that a lot of her friends back in Los Angeles had also been competitors. No one had time for get-togethers. Or a willingness to get too friendly with someone who could steal your job. Or maybe it was a Fool's Gold thing.

There were seven of them around the table today. Madeline, a pretty blonde who was part-owner of Paper Moon—the local bridal gown boutique. Destiny, a recent transplant and songwriter, Bailey, the mayor's assistant, Patience, the owner of Brew-haha and someone Maya remembered from when she'd been a teenager, Phoebe, and Dellina, Phoebe's wedding planner and another local.

"I swear it was him," Madeline was saying. "In the flesh. I thought I was going to die."

"You sound like you're fifteen," Patience told her with a grin. "I said that with love, not judgment. Jonny Blaze, here in town? There's going to be a lot of swooning."

"He's *so* good-looking," Madeline told them. "And that body. Those muscles are real."

"You want to trace every inch of them?" Maya asked, reaching for a chip from the large platter of nachos that had been delivered.

"Twice!"

Everyone laughed.

Phoebe smiled at Madeline. "He's very nice. Single, I think. Want me to introduce you?"

Madeline shook her head. "That would ruin the fantasy. What if he's not as great as I think he is?"

"What if he's better?" Maya asked.

"Is that likely? I don't think so."

Everyone laughed.

Conversation flowed easily. Maya watched Phoebe

chat with the other women and liked the changes she saw in her friend. Gone was the tension. Instead, her friend was relaxed and happy. Fool's Gold looked good on her. Or maybe it was being in love with Zane. Because love sure brought a glow to Phoebe.

Had she looked like that back when Del had been her world? Maya hoped so. Although she'd been terrified, she'd loved him as much as she'd been able. Certainly more than she'd ever loved another man.

Working with him now was nice, she thought. Easier than she would have guessed. He was a good guy. Funny, charming, a fantastic kisser.

Thinking about their kiss made her smile. If she couldn't forget that chaste lip encounter, then she should be grateful he hadn't taken things further. Had they done more, she would be so distracted she wouldn't be able to get anything done.

It wasn't him, she told herself firmly. She'd just been too long without a good kissing. As soon as she got her act together and found a boyfriend, she would be fine. Or so she hoped. Because it would be foolish to still have a thing for Del. He was so over her as to practically think of her as his little sister. At least that was how he acted. Which was a good thing, right?

She shook off Del thoughts and turned her attention back to the lunch conversation.

"…super busy," Dellina was saying. "We are a town that likes to party."

"Which makes you the person to call," Phoebe told her. "I'm glad I was able to get you while you still had time."

"Me, too," Dellina told her with a smile. "Weddings are my favorite."

"Do you have many this fall?" Maya asked.

"No more than usual, but I sure have a ton going on over the holidays. The Hendrix family is planning a Christmas reunion blowout that is getting more complicated by the day. Score is being their usual PR selves and hosting a huge customer event in mid-December."

Patience laughed. "Ask your handsome husband to help with that one."

"Believe me, I will."

"When do you get to celebrate the holidays?" Maya asked. "It must be tough with so much going on."

"It is," Dellina admitted. "Sam and I are going somewhere warm and beachy in mid-November. Before the madness strikes. No cell phones, no internet. I can't wait."

Madeline sighed. "Sounds heavenly."

Maya leaned toward her. "What are the odds that you're picturing Jonny Blaze on a beach right this second?"

Madeline raised her eyebrows. "Excellent, in fact. The man moves me. It makes me shallow, but I can live with the flaw."

"I really can introduce you," Phoebe said. "I think Jonny needs a nice girlfriend in his life. He doesn't date much."

Patience grinned. "I'm not sure Madeline is interested in dating him."

Destiny turned to Maya. "I heard you used to live here. Back in high school. Is that right?"

"Uh-huh. For a couple of years. My mom and I moved here from Las Vegas. There was some culture shock for sure."

"I would guess. Are you enjoying being back?"

"Very much. I like the small town vibe."

"Me, too. I'm a recent transplant. There's something about this town."

Patience leaned toward Maya. "I heard that Eddie and Gladys can't do their butt contest anymore. Please say that isn't true. I love the butt contest."

"Don't tell them you love it," Maya muttered. "I'm trying to get them under control."

"Good luck with that," Dellina told her.

"I love them, too," Phoebe admitted. "They're so adventurous. Remember how great they were on the cattle drive? They weren't afraid of anything."

"You say that like it's a good thing," Maya told her, then sighed. She had a feeling there was no winning on the Eddie-Gladys front. They were like bad weather. Easier to hunker down and endure than try to fight the inevitable.

"Oh, I heard you're going to help out with the Saplings," Patience said. "That's so great."

It took Maya a second to figure out what the other woman was talking about. Because she had no plans to help with trees.

"You mean the little girls in the Future Warriors of the Máa-zib?" Maya asked. "Yes, I was asked to give a talk on how to use a camera."

Patience smiled. "I know. My daughter is a Sapling now and you'll be talking to her grove. The first year they start out as Acorns. The second year they're Sprouts, then Saplings and so on. We're all excited about the afternoon. It'll be fun."

"I hope so," Maya murmured, thinking she wasn't sure she was qualified to teach several eight-year-olds how to do anything, but she would do her best.

DEL STUDIED THE two paths that cut through the forest. The one on the left headed straight up the hillside and looked a lot less used. As he wasn't looking for company, he picked that one.

The afternoon was clear and warm. Although it was still technically summer, he'd seen more than a few leaves had started to turn. In a month or two the whole mountainside would be red and gold with changing leaves. A beautiful sight he wouldn't be around to see.

While he was glad he'd decided to come home to see his family he couldn't say he would be sorry to leave. He was already feeling restless. There was a whole world out there and he needed to be in it. The only question was what to do with himself when he got there.

Even as he turned over possibilities, he found himself feeling he should talk to Maya. She would have a sensible solution. Or if not, she would be willing to brainstorm with him. She was smart, with enough creativity to keep her interesting.

Thinking about Maya meant remembering their

last conversation. When she'd admitted never seeing a successful romantic relationship until moving to town.

He'd grown up with parents who were embarrassingly in love with each other. Even when he hadn't understood why his mother put up with his father's drinking and moodiness, he'd never questioned her devotion to him or Ceallach's to his wife. They were a single unit made up of two halves. Like a coin. Without one, there couldn't be the other.

He might not be interested in a traditional relationship for himself, but—

Del circled around a tree and paused to grab his water bottle. There was no point in lying to himself. He *did* want something traditional. Maybe not exactly what his parents had—he wanted a relationship of equals—but still, the together forever appealed.

He supposed in his and Maya's case, they'd both been too young. She'd been dealing with things he couldn't possibly have understood. She'd reacted to her feelings and he'd been caught in the fallout. With Hyacinth, well, he'd chosen badly there.

Which left him with a problem. He knew he wasn't the kind of man who would be comfortable in one place for very long. He wouldn't mind a home base, as long as he didn't have to spend much time there. But how was he supposed to find someone who shared that dream with him? Hell, he couldn't even figure out what to do with his life, let alone find his damn soul mate.

He dropped the water bottle into his backpack and

continued up the trail. The path was rocky and steep, just challenging enough to be interesting. The hike might take longer than he'd planned, but he had plenty of time. Not to mention GPS so he wouldn't get lost. One of the advantages of the new search-and-rescue program was cell towers all over the mountains. With a smartphone even the most tenderfooted of tourists should manage to find his or her way back to civilization.

Or not, he thought humorously, considering how many search-and-rescue calls there had been this summer.

He wondered if he and Maya should talk about interviewing the search-and-rescue people for their videos. Although maybe talking about getting lost wasn't good for tourism. He knew Maya would get the humor of it, though. She always did.

He thought about what she'd told him. Although he believed her, he had trouble imagining what it must have been like never to have seen two adults in a happy relationship. No wonder she hadn't been able to deal with the two of them falling in love. Her past also explained her close relationship with his mother.

After he and Maya had broken up, he'd thought it was strange that she stayed in touch with Elaine. Now he knew it had something to do with her upbringing. Elaine would have provided stability and caring—two things Maya would have needed. She would have been the nurturing mother Maya had never had.

Maya could have told him the truth, he thought. Been honest. He would have understood. But she'd held back and they'd never had a chance. Ironic that the first woman he fell for kept just as many secrets as his family did. Was there anybody out there who told the truth? Although he supposed he was being hard on Maya. She'd been a kid and scared.

How would things have been different if he'd known she was afraid? If he'd been able to see her breakup as fear talking rather than her heart? Would he have been able to explain that to her? Would she have listened? Told him what she was thinking and feeling? And to what end? Could they have made it, like the old people on the mountain?

Questions that would never have an answer, he told himself. What was done was done.

He continued to head up the mountain. About a half hour later, he paused as he heard an unusual sound. It was man-made. A chain saw? Del swore. Was some moron illegally cutting down trees?

He turned toward the noise. Following it was easy. Fifteen minutes later, he stepped into a clearing and stumbled to a stop. The grinding, biting sound did come from a chain saw, but the person wielding it wasn't cutting down trees. And he wasn't a stranger. Del stared as his brother Nick used the machine to make unbelievably delicate cuts in a trunk that had to be at least ten feet high.

Nick was wearing goggles and gloves to protect his eyes, hands and forearms. He stood on a nest of sawdust. Although it was too soon for Del to know what the sculpture was going to be, he knew it would be huge.

Behind his brother he saw a tall building. Wide double doors stood open and inside were dozens of completed sculptures. Bears and deer, each so lifelike that it seemed any one of them could take a single step and be alive. He saw a dancing girl, standing *en pointe*, her arms held above her head. A woman holding a baby in her arms.

The work was brilliant, and more impressive considering the medium and how the sculptures were achieved.

He thought about his father's criticism that Nick was ignoring his gift and knew the old man was wrong. Which meant Nick hadn't told him what he was doing. Based on the location of his work space, Del wondered if anyone knew what was going on.

Slowly, carefully, he backed up until he was in the brush again, then turned into the forest and continued on with his hike. He wasn't sure if he was going to confront his brother about what he'd seen or let it go. Because not telling anyone was kind of a Mitchell tradition.

MAYA HAD NEVER had a garden before. Her apartment in Los Angeles had come with a tiny balcony that she'd never once used. Her office had windows and a view, but she'd never been in it long enough to consider a houseplant of any kind. But now that she had a house, she was determined to make the plant thing work.

Her rental came with a perfectly nice yard. There was a lawn, along with hedges and other green plant things. But there weren't any flowers. So her first week in town she'd gone to Plants for the Planet—a local nursery. She'd bought three big pots and flowers to go in them. The lady at the nursery had promised geraniums couldn't be killed, so Maya had chosen them.

Now, in the quiet of the evening, she carefully watered her plants. It had been warm and she didn't want them dying from the heat.

So far the week had been a good one, she thought. She and Del had made progress on the videos, she was caught up in her other work and the house was ready for Elaine to spend a couple of days with her after her surgery in the morning.

As soon as she thought of Elaine, she felt tension in her body. Not only worry about the cancer, but a sense of foreboding about keeping the secret. While she respected Elaine's reasons, Maya knew in her gut the other woman was wrong not to tell her family. They loved her. They would want to be there for her. Sure Ceallach could be difficult, but as much as he was an artist, his wife was his world. He would be devastated when he finally found out what she'd kept from him.

Maya also knew that she could offer advice, but ultimately the decision was Elaine's. Maya would be her friend, help where she could and do her best to keep her mouth shut about the rest of it.

Which was what friends did, she reminded herself. This was what she'd come home for. Plants to be watered, friends to hang with. There was a rhythm to her days that was a lot less frantic than it had been back in Los Angeles.

She finished and went back inside. She had her favorite shows she'd recorded and there was a book she'd been wanting to read. But instead of reaching for either, she crossed to the small built-in bookcase and pulled out a worn scrapbook. She settled on the sofa, sat cross-legged and opened the book.

She'd been seven or eight when she'd started the scrapbook and she thought maybe she'd put in the last pictures when she'd been in her early twenties. Probably right after college.

The pages were simple. They were covered with pictures of places in the world she wanted to go. The first choices were obvious. Paris was represented by the Eiffel Tower. London by Buckingham Palace. But as she'd gotten older, her dream destinations had grown little more unexpected. There was a photograph of a café outside of a mountain village in Peru. The shore of the Galápagos Islands. She'd always planned to get there.

But working in local television didn't exactly lend itself to exotic travel. Vacation plans were often disrupted by unexpected events. She hadn't minded so much when there was actual news, but she'd had to cut short a trip once because of a rumor that Jennifer Aniston got engaged.

No more canceled trips, she thought. She could take an actual vacation. Go somewhere interesting. Not that a two-week trip was the same as really immersing yourself a place, but it was a start.

Her cell phone rang. Phoebe's face appeared on the screen.

Maya smiled as she answered. "What's up?" she said when she pushed the green button. "Wedding crisis?"

Phoebe laughed. "Okay, so you're not watching Eddie and Gladys's show."

Maya held in a groan. She reached for the remote and turned on her TV. "What are they doing now? Tell me it's not frontal nudity."

"It's not. You'll see. And then you'll have some explaining to do. How come I didn't know?"

"Know what?"

The TV came on. Maya flipped to the Fool's Gold cable access channel. Eddie filled the screen.

"I know," the old woman was saying. "You want to see it again. Here goes."

As Maya watched, a video came on. It was blurry at first, then came into focus.

Her mouth dropped open as she saw Del and herself standing in a meadow. *The* meadow. Where they'd done the intro shoot. Where they'd kissed. Where she'd accidentally left the camera on and hadn't bothered to erase the footage.

"No," she moaned. "No, no, no."

"Yup," Phoebe said cheerfully. "First you tell each other you were in love and then you kiss. It's very hot."

Sure enough, that was exactly what happened.

She watched her videoed self say, *"I did love you."*

"I loved you, too. Talk about a lot of confessions for an early-morning shoot."

And then it happened. In front of God and the entire town. Del leaned in and kissed her.

Maya dropped her head to her free hand. "Kill me now," she murmured.

"I think it's too late for that. At least it's not frontal nudity. That has to be something, right?"

Maya curled up in a ball and wondered if it was possible for the earth to swallow her whole. "You think anyone else has seen this?"

"Just, you know, the entire town."

CHAPTER SEVEN

MAYA TOLD HERSELF that having a private moment of her life go viral was a good thing. It distracted her from worrying about Elaine.

The waiting area of the surgery center was pleasant enough. Lots of comfortable chairs, a huge aquarium filled with serene fish, free Wi-Fi and a big television currently tuned to *Good Morning America*. The hosts had already teased the clip of the video that apparently had exploded on social media overnight.

Maya had been fielding text messages and was also getting calls, although not taking them. She didn't want to leave the surgery center until she knew Elaine was okay and she wasn't about to talk on the phone in front of other people.

She glanced up at the screen just in time to see the video being played. On a personal level the whole thing was cringeworthy. She didn't like having a private moment exposed to the world. She felt vulnerable and exposed—not that anyone was paying attention to the show or her. No doubt they were as worried about their loved ones as she was about Elaine.

But professionally, she had to admit that the shot

was framed perfectly. The wildflowers, the trees—it was beautiful. It was also her kissing Del.

For a second, she could feel his mouth on hers. The tender pressure, the heat. Yearning filled her. In part for who they had been back then and in part for what could never be now. Whatever friendship they'd found, the romance had been lost. All heat and tingles aside, they weren't going back. There was only forward, and that path seemed to be leading directly to friendship land. Despite those sweet kisses.

She hadn't heard from him yet, so wasn't sure if he knew. Although it wasn't as if she'd reached out to him, either. She knew he wouldn't be thrilled, but she also wondered how much he would care.

"Maya?" The nurse smiled at her. "You can come back now."

Maya followed her to the recovery area and found Elaine sitting up. Her friend was pale, but otherwise looked okay.

Maya took her free hand and squeezed. "Hey. How are you feeling?"

"Not too bad." Elaine smiled. "The doctor says the tumor was very localized. So we can stick with the original plan. A few days to recover, then six weeks of radiation."

Maya squeezed her fingers, thinking a hug right now wasn't going to be the best thing. "That's exactly what we wanted to hear."

"I know. I'm so grateful."

The nurse turned to Maya. "Elaine tells me you'll be taking care of her tonight."

"Yes. She's staying with me."

"Good. The postsurgical instructions are pretty simple. I'll go over them with you. I gave them to Elaine before her procedure, but it's always good to have someone else following along. Plus, we'll send her home with written instructions."

"I'll make sure she does everything she's told."

BY NOON, ELAINE was settled in Maya's guest room. She'd had some soup and crackers and taken her pain medication. Sophie jumped up onto the bed, then curled up next to Elaine, as if understanding this was a time to be quiet.

"I'm fine," Elaine said firmly as she stroked her dog. "Exhausted, but fine. I didn't sleep at all last night. In fact, I haven't slept for a couple of nights. So I'm going to stay right here and rest. I want you to leave."

They'd been having the same conversation for about fifteen minutes. Elaine wanted her to go to work for a few hours, and Maya didn't want to leave her friend.

"It's a small incision," Elaine continued. "I don't even have a drain. There's nothing to do. I can shower in the morning and resume my normal life. No strenuous exercise for a week and then I'm healed."

Except for the fact that she still had to deal with radiation and having cancer, Maya thought.

"I'm here to take care of you," Maya insisted.

"You're making me nervous. You hover. Go and

let me sleep. Come back in two hours and let Sophie out. That's all I ask."

"I'll wait an hour, then walk Sophie. If you're still okay, then I'll go."

"You're very stubborn," Elaine murmured, her eyes already closing.

"It's one of my best qualities."

Elaine had fallen asleep almost immediately. She'd barely stirred when Maya had taken Sophie out for a quick walk. The dog had immediately done her business, as if wanting to get back to her human's side. Elaine didn't even notice when Maya had touched her forehead and cheek to see if she was too warm.

After writing a note to say where she was and making sure fresh water and Elaine's cell phone were on the nightstand, Maya had let herself out and walked to her office.

Now she set the alarm on her phone so she didn't get caught up in work. She would head home in ninety minutes to look in on her friend.

Maya circled by the editing room on her way to her office. The editing room door stood open and Eddie Carberry sat in front of the computer. Even more surprising was the fact that the older woman was looking at Maya's footage from a previous shoot.

"Oh, my God. It was you."

Eddie looked up, her expression more triumphant than repentant. "I have no idea what you're talking about."

The interview played in the background. Considering the clip had been on Eddie's show, her being the one to find it shouldn't have been a surprise, but it kind of was.

"You've been going through my footage."

Eddie glanced back at the screen. "It's good stuff. You have a real eye. That kiss was a find."

"You stole it."

"Copied. You still have it yourself. So it wasn't stolen. Besides, now you're famous."

For kissing Del. Something that would have rocked her world a little more if she hadn't been dealing with Elaine's cancer surgery.

"Don't do that again," she said firmly.

"Why not? You should thank me."

How could this little old lady with her short curls and bright eyes be so confident? Was it an age thing? Personality?

"I'm not thanking you for stealing my stuff."

"I got you on national TV. That's a trick. And it was good publicity for the town, which is actually your job. Yup, I think some flowers are in order. Maybe a box of chocolates. See's are my favorites. Gladys likes them, too."

Maya felt as if she'd stepped through the looking glass. "I'm not sending you flowers or chocolates."

Eddie sniffed, then stood. "If you're going to be like that."

"I am."

"You should be more appreciative of what people do for you."

Maya watched her leave, then went over to her computer and activated the security program. As soon as it was up, she put a password on her files, then walked to her office.

She was still trying to make sense of everything that had happened in the past eighteen hours when Del walked in. The second she saw him, she had an overwhelming urge to step right into his arms and have him hold her until she knew everything was going to be okay. On the heels of that came the need to tell him that his mom was fine. That he shouldn't worry. Only he didn't know anything was wrong with her and Maya couldn't tell him.

"Okay, that's not a happy face," he said, leaning against the doorframe. "You're upset." He moved toward her. "It's not what I would have chosen, either, but it's no big deal. In a way, it's funny."

"The kiss," she whispered, knowing he couldn't be talking about the cancer, even though that was what she was thinking about.

He moved into her office and shut the door. "Is someone going to get angry?"

"Someone? Like a guy?"

The corner of his mouth turned up. "If it's not a guy, can I watch?"

She started to laugh, then had to fight unexpected tears. The latter were because of his mom, she thought. The surgery, the fact that the doctor was optimistic. Once again she wanted to walk into Del's arms and be held. She also wanted him to know what was going on. But she'd promised. A promise that sat like a rock in her stomach—and on her conscience.

"There's no girl or guy," she said, hoping her tone

was light enough. "I was surprised by the clip. I'm sure you were, too."

"Completely. I've been getting a lot of jokes from my friends."

"I can imagine. You'll also be getting a lot of fan mail. You looked good on-screen."

"So did you."

Kissing. They'd been kissing.

"It was Eddie Carberry," she said to distract herself. "I found her going through my material."

"Not a surprise. She's impressive."

"I put a password on the files."

He laughed. "Good for you. Make her work for it."

"My plan is that she won't have access to it anymore."

Maya moved to her desk. Del took the visitor's chair. He studied her.

"You sure you're okay?"

"Just tired. I was in shock last night. I couldn't believe it. How did you find out?"

"Ryder Stevens saw it online and emailed me. Did you know Eddie and Gladys's show has an internet following?"

Maya rubbed her temples. "No, and I didn't need to. At least the internet is an open system and we don't have to worry about the FCC there."

"You're not mad at them, are you?"

"No. Surprised. Flummoxed by them."

"They're uncontrollable."

"You don't mind about the kiss going viral?"

His gaze shifted. For a second she would have

sworn he was staring at her mouth. She felt a flash of heat followed by longing.

They could do it again, she thought. A real kiss this time. With bodies pressing and tongues... Well, she could use a little tongue in her life.

But that wasn't going to happen. She and Del were friends. They worked together. He liked her, they got along, but she was pretty sure he had no sexual interest in her. As for her feelings, they were, ah, nostalgic. That was all. She was reacting to the past.

"At first I was a little uncomfortable, but what the hell. Stuff happens."

She smiled. "You like the attention."

"Some. While you like being behind the scenes."

"I do," she said slowly, immediately thinking about her network dreams.

"What are you thinking?"

"That I put so much energy into getting a network job. I wanted to be on camera. To be the star. But you're right. Looking at the video, I didn't like the attention, but I did appreciate how good the shot was."

That couldn't be right, could it? Had she been chasing the wrong dream all this time?

"Regretting your decision to come here?" he asked.

"No. I was so tired of the gossip show. I couldn't have done it anymore. This is nice."

But maybe not permanent, a little voice in her head whispered.

"It's good to be happy in your work," he said.

"It is. What are you doing this weekend?"

"Hanging out. You? Oh, that's right. You have your

girls' weekend with my mom. What does that entail? Mani-pedis?"

"I'm impressed you know what a mani-pedi is," she said, dodging the question. Because her girls' weekend would consist of making sure her friend was recovering.

"I'm well traveled," he told her, coming to his feet. "You sure you're okay?"

"Yes. We are now world famous kissers. I'm sure we can both use that to our advantage."

He grinned. "I know I will."

DEL LEFT THE studio offices and headed for The Man Cave to see Nick. Maybe a little one-on-one time with his middle brother would give him some answers as to why Nick felt he had to hide what he was doing. Because Del sure didn't get it. Ceallach might not approve of the medium, but he would be happy to see the art being produced. So why not let the old man know?

He crossed the street and turned at the corner. Everyone had their reasons, he supposed. Very few actions were random. Like his coming home. It had been a deliberate choice and he had a feeling he'd made it for reasons that were not the ones he'd first thought.

He walked into the bar and saw Nick wasn't alone. Aidan was with him. *Two for the price of one*, Del thought as he approached them, wondering if Aidan would walk out the second he saw him. Their last conversation hadn't ended well.

"It's TV's newest reality star," Nick said from behind the bar. "Back only a couple of weeks and already making time with Maya. Everything old is new again."

Del accepted the ribbing. "It wasn't like that."

"It looked like that," Aidan said, grabbing a handful of peanuts from the bowl on the counter. "It looked a lot like that."

It had been a nice kiss, Del thought. When he'd first seen the video, he'd been shocked and a little embarrassed. But even though it was a personal moment, he wasn't ashamed. Hell, he and Maya looked good together. His only regret was that they hadn't done more. Not on camera, of course. But later. Privately. One on one. Naked.

She'd always looked good naked and he had a feeling time had been especially kind to her. They both had some years on them, which meant experience. Making love with her had been fantastic before. He would guess it would be even better now.

"What can I get you?" Nick asked.

Del pointed to Aidan's bottle and sat down at the bar. "What he's having."

Aidan glanced at him. "Did you figure out what happened with the video? How it got online?"

"Eddie Carberry got into Maya's files."

Aidan shook his head. "You've got to admire her and Gladys. They move with the times."

"That's what I said. We should all be so determined when we're their age." Del found himself watching Nick, thinking about his brother's secret.

Not that he was going to ask. Instead, he turned back to Aidan. "How's business?"

Aidan's expression immediately went tight. He put down his beer. "Go to hell," he said, and walked out.

Del stared after him, then turned to Nick. "What did I say?"

"You have to ask?"

"Yeah, I do. I know he's pissed. So let's talk about it. Walking away doesn't accomplish anything."

"So speaks the man who ran."

Not how Del would have characterized his leaving town, but he could see how it would have looked that way. "Maybe I learned from my mistakes."

"I'm not the one you're fighting with. No point in telling me."

Del stared at Aidan's abandoned beer, not sure how to handle the situation. "I don't suppose he's like this with everyone."

"Nope. Just you."

"Great. I guess I'm going to have to talk to him."

"You just tried that. It didn't go well."

"What do you suggest?"

"Not a clue." Nick leaned against the bar. "Regretting coming home?"

"Sometimes. There's a big world out there that's a whole lot easier to deal with than family." He took a drink of his beer. "You know, if Aidan's so unhappy, why doesn't he just sell the business and leave? Dad's not drinking anymore, so he's not going to go on a bender and destroy a year's worth of work. No one needs the income to put food on the table."

Nick straightened. "It's even easier than that. Aidan bought out Mom a few years back. The business is just his now."

"So why doesn't he leave, if it's so awful? Or does he enjoy spending his days thinking about how I ruined his life?"

"You'll have to ask him."

"He's not here."

"Funny how that works."

Del looked at Nick. "Anything you want to talk about?"

"My life's an open book."

"Written in invisible ink."

Nick chuckled. "See what you missed while you've been gone? Speaking of being gone, where are you off to next?"

"I have no idea."

"No great adventure calling?"

Del shook his head. "A few people have been in touch, wanting me to develop the next hot piece of equipment, but I'm not that guy. The sky board I worked on was just one of those things. I didn't like what was on the market. But I don't wake up in the middle of the night with ideas for inventions."

"You need to follow your passion," Nick told him.

If Del had been drinking, he would have choked. Seriously? This from a guy with a secret life?

"I'm not an entrepreneur," Del said instead. "I have no desire to discover a better way to reinvent the wheel."

"Ever think about settling down in one place?"

"Now and then. I'm not sure I mean it."

"What would you do if you had to stay in one place?"

"I'd be a teacher."

Nick raised his eyebrows. "I didn't see that one coming."

Del rested his elbows on the bar. "I like kids. I like sharing the world with them. That was one of the best parts about my travel. Going into classrooms all over the place and talking about what I'd seen. Showing them."

"Pictures?"

"Sometimes. Videos. Or telling them stories. Kids want to know what it's like everywhere. They're curious. Open."

Del thought about the videos he shot. They were a start, but not a good one. He had a vision, but not the ability to see it through. Since selling his company, he had capital. Maybe he should hire somebody. Start some kind of travel production company.

He reached for his beer and knew that wasn't the answer. Even though it might get him where he wanted to go, it didn't feel right.

For a second, he wondered about Maya. She was brilliant. Dedicated. But she was also committed to Fool's Gold. And working together for a few weeks wasn't the same as an ongoing business partnership. Because of their past, he didn't know if he could trust her. Not completely.

"A teacher," Nick said. "I never would have guessed."

"I'm not planning on settling down, so I don't see it happening." He finished his beer, then passed Nick the bottle. "You like working here?" he asked, motioning to the bar.

"Sure. The hours are good and the pay is decent and I spend my time hanging out with people I like."

Del wondered which was the most important. Based on what he'd seen of his brother's sculptures, he would guess the working schedule that freed Nick's mornings and early afternoons. When he could be outside, creating. Because for so many artists, it was all about the light.

"You hear from the twins much?" he asked.

"Not really," Nick said, getting him another beer. "Mom said they'll be back for Dad's birthday. We'll see if that really happens."

"They took off, what? Three years ago?"

Nick nodded. "Right after Dad's heart attack. One day they were here, the next they were gone. Sort of like you."

Del sighed. "You're never letting that go, are you?"

Nick grinned. "As long as it bothers you, we're all going to keep poking at the wound. You know that, brother."

"Yes, I do."

It was the law of the Mitchell jungle. Only the strong survived. Or left. Of course, he was assuming that getting out was a sign of strength. Ten years ago, he'd known he hadn't had a choice. But things were different now. He was a grown man with a lot of success. He was more confident. He had money in the bank and he had options. But he also had questions, and as of now, no way of getting answers.

CHAPTER EIGHT

MAYA OPENED THE back door of her car and Sophie jumped down. "You'd go with anyone for a car ride, wouldn't you?"

The beagle gave a happy wag of her tail, before heading into the house. Elaine turned to Maya.

"Thank you for everything. I appreciate your help."

"You're welcome. You're sure you're okay?"

"I'm fine. I'm not really in any pain. You're a good friend."

Maya hugged her, careful to avoid the side with the still-healing incisions. "I'm here for you. If you need anything, call me."

"I will." Elaine straightened. She gave an impish smile. "I'm going to tell Ceallach that I have a hangover from our girls' night. That way I can relax for the rest of the day and he'll fuss. It'll be good for both of us."

Maya nodded, even as she thought that what would be good for the family was Elaine to come clean. But it wasn't her problem and she would do well to remember that. She'd supported her friend and would continue to do so. Even if she didn't like keeping the secret.

Maya drove home. On the way, she considered what she was going to do with the rest of her day. She had the usual weekend chores—laundry, a bathroom to clean. Neither of which sounded especially inspiring. Or interesting.

She pulled into the driveway and noticed the plants on her front porch. They'd looked a little pale a few days ago and now were hanging down as if they'd died in the night.

"What on earth?"

She'd never had plants before, so didn't know what she was doing wrong. She studied them, thinking they looked desperately sad. She'd been faithfully watering them. Had they needed food or something? Was she starving her plants?

"Those don't look good."

She glanced up and saw Del standing on the sidewalk. At the sight of him, her entire body seemed to get a little lighter. Tiny tingles ignited in her stomach and fingertips. She hoped she didn't look as happy to see him as she felt.

"I don't know what I did wrong," she admitted. "Any gardening experience in your past?"

"Sorry, no."

"Me, either."

"You done with your girls' weekend?" he asked.

"Yes. I just took your mom and Sophie home. I was going to get replacement plants."

"Want some company?"

The unexpected question had her nodding. "Yes, please. You can carry the plants back."

"What about equality between the sexes?" he asked, his voice teasing.

"What about bite me?"

Del laughed. "Let's go."

She joined him on the sidewalk and they went north on Brian Lane. The neighborhood was quiet, with smaller, one-story houses and wide lawns.

"There's such a suburban feel to this part of town," she said. "However do you survive?"

"I like the suburbs."

"No, you don't. You're world traveler guy. You're probably counting the days until you leave."

"I'll be ready when the time comes, but it's okay to be back. Sort of."

"What does that mean?"

"Aidan's not talking to me. I know he's mad I left ten years ago. That, I get. But Nick told me that Aidan bought Mom out of the business. He owns the company outright. So if he's so unhappy, why does he stay? He could sell and go somewhere else."

"Have you asked him about that?"

"He doesn't stay in the room long enough for me to have a conversation with him."

"How hard have you tried?"

Del was silent. Maya shook her head. "You're such a guy. Maybe he needs to see you make a little effort. I don't pretend to understand all your family dynamics, but what I can tell you is that people want to feel like they're being heard. Maybe he needs to know you're interested in listening to his side of things."

Del nodded. "Maybe." He looked at her. "Was I wrong to go?"

Not a question she was comfortable with, mostly because she felt responsible for what had happened. "You were young and hurt and feeling trapped. Leaving made sense."

"I don't think I would have been happy here. It was too easy to be somewhere else."

"Anywhere else," she corrected. "It's not like you settled down at all. Some people like to be on the move. You're one of them." She came to a sudden stop. "It's not my fault. You leaving. It would have happened anyway."

He faced her. "Maya, it was never your fault. Did you think it was?"

"I've had guilt."

"You shouldn't. You didn't want to marry me. That's okay. You get to choose."

They'd already been over what had happened. She'd apologized and he'd accepted her apology, so she wasn't going to go there again. But this was an interesting twist on what they'd gone through.

"You wouldn't have been happy married to me," she said. "Not if it meant staying here. Wow, that would have been interesting."

"Me bugging you to leave town? Would you have gone?"

"I don't know."

They started walking again.

"Because you want to be in one place," he said.

"Why do you think that?"

"You moved to LA and never left. Now you're here."

"A lot of that was about my job."

"I'm not saying it's bad." He motioned to the houses they passed. "Settling down is normal. I'm pointing out that you've never had a burning desire to see the world."

She thought about her scrapbook. Were those actual dreams or just idle wishes? "Travel sounds fun," she admitted. "To always be seeing new places. What's your favorite part of going somewhere different?"

"Meeting the local kids. They're curious about everything. Especially America."

"Sure. They've seen snippets from TV shows and movies, but that's not real. It's too bad there's not a way to share what things are really like. Sort of like those day-in-a-life documentaries, but geared for schoolkids. Here's a school day for a regular kid in Baltimore. Here's a school day for a regular kid in Melbourne. If they had the same format, students would get the rhythm of them right away. Know there was going to be a section on sports, or lunchtime. Children like repetition. It's one of the reasons they like to hear the same story every night, to watch the same…"

Maya realized Del was no longer next to her. She turned and saw he was back a few feet, looking bemused.

"What?" she demanded.

"It's a good idea," he said, walking toward her.

"The idea of using a consistent format is a good one. You're right about the repetition. I never thought of that. It could be an ongoing series."

"Sure. Focus on regular kids at first, then expand. What is it like to be the daughter of the president? The son of a movie star or sports hero? To live on the streets in India? Seeing is believing."

He caught up with her. "You're good."

She smiled. "I can brainstorm with the best of them. Believe me, when your topic is celebrity gossip, you find ways to make the most mundane seem interesting."

They started walking again. She thought about the potential for the project. There were so many ways to make it appealing, and not on a big budget, either. Not that Del needed her help.

"I never meant to get stuck in LA," she said, knowing it didn't matter, but needing him to know. "I always thought I would end up somewhere else."

Which could have been the problem, she admitted, if only to herself. Ending up wasn't the same as executing a plan. It was still being tossed around by circumstances.

"Now you're here," he said. "That's somewhere else."

She nodded, thinking she should be grateful for that. They turned left on Second. But this job had just kind of happened. She hadn't been looking for it. Mayor Marsha had come to see her. What was up with that? Maya always prided herself on getting the details right in her stories, but not in her own life.

"What are you thinking?" Del asked. "You're looking fierce."

"Just thinking about not making decisions. Inaction is its own plan—not a good one, but there is always an outcome."

"Wondering if you should have actively planned more?"

"Maybe. Or at least thought about what I wanted." She drew in a breath. "A network job, which isn't going to happen. So I'm a behind-the-camera girl now."

"One of the best."

She smiled. "Thanks. I'll accept the compliment, even though you have no point of comparison."

"You're better than me."

She pressed her lips together.

"Hey," he said, in mock annoyance. "I'm not that bad."

"You're perfectly adequate. Better than most with your level of training."

He put his arm around her and drew her against him.

"Stop trying to shield my feelings," he teased. "Just tell it to me straight."

She smiled up at him. "You're a dabbler. A cute dabbler, but a dabbler all the same."

He was close enough to kiss her, she thought, aware of his body pressing against her and his mouth tantalizingly close. Despite being in the middle of town, on a public sidewalk at two on a Sunday afternoon, she could use a good kissing. Del's kisses were special.

But instead of drawing her nearer, he released her and pointed to the sign. "We're here. Let's go find out why you're killing plants."

Better to keep things light, she told herself, even though she knew she was lying. Did Del not want to kiss her? Was she not appealing to him? Funny how ten years ago there had been so much passion between them, it had been hard to see anything else. Now, while she still felt quivery whenever he was around, she was just as intrigued by the emotional connection. In some ways, that was even more powerful. And potentially dangerous. Especially if it was only a one-sided sensation.

DEL COULDN'T GET Maya's idea out of his head. He only half listened as she discussed her recent plant homicide with one of the employees at Plants for the Planet. He was too busy thinking about possibilities.

The way she'd talked about the ongoing video series had brought so many of his disparate ideas into clear focus. He liked the concept of a consistent format, using different kids from all over the world. There were universal elements—school, family, sports. Once the kids saw the connection, they could experience what other students were going through. After commonality came the ability to relate. It was easy to hate or fear otherness, but if the person was just like you, there was a bond.

Was there a market for that kind of material? he

wondered. He knew school budgets were tight. If he had the right financing, plus his own money, he could offer the program for free. Because what was important to him was the message.

Something to think about, he told himself.

Maya stood by the cash register. He walked over and took the box of plants in front of her. She looked more worried than happy.

"They're replacing them for me for free," she said. "It's their guarantee. I don't want to take advantage of them. I mean, what if I did something wrong?"

"It's four plants," he told her. "Go with it. If these are fine, then it's the plants. If these die, it's you, and you can pay them for these, along with some new ones."

"If these die, I should give up on growing things," she said, following him out of the store. "I knew I wasn't very good at relationships, but I would hate to have that concept play out in ongoing plant death."

"Why would you say you're not good at relationships?" From what he'd seen, she was friendly and well liked. He enjoyed her company.

"The usual reasons. I'm going to be thirty in a couple of years and I'm not married. I haven't had a long-term boyfriend in…a while." She glanced at him, then away. "Zane."

"Your stepbrother? What does he have to do with anything?"

"You're not the only one with weird family relationships. Zane and I have been circling each other like wary adversaries for years. I've always talked about him having a stick up his ass. I thought he was too hard on his little brother and a grumpy guy who needed to live a little."

"And?"

"It's possible I was wrong."

"You?"

She flashed him a smile. "I like that you're pretending to be surprised, even though we both know you're not. Yes, me. Chase has always been a handful. Even though I knew that, I always took his side against Zane. A few months ago, Chase went too far. I won't get into the details, but the upshot is he needed to learn a lesson and Zane was determined to teach him. There was a fake cattle drive and—"

"Did you say fake cattle drive?"

She laughed. "Yes. Chase took money from tourists after promising them a cattle drive. He was going to pay the deposits back and couldn't, so Zane decided to create a fake cattle drive and made Chase handle all the crappy jobs. It was a good solution."

"Except for the guests."

"They did get to spend several days herding cattle. It was actually a really good time. Except for the flood at the end."

Del looked at her. "You're making that up."

"I'm not. There was an article about it in the local paper. Anyway, my point is, Chase really screwed up. He's a teenager, so it's kind of expected, which was what I would have said to Zane. Actually I did say it. But Zane was right. Chase needed to be taught a lesson. It made me think that I might have been too much on Chase's side and not supportive enough of Zane. That would be an example of me messing up in a relationship."

"Not a really good one," he told her as they approached her house. "On the scale of transgressions, it's not impressive."

"Why do you get to say?" she asked.

"Because I'm me."

Maya laughed. The sound was happy, and oddly, it pleased him to hear it.

"How are things with Zane now?" he asked.

"Better. I'm less judgmental and he's less crabby. Phoebe's the reason he's different. They're crazy in love and getting married in a few weeks."

Her voice sounded wistful. Del supposed it wasn't a surprise. Most people wanted a relationship they could count on. Someone to watch their back. He did, too. He just wasn't sure how to find it.

They set the new plants on the porch.

"You have gardening tools?" he asked.

"Sure."

"Go get them. I'll help you swap out dead for alive."

"Thanks."

She went into the house. For a second he thought about following. About stopping her in the kitchen or hallway and pulling her close. Holding her would be good. He'd always liked the feel of Maya in his arms. Then he could kiss her. Really kiss her. Not like before, but a kiss that rocked both their worlds and left them breathless. Because Maya breathless had always been one of his favorite sounds.

Only he didn't, because sex would complicate things. He shook his head. He was the only one here—no reason to lie. Sex would put what they had at risk. Sex would take away the easy and make their relationship awkward. He liked what was going on with Maya. He liked working with her, hanging out with her. He liked having her as his friend again. As much as he would like to get her naked, this was better.

She returned onto the porch with a tool in each hand. "Tiny shovel or weird claw thing?" she asked. "You're my guest, so you get to pick first."

Because Maya was nothing if not fair, he thought, reaching for the spade.

"This is a man's tool," he told her.

She batted her eyes. "And here I thought it would be bigger."

PAPER MOON HAD started life as a bridal boutique. In the past couple of years, the store had expanded to include a clothing store that specialized in unique fashions made by little-known designers. Maya had been meaning to stop by to spruce up her wardrobe or at least find a few things with a little color in them. Her work uniform had consisted of a lot of black. And while that worked as a TV producer in LA it wasn't exactly Fool's Gold friendly.

Now she found herself in the bridal side of Paper Moon, waiting to try on her bridesmaid's dress.

"I know you wouldn't do this for just anyone," Phoebe told her.

"I wouldn't, but I would do it for you in a heartbeat." Maya smiled. "You're getting married and you asked me to be in the wedding. That's so cool."

"You really think so?" Phoebe sounded anxious. "I don't want you to think it's silly."

Maya hugged her. "Never. I'm so happy for you and Zane. The wedding is going to be beautiful and you'll be the most perfect bride ever."

Phoebe blushed. "I doubt that."

"We can take a vote."

Madeline walked into the large dressing room. "What are we voting on?"

"Phoebe being the most beautiful bride."

"Of course she will be." Madeline hung up the pale blue dress. "All my brides are. I take my work very seriously."

Phoebe's worry faded as her expression turned impish. "Despite how you're stalking Jonny Blaze."

Madeline grinned. "First, I'm not stalking him. Second, I can multitask. I'm a great multitasker." She opened her mouth, then closed it. "OMG, did you invite him to the wedding?"

Maya laughed. "I can't figure out if your panic is that he'll be there or he won't."

"I'm not sure, either," Madeline admitted.

"Sorry to disappoint," Phoebe said. "I did invite him, but he's going to be out of town. Filming on location."

Madeline waved her hand in front of her face. "Good. I would hate to embarrass myself. Plus, it's your wedding. The day should be about you and Zane and not me and my movie star crush."

"You could be the entertainment," Maya told her.

"Um, no." Madeline motioned to the dress. "Put that on. If it looks half as good as I think it's going to, you'll both be thrilled."

Phoebe and Madeline stepped out of the large dressing room. Maya quickly stripped down to a bra and panties, only to realize there was no bra-wearing with this dress.

The design was simple. A sleeveless bodice in a faux wrap style and a long slim skirt. The back had crisscross straps and a flowing bow. The fabric was soft, with a slight sheen to it.

Maya slipped into the dress, then closed the side zipper. There was a bit of support in the front. She was on the small side, breastwise, so the style worked fine. She put on the nude pumps she'd brought along for the fitting, then stepped out into the main viewing area of the store.

Phoebe sighed and clutched her hands together. "I love it. Do you love it?"

"It's beautiful," Maya said. "But you're the one who has to decide. This is your day."

While Zane and Phoebe wanted a traditional wedding with all their friends and much of the town in attendance, they were also keeping things simple.

"The dress looks great," Phoebe said. "Madeline?"

"I love it," her friend told her. "It goes great with your bridal gown. The wrap style is similar but the skirts are completely different. They'll complement each other without competing."

Maya stepped up onto the raised platform in front of the half circle of floor-length mirrors. As she turned back and forth, she could see herself from every angle.

"I need to start working out," she murmured, eyeing her butt.

"Stop," Phoebe said with a laugh. "You're tall and skinny and if you weren't my best friend, I could easily hate you."

"You're glowingly in love," Maya pointed out. "I get to worry about my butt if I want to."

Madeline ignored them and stepped onto the platform. She handed Maya a small basket of clips, then pulled and tucked and secured, showing them both how the dress would look when it was tailored.

Maya was impressed. The gown went from pretty to knockout in less than a minute. "This is great. Phoebe?"

Phoebe nodded. "I like it. Yes, that's the one."

"I agree," Madeline said with a satisfied nod. "Okay, Maya, you just hang out here. I'm going to get Phoebe into her dress and we'll see how you two look together."

Maya stepped off the platform and returned to her dressing room. She pulled out her phone to check on her email and saw she had a text from Del.

Why aren't you at work?

She grinned and texted him back. I'm trying on bridesmaid dresses for Phoebe's wedding. I'd invite you to drop in, but all this lace would turn you into a woman.

A few seconds later, he responded. Neither of us wants that. What if I'm prettier than you?

She laughed. I don't see that as the bigger problem. She paused for a second, then impulsively asked, Want to be my plus-one for the wedding?

Will I like the dress?

She laughed again. Pretty sure you will.

Then I'm in.

She heard Madeline walk by and dropped her phone into her bag, then went back to the viewing area to wait for Phoebe.

Her friend came out a few seconds later. Maya sighed. "Wow," she said. "Just wow."

Phoebe bit her lower lip. "You like it?"

"I love it."

The gown was simple, with a wrap bodice, like Maya's. But instead of the slim skirt, Phoebe's dress billowed out in a traditional ball gown style. There were embellishments on the straps and at the waist, along with a beautiful sheer overlay on the full skirt.

"Mermaid gowns are the big thing right now, but I'm too short. I think this style suits me better."

Maya nodded. "It's perfect on you."

Phoebe stepped up on the platform and turned toward the mirrors. Maya watched her, delighted with the dress and her friend's obvious happiness.

Madeline had pinned up Phoebe's brown hair and secured it with a few combs. She walked in with several veils draped over her arm.

"Don't you love it?" she asked as she handed the veils to Maya, then got on the platform and smoothed out the skirt. "The chapel-length train is perfect. You're that sexy combination of petite and curvy. This dress accentuates all the good stuff. You look like a princess."

Maya nodded. "Zane is going to be overwhelmed."

"I like that," Phoebe said shyly. "He overwhelms me all the time."

Madeline worked her magic with the clips, making the exquisite gown fit even better. She then chose one of the veils.

"This one is my favorite," she said, securing it into place. "You wear it down. There's no piece to cover the face, but that's more popular these days. The embellishments match what's going on with your dress, which will be pretty."

She fluffed the veil, then stepped back.

Maya smiled. "It's beautiful."

"I like it a lot," Phoebe said.

Madeline didn't look convinced. "Hmm, this isn't the look I was going for. You know, I have another one in the back. I special ordered it, then the bride picked something else because it wasn't the one for her. I've been saving it for the right dress and bride.

I'm thinking it might be you. Hold on. It's gonna take me a second to find it."

Madeline hurried to the rear of the store and went into the storeroom. Maya walked toward the mirror.

"You're dazzling," she told her friend.

Phoebe nodded, then surprised her by wiping away tears.

Maya stepped up next to her. "What's wrong?"

Phoebe swallowed. "I miss my mom. I know it's silly. It's been years, right? I don't remember much about her at all. So it's the concept, not the person. But I wish she was here, to help me buy my dress and to see me get married."

Maya reached for her friend and hugged her. "It's not silly. Of course you miss her."

Phoebe shook a little as she fought tears. "I guess it's all the emotion."

"Sure, and the tradition of what you're doing. You love your parents. Just because they're gone doesn't mean you stop loving them."

Phoebe nodded. "Thanks. I know I'm going to have a new family now. With you and Zane and Chase. And I'll have kids. So it's not like she's gone forever. She'll be part of her grandchildren."

"She will," Maya promised, understanding Phoebe's pain intellectually if not viscerally. Her mother was gone, too, and Maya couldn't begin to imagine missing her. But her relationship with her mother had been different from that of Phoebe's with her own mom.

It was like the way Maya felt about the town. Fool's Gold had taken her in and encouraged her. Without the support of her friends and teachers, she wasn't sure she would have found the courage to go after her dreams. To make it to college, not to mention pay for it. She still didn't know who had funded her scholarship, but that wasn't the point. She'd been nurtured, and when she left, she'd missed the support. Phoebe had been loved by her mother, so now, getting married, she missed her.

"You're good to me," Phoebe said, straightening. "Thank you."

"You're my best friend. You couldn't escape me if you tried."

CHAPTER NINE

"Thanks," Aidan said grudgingly. "I owe you."

Del waved off the words. "I'm happy to help."

Aidan shoved his hands into his jeans front pockets. "Two of my guys are out sick with whatever's going around, and Rick's still recovering from falling off the mountain. Mom can usually fill in, but she's not feeling well, either."

"Like I said, it's no big deal."

"You don't have a shoot or something?"

"Nope, I'm all yours."

Del studied his brother. They looked a lot alike. When they'd been kids, it had been easy for strangers to pick out the Mitchell brothers. Back then the boys had thought the similarities were funny. Now they simply existed. But even though Del and Aidan shared traits on the outside, he wasn't so sure they had much else in common.

He'd been pleased when his brother had called and asked for his help today with a local tour. Not only was he happy to fill in, he was hoping that by being there when his brother needed him, he could open the lines of communications.

Aidan handed him a stack of maps. "It's a pretty

simple walking tour of the town. You hit the high-lights, talk about the history. We have a deal with Brew-haha. Patience will have drinks and pastries for everyone there. Once they have their drinks, you give them the store maps and leave them downtown to shop. Oh, and tell the guys about the sporting goods store over by The Christmas Attic. After an hour, they get lunch from Ana Raquel. She has the food truck by the park. Once the folks have their lunch, you're done."

Del studied the map. It was similar to the one he'd used when he'd been in charge of the company. There were a few modifications, but nothing he couldn't handle. "I got it," he said. "I even remember my town history."

Aidan didn't look convinced. "It's just that I have a three-day river rafting trip heading out in a couple of hours that I need to get started. Then I'm taking a group for camping and bird-watching for two days."

Del stared at his brother. "You go bird-watching?"

For the first time since Del had arrived, Aidan smiled. "Naw. I go camping. Some university profes-sor guy comes along for the bird-watching." Aidan sighed heavily. "We have a lot of birds in the area and now I know about all of them."

"Bummer."

"Tell me about it." He glanced toward two women in their twenties in the waiting area of the tour office. They were both wearing shorts and hiking boots, with backpacks resting beside them.

Pretty enough, Del thought, watching his brother

eye the women. "Compensation for having to listen to lectures on birds?" he asked.

Aidan raised a shoulder. "Very possibly."

An interesting life choice, Del thought, knowing that kind of serial hooking-up wasn't for him. Unlike his brother, he wasn't into the thrill of the chase. He was, at heart, a one-woman guy. The trick seemed to be finding the right woman.

Aidan reached for a piece of paper on his desk. "Okay, here's your group. They'll be here at nine-thirty. There are ten in all."

Del studied the sheet. There were the names, along with the route Aidan wanted him to take. It hadn't changed all that much in the past ten years. The tour started by the lake, went by the park, then to City Hall and Brew-haha and ended by The Christmas Attic.

"Easy enough," he told his brother. "I got this. Don't worry."

"Okay, thanks. I appreciate it."

"Sure thing."

He knew Aidan was expecting him to say more. Maybe mention that they hadn't been spending any time together. But a busy morning with tours heading out wasn't the time. He would approach Aidan later.

"I'll go grab a coffee and be back at nine," he said.

"I'll be gone by then. Millie will get you started."

Millie was the fiftysomething woman working the counter. Del had already met her.

Del waved once and left. He left a message for Maya, explaining why he wouldn't be joining her on their planned editing session. After that, he spent a few minutes on his smartphone, reviewing town history. He had a feeling that once he started talking, it would all come back to him.

He wanted to do a good job for Aidan—so his brother could stop being so pissed at him. Since coming home, he'd started to realize how much he'd missed his family. The fault was his—he'd been the one not to stay in touch. His initial goal had simply been to avoid the place where his world had crashed around him. Now he saw he'd taken that too far.

At eight forty-five he was back in the office. He checked in with Millie, then introduced himself to the tourists who would be on his tour. A little before nine Maya walked in.

She had on a pink sundress and flat sandals. Her long blond hair had been pulled back in a braid. She looked pretty, and while technically the dress didn't show anything it shouldn't or come close to being short, she looked amazingly sexy.

"What are you doing here?" he asked, hoping his pleasure at the sight of her wasn't obvious to everyone around him.

"I got your message. You haven't done this in ten years," she told him. "I thought you could use help."

"Like you know more about this town than me?"

She smiled. "I was always better with the in-town tour groups and you know it."

She had him there. He also wasn't going to refuse her company.

By nine they had their tour group and were heading out to walk the town. The morning was warm, the sky blue. Up in the mountains, leaves were starting to turn, but not in town. Not yet. Fall would come soon enough.

Maya gave a brief history of the Máa-zib tribe—their place of origin and how scholars believed they came to be in the area.

"But for me," she was saying, "the *real* history of the town starts later than that. In 1849 an eighteen-year-old young woman named Ciara O'Farrell was on her way to an arranged marriage to a much-older man she'd never met. She escaped the ship in San Francisco and headed east. Using the little money she had managed to save, she bought land rights in the foothills of the Sierra Nevada."

"Oh, I know where this is going," a woman said with a sigh. "It's going to have a happy ending, I just know it."

Maya laughed. "You're right. The ship's captain, Ronan McGee, goes after her. He'd promised her father to deliver her safely to the wedding. When he finally catches up with her, Ciara refuses to go with him. She has a dream. Ronan says the dream is sheer folly, and then he promptly falls in love with her. They settle here, in Fool's Gold."

Maya motioned to the lake. "Lake Ciara is named after her, of course. Some of you are staying in Ronan's Lodge, which was their home. A big, beautiful mansion that people called Ronan's Folly. Many of the streets in town are named after their ten children. Ronan and Ciara lived a long and happy life here."

Del listened to the history of the town and wondered how she'd remembered it all so easily. He could cough up a few facts on the Máa-zib artifacts in the museum, but he'd forgotten about Ciara and her determination to make her own way in the world.

He had a feeling he would have liked the young woman. Or at least have admired her willingness to strike out in a time when women were expected to do what their fathers and older brothers told them.

"Do they still have relatives here in town?" a woman asked Del.

"The grandchildren were all girls," he told her. "So the name died out. But many of their descendants still live in the area. My family has a few McGees in our history, as does the Hendrix family."

"That's so nice," the woman said with a sigh. "History and family traditions."

Maya grinned at him, then launched into a story about the 1906 San Francisco earthquake and how a subsequent landslide revealed a cave filled with Máa-zib artifacts, including gold statues and jewelry.

When they stopped for coffee and pastries at Brewhaha, Del moved next to Maya.

"Nicely done," he told her.

"This is fun. I haven't played tour guide since that summer. I had no idea I'd remember everything, but apparently it's stored right next to the lyrics to songs that used to drive me crazy."

His cell phone rang. He glanced at the screen and saw it was his attorney. "Can you handle this crowd for a second?" he asked.

She pointed to the door. "Go take your call. I'll make sure everyone gets their coffee."

He stepped outside and answered. "This is Del."

"You're avoiding me," Russell said. "You know that makes me nervous."

"You're a lawyer. Everything makes you nervous."

"That makes me a good lawyer. Have you decided?"

Just before returning to Fool's Gold, Del had yet another offer to be part of a start-up. The ideas were good and he liked the guys involved. "I think they're going to be successful," he began.

Russell groaned. "That's a no. What is it with you?"

"I'm not an entrepreneur."

"I'm getting that. Del, you're too young to retire. You need to do something, and honestly, I can't see you taking a job somewhere. It's not your style."

"I know. I'll figure it out."

"And I'll tell them thanks but no thanks."

Del hung up. He turned and saw Maya watching him from the entrance to Brew-haha.

"Want to talk about it?" she asked when he rejoined the group.

"Not much to say. I got an offer to be part of a start-up and I said no."

"I figured that. Any particular reason?"

"It's not what I want to do. I've been lucky. I don't have to take just anything. I can choose."

He waited for her to ask what that would be but she

didn't. Instead, she held out a latte. "Patience said to tell you it's how you like it."

"She's a good woman."

"Yes, well, you get to return the favor in a couple of days when we have to go talk about cameras with her daughter and her grove of Saplings."

"I thought you were going to do that."

She smiled. "I am and you're coming with me."

He chuckled. "So that's why you decided to help out today. So I'd owe you."

"That is very possible."

TWO DAYS LATER Maya was incredibly grateful she'd asked Del along. In theory, facing eight girls shouldn't have been a big deal. And it wasn't. It was terrifying. Maya stared into their pretty faces, watching them watch her, and knew that if she was by herself, she would have been a stuttering mess. Ridiculous but true. Talking about the town was one thing. She supposed it was because history was impersonal. Explaining how to use a camera seemed more personal somehow. Or maybe it was a passion thing. While the history was interesting, she didn't care about it.

But with Del to make jokes and deflect some of the attention, she found that she wasn't all that nervous. Not if she kept focused on what she was doing.

"Filters are a great way to manipulate a picture," she said. "There are lots of free apps for your smartphones that can change a regular picture into something more fun." She paused. "Be sure to check with your parents before downloading any apps, okay?"

One of the Saplings raised her hand. "Not all apps are kid appropriate," the girl said firmly.

"That's right. Now with your digital camera, you do the editing on your computer. With a couple of good programs and your mouse, you can work magic."

She'd hooked up her laptop to the screen provided. The meeting room where the Saplings met was surprisingly nice. There were desks and chairs, an area where the girls could sit on cushy carpeting and a craft station.

Maya clicked with her mouse and rotated the picture on the screen. It was a group shot of all eight girls. She'd taken it when she first arrived and now used it to demonstrate different ways to make an image more interesting.

She changed the picture to black-and-white, brightened the lighting, added a few special effects, then turned the girls loose on the computer.

She and Del had their smartphones with them. Each took a couple of girls and used pictures already on the phone to demonstrate different apps.

"This is fun," one of the girls said. "We were worried because Taryn's away for a while."

Maya knew that Taryn was one of the Grove Leaders. Her husband, Angel, was the other.

"Taryn had a baby, didn't she?" Maya asked.

"Uh-huh. A boy. Bryce. He's really cute. She'll be back soon. It's nice that they have a baby." The girl, Chloe, glanced pointedly at the man next to Angel.

Kenny, Maya thought, remembering him introducing himself when she and Del had arrived. Chloe's stepfather.

The eight-year-old narrowed her gaze. "*I'd* like a little brother or sister," she said loudly.

Kenny groaned. "I'm working on it. I'm working on it."

"Work faster."

Angel snickered.

Maya quickly pointed at Del's phone. "Oh, look. He has pictures from his travels. Del, show us the pictures."

Del hadn't heard the baby conversation so looked a little confused, but he nodded, anyway.

"Sure. Let me hook my phone up to the computer."

He pulled a cord from her tote and plugged in his phone. Seconds later, a slide show started on the big screen. The girls all stared at photos of mountains, capped in snow. They laughed when they saw a big yak.

"Where is that?" one of the girls asked.

"Tibet. Who knows where that is?"

Del went through about a hundred pictures. He explained about life in the village and talked about the different kids he'd met. The girls were enthralled— their photograph-editing session forgotten.

Maya watched and listened. She knew that a video would be even more compelling than still pictures. Del was on the right track with his idea to create videos for schoolkids.

She found herself wondering what it would be like to be a part of that. Not that he was asking. Or she was offering. Fool's Gold was her home now, but it would sure be nice...

DEL TYPED ON his laptop on the porch of his cabin. Call him crazy, but he couldn't get China off the brain. The country was geographically massive and diverse, and they were changing economically. Rural villages were giving way to factory jobs. Was it like postwar America in the 1950s or completely different? How did the rapid changes affect the children of the country?

China, he thought again, typing in the document. That was where he wanted to start with his video series.

Travel could be a challenge. Many areas were completely open for travel by westerners, but there would be parts that wouldn't be. He made a list of people he knew in the State Department. Maya might have some contacts. Celebrities often traveled to unexpected places.

He would need her help with equipment. How little could he get by with? Probably some kind of satellite uplink would be best, so he could send footage back to a safe location, in case some local official took issue with what he was doing and confiscated their cameras.

The team would have to be small. In a perfect world, it would be him and Maya and—

He stopped typing and stared at the lake. Him and Maya? No. That wasn't happening. They weren't together, or even business partners. He was helping her with the town videos because the mayor had asked him. The fact that he'd gotten sucked in deeper than he'd planned was just one of those things. Working with Maya was fun. They got along. But he wasn't taking her to China with him.

Still, they'd been good with those kids the other day, he thought. And on the tour. They worked well together. They understood and respected each other. Because of their past, he thought.

Once again he wondered how things would have been different if he'd realized she'd broken up with him out of fear and not because she didn't care. If he'd been able to see that, to reach out to her. Would they have stayed together? He could have transferred to her college. And then what? He wouldn't have enjoyed settling in LA any more than he would have been able to stay here. So eventually he would have had to leave.

Would she have gone with him? *A question with no answer*, he thought. Because the past was done and there was no changing it.

He looked up at the sound of an SUV driving toward his cabin. He recognized the battered vehicle and saved his work before closing his laptop. What he wanted to do was slip out the back door and not be seen. Only the cabin didn't have a back door and he was too old to be hiding from his father.

So instead he waited and watched until Ceallach walked up the front steps and took the seat opposite his.

"So this is where you're staying."

"It is."

Ceallach looked around. "Too many people."

Del didn't bother saying the people around him were a part of what he liked. His father wouldn't get it or care.

"How can I help you, Dad?"

"Something's wrong with your mother."

That got Del's attention. "What do you mean?"

"I don't know. She's a woman. A mystery. But there's something. She's not herself." He hesitated, as if he were going to say more.

"Do you think she's sick?"

Ceallach shook his head. "She's more quiet than usual. She's gone a lot. Into town. I've asked her what's going on, but she says she's fine. I have to do something."

"Okay," Del said slowly. "Like take her away for a vacation?"

"Don't be ridiculous. I have to work. She hasn't said anything to you?"

"No."

"She knows I'm working on several commissions. Big jobs. It's not like her to distract me."

Because it was all about the art, Del thought grimly. All about Ceallach. He was the center of the known universe and life revolved around him.

"These are important commissions," his father added defensively, as if he knew what Del was thinking.

"I'm sure they are."

"One's for the French government. I have to be in my work. Elaine understands that."

After thirty-five years, she wouldn't have much of a choice.

Del had often wondered what it was about his father that had drawn his mother in the first place. She'd been a small-town girl. He was sure there were those who thought she'd been overwhelmed by Ceallach's fame. Even in his early twenties, he'd been famous and successful.

Del suspected that hadn't impressed her. She would have been drawn to something else. Maybe Ceallach's passion? Not that Del wanted to think about that too much. But whatever the appeal, she had been loyal and loving through all the difficult times. Even when his father's art messed with his head and the drinking had made it worse—she'd been there.

As a kid, Del had wondered how much of his father was in him. He was sure his brothers worried about the same thing, although they never discussed it. Would they grow up to be like him?

Nick and the twins had inherited Ceallach's artistic ability. Del and Aidan were more like their mother. Del saw some of his father in himself. The videos were probably an offshoot of the other man's talent. The restlessness that Ceallach harnessed into his glasswork had manifested in other ways in Del.

He hoped he didn't have his father's selfish streak. That he was more accepting of people. Difficult to know when it came to himself.

"What are you doing?" his father asked. "You have a job yet?"

"Not right this second," Del said. "I'm still considering my options." He thought about mentioning that he'd sold his company for enough money that, in theory, he never had to work again. At least not very hard. But his father wouldn't see that as a positive. "I've had some offers."

"In business." Ceallach's tone was dismissive.

"Yeah, Dad. In business."

"A necessary evil."

"But without the intrinsic value that art brings to the table."

His father brightened. "Exactly. Men of business don't understand the genius required for art."

"What about women in business?" he asked, thinking Maya would appreciate the joke. His father, not so much.

Ceallach stared at him.

"Women in business?" Del repeated. "Because women and men do the same jobs these days."

"Ridiculous. Your mother always knew her most important job was to support me."

Which was probably true, Del thought, hoping his mother was happy with her choices. He wouldn't want that, a woman who simply served him. While the theory of it was kind of fun, the reality would be very different. He wanted someone who was there for him as much as he was there for her, but he also wanted more. A partner in his work. Someone who cared as much as he did about what they were doing. *A collaboration*, he thought.

Something else his father wouldn't understand.

"Are the twins coming for your birthday?" he asked.

Ceallach dismissed the question with a shake of his head. "I have no idea."

"Where are they?"

"You think I have time to keep track of things like that?"

"Okay, I guess you also don't know why they left town, then?"

His father shifted in his seat and looked away. "I have no idea."

The statement was so at odds with the other man's body language that Del nearly started laughing. Obviously Ceallach knew exactly why the twins had run off, but he wasn't saying. Which was pretty typical for a family that loved to keep secrets, he thought.

"I hope they're coming to the party," he said. "It would be good to see them."

He thought maybe his father would agree, but instead Ceallach stood. "I have to get back to work. Goodbye."

Not the most satisfying of meetings, he thought as the older man walked away. He still didn't know exactly why his father had stopped by, except maybe to talk about Elaine.

Del stood and moved around the porch. Restlessness threatened. Not to leave town—he wasn't ready for that just yet. But for a calming force. A place to be that always made him feel better.

Maya, he thought with relief. He needed to see Maya. Then everything would be fine.

CHAPTER TEN

"You won't believe the stuff we're building," Chase said, his tone excited, his hands barely able to keep up with his words. "We're so over the robot cat. My team's working on an underwater robot that does welding. It has to be light enough to be easily maneuverable, but also able to work with everything that goes with underwater welding. Just dealing with the currents. Because they're always changing, right? And the tides have an influence."

Maya smiled at her younger stepbrother. "You exhaust me."

"It's 'cause I'm so smart."

She laughed and hugged him. "That's part of it."

Chase hung on for a second. "Have you seen Zane? He's happy. It's weird, but I like it."

"As much as you like your nerd camp?"

The seventeen-year-old straightened and grinned. "Even more, but don't tell him."

"I won't. I promise."

Chase ran off to the house. Maya turned to Del. "He's happy."

"I can see that. The camp sounds intense."

"It is."

They were out by the barn, at the Nicholson family ranch. Tonight was the rehearsal dinner, which meant a small group. Maya and Del, Zane, Phoebe and Chase. Dellina was also there with her husband, Sam. The wedding would be a big affair with half the town showing up, but tonight was more intimate.

"Chase was lucky to get in," Maya said, heading toward the goat pens nearest the main house. "Apparently there's a long waiting list. But a spot opened up in the second session and Zane pulled some strings. I decided not to ask. I was thrilled that Zane was being so supportive."

"Wasn't he always?"

"Yes and no. Zane worried that Chase didn't take life seriously enough. Chase isn't that guy. He's gifted when it comes to electronics and inventing things, but not one for following the well-traveled path in life. Zane saw him as a screwup and Chase kind of was. They both had the best of intentions but neither could see the other's side."

They paused by a pen of adolescent goats. She looked at Del, liking how he was watching her. She wanted to read desire in his gaze, but even if they were just going to be friends, she was happy. Being around him always made her feel better.

"Over the summer that changed," she continued. "They had a couple of big fights, then had to pull together to save the cattle on that trip I told you about. Along the way Zane fell in love. It changed him in the best way possible. He'll always worry about Chase, but he's learning to trust a little. And Chase is acting more responsibly."

"A win-win?"

"Exactly."

He pointed at the goats in the pen. "Want to talk about these guys?"

"They're goats."

"I can see that."

"Cashmere goats and they bite."

He grinned. "You know that from personal experience?"

"I've been nipped a time or two. They're being kept close to the house while they're still young. They'll head out with the herd soon."

"There's a herd?"

"More than one." She pointed to the small animals. "The females are probably close to forty pounds now. The males a little bigger. Technically there's no purebred cashmere goat. All goats can have the gene to produce down." She paused. "How much goat information are you looking for?"

He leaned against a fence post and crossed his arms over his chest. "How much you got?"

He was tall and broad-shouldered, she thought, doing her best not to swoon. Handsome. There were tingles whenever she looked at him. Foolish, but unavoidable. She wanted to step closer and have him hold her. Kiss her. Touch her. Sure, it would give the goats something to talk about but these ones were teenagers. No doubt they could relate to the need to get into trouble.

"Solid-color goats are preferable to multicolored. As you can see, Zane has all solids here. Their coats have a coarse outer layer, with the down underneath. Each adult goat will produce three to four ounces of down."

He frowned. "That's it? Three ounces?"

"Uh-huh. That's enough to knit about a third of a sweater. Which is why high-quality cashmere is so expensive."

"You know a lot about goats."

"I lived here for two years and I paid attention. I can tell you about the cattle, too, if you want." She held in a laugh. "Zane sells bull sperm."

Del took a step back. "I don't think I want to know about that."

"Most men don't." She looked at the big house, the tent set up for the wedding, the mountains in the distance. "It's beautiful here."

"Different from Las Vegas?"

She nodded, remembering her shock the first time she'd seen the ranch. "I didn't know places existed like this. Not real places. I thought they were only on TV or in the movies." She looked at him. "I'd never seen snow before we moved here. Not piled up on the ground."

"You'd probably never seen a goat before."

"Maybe once at a petting zoo." She looked past him. "I liked how green everything was. And the quiet. It was safe here."

Because things hadn't always been safe with her mother, she thought. As she'd gotten older, a few of her mother's boyfriends had started paying attention to her. While it wasn't anything she'd wanted or sought out, her mother had always blamed her.

"Gotta love the town," she said, rather than go down a dark path to her past. "You, on the other hand, probably took the charm for granted."

"Sure. I was a kid. That was my job."

They started toward the barn. "I remember when we used to come out here," Del said as they approached the large, red building. "Remember going up into the hayloft?"

She nodded. Hay hadn't been stored up there in years, so it was mostly open and empty, with some old ranch equipment and a bunch of boxes containing who knew what. But for her and Del, it had been quiet and private. Something they'd been interested in a lot that summer.

They stepped into the barn. It was cool and dim. Light filtered in through the door and a couple of windows. Memories jostled with shadows.

"Zane would have killed us both if he'd found us," she said, automatically lowering her voice. Because back then they'd been careful to be quiet.

"He cared about you," Del told her. "Despite how you two didn't get along."

"He did. I just couldn't see it that way. He was so annoying back then." She looked at Del. "Do you know the only reason he met Phoebe is because I begged her to come on the cattle drive? I was worried about Chase and couldn't get up here right after their big fight. Phoebe had some time so I asked her to come protect Chase. It was a completely selfish motive."

"Not selfish if you were looking out for your brother."

"Looking out for one at the expense of the other." She sat down on a bench. Del settled next to her.

"It all worked out in the end," he said.

"It did. I even joked with her about being a distraction for Zane. We both thought I was kidding. But she turned out to be the one." Life was funny that way, she thought. "If Zane hadn't been such a stick up the butt, I wouldn't have sent Phoebe here and he might never have met her. Looking at them together, I know that would have been a really sad thing. They're a great couple."

She hoped her envy didn't color her voice. She was thrilled they'd found each other, but she would like a little of that magic, too. Being happy with someone. Knowing you'd found the one. She wanted permanent.

Strange how she'd never found that. She'd dated some, but really hadn't found anyone who interested her. Not in a significant way. That combination of friendship and sexual attraction seemed elusive.

"Love is strange," Del said. "Look at my parents. They've been together for thirty-five years. I can honestly say, I don't know what my mom sees in my dad. He's not the nicest guy."

"She loves him and he's good to her."

Del looked at her. "You're leaving out the most important part of that sentence."

"Which is?"

"He's good to her, in his way."

Maya exhaled. "I knows it seems like that, from your perspective," she began.

"Not from yours?"

They were treading on dangerous territory. Elaine was her friend, but she was also Del's mother. "I know he's the only man she's ever loved. I know she's never regretted any part of their marriage. I know she loves him and he loves her. Is it a relationship I would be happy with?" She shook her head. "No. I'd want more of a partnership."

"Equals," he said firmly. "I agree. My dad stopped by a couple of days ago. He wanted to talk about Mom. He thinks there's something going on with her, but doesn't know what. I would applaud him being aware enough of her to notice, except the context of his concern was all about him. How she knows her place is taking care of him for his art." He leaned back against the wall. "Maybe it's an age thing."

Maya was less concerned about that than what was going on with Elaine. She wasn't surprised Ceallach had noticed something was wrong with his wife. The woman was fighting cancer. She *had* to be acting differently at home.

Loyalty to her friend battled with her dislike of keeping such a huge secret. If she thought about it too long, she got a knot in her stomach.

"Did your dad say what he thought was the problem?"

"No. He was pretty vague about it."

"If he's worried, he should talk to her."

Del stood. "That's not the Mitchell way," he reminded her, holding out his hand and then pulling her to his feet. "You know we love our secrets."

"Yes, I do." She tilted her head. "So what secrets are you keeping?"

"None that are interesting."

"I suspect there are a few that would raise some eyebrows."

He chuckled. "My life is an open book."

"Even when it comes to Hyacinth?"

She hadn't planned the question. She hadn't even been thinking about the other woman. At least not consciously. But apparently she had been on her mind.

"That wasn't the most subtle transition," he said. "What do you want to know?"

"How did you meet?"

"Through friends. We were at the same party. It was one of those things."

"I can imagine. She's very beautiful."

Hyacinth was a petite firecracker on skates—Maya would guess she was even more impressive in person. She had a bubbly, slightly irreverent personality that made her a favorite subject for interviews.

"You were in love with her." Maya made the words a statement rather than a question.

"I was."

"And now?"

Del studied her for a second. "No. It's long over. We wanted different things. I was too traditional for her."

"Traditional as in marriage and kids?"

"Traditional as in one man, one woman."

"Oh."

Del shrugged. "It happens. She liked variety. A lot of variety. I realized I either had to accept that or move on. It's not in my nature to share the woman in my life."

She never would have guessed that was what broke them up. "You know that for most people, being a one-woman man is a really good thing."

"I've heard rumors." His dark gaze settled on her face. "What about you? Any embarrassing secrets in your past?"

"I'm oddly boring that way. There was that one night with the wrestler, but you don't want to know about that."

He grinned and put his arm around her, then guided her out of the barn. "Even though I know you're making it up, tell me the story, anyway. Good-guy wrestler or bad-guy wrestler?"

"Bad guy, of course."

"That's my girl."

THE DINING ROOM in the ranch house was awash with twinkle lights. Large displays of flowers filled the corners and marched down the center of the table. Every place setting had a stemless wineglass with Zane and Phoebe's names engraved, along with the wedding date. The traditional dining room chairs had been covered with pale blue linen toppers, and soft music played from portable speakers.

"You outdid yourself," Maya said. "I'm feeling a strong combination of wow and envy."

Dellina, the pretty brunette who had planned both the wedding and the rehearsal dinner, sighed. "Thank you. Envy compliments are my favorite. When it's your time to do the marriage thing, call me."

"Sure," Maya said, thinking she needed a relationship first.

The rehearsal had gone smoothly. It helped that the wedding party was small. Now they were going to enjoy a nice dinner before all the craziness started in the morning.

Maya followed Dellina back to the living room, where the small group had gathered. Phoebe was talking to Chase and Del. Dellina moved to her husband's side, while Zane approached Maya.

"She's throwing me out," he complained as he handed her a glass of champagne.

"Just for the night. Tomorrow you'll be married and with each other forever."

Zane watched his bride for a second, before looking at Maya. "Thanks to you."

"Yes, you owe me. Remember that the next time I annoy you. That should be in about five minutes."

He didn't smile at the joke. "I do owe you. You're the one who brought Phoebe into my life. Without you, I probably wouldn't have met her."

Maya swallowed against a sudden rush of emotion. "Don't you dare break the tear seal," she told him. "If I start crying, you know Phoebe will be next."

Zane winced. "Good point. How about those

49ers? I think they have a real shot at the Super Bowl this year. What about you?"

Maya chuckled. "I'm sure they'll go all the way."

Zane moved close and lowered his voice. "I'm going to risk the tear seal and say you know you're always welcome here, right? You're family. I know we've had our differences, but they're behind us now and you'll always be a part of things."

"I know." She swallowed, fighting tears. "I wish we'd had this talk ten years ago. I might not have stayed away for so long."

"Me, too. But maybe we both needed to grow up. You more than me, of course."

The need to cry evaporated as she laughed. "I can always count on you to put me in my place."

He kissed her cheek. "No. You can always count on me. Period." He nodded at Del as he approached, then went off to talk to Phoebe.

"You doing okay?" Del asked.

She tucked her arm around his. "Yes. Just bonding with family and trying not to cry. You?"

"I've sobbed at least twice since we arrived. Did you see the flowers in the dining room? They're so beautiful." He waved his free hand in front of his face. "I just love weddings."

"Mock me all you want," she told him. "I'm having a moment here."

"You should enjoy it. Zane's a good guy. I'm glad he found the right woman."

"Me, too." She sipped her champagne. "I hope this isn't too intense for you."

"It's nothing. At my house there was lots of yelling and the occasional fight broke out."

"I guess that comes with having five boys so close in age."

"My mom was doing most of the fighting."

Maya laughed. "I'm serious."

"Okay, serious it is. We fought a lot. And then we made up."

"Are things better with Aidan?"

Del considered the question. "Some. He's avoiding me less."

"You helped him out. That has to mean something."

"So you'd think." Del pointed to where Chase and Zane were talking. The two brothers were laughing, obviously at ease with each other.

"I want that," Del admitted. "Before I leave, I want to have one good conversation with Aidan. I want to know things are okay between us."

He kept on talking, but Maya had stopped listening. All she could hear was his phrase, "Before I leave."

Because that was what was going to happen. Del was going to leave. He'd come back for his father's birthday party. Once that was over, he had no reason to stay.

While she'd always known his stay wasn't permanent, somehow she'd forgotten. Del was a part of her days now. A part of her work. Having him gone was going to be awful. But he was a man who needed to be on the move, and getting him to stay, well, that wasn't going to happen.

Last time she'd been the one taking off. This time it was him. But the end result was going to be the same. Once again, she and Del would be apart. She knew she was going to miss him. The question was, how much?

As EXPECTED, MUCH of the town turned out for Phoebe and Zane's wedding. Del mingled with the other guests before the ceremony started. Maya was busy helping the bride do whatever it was brides did before they got married. He spotted his brothers and headed over to talk to them.

"Nice suit," he said to Nick, then turned to Aidan. "You, too."

Both brothers had on dark suits with ties. Aidan tugged at his collar. "Damned social conventions."

Nick looked comfortable in his fancy clothes. "I like getting dressed up every now and then. Besides, it's for Zane."

Aidan grumbled something under his breath, but Del suspected he was a lot less annoyed than he let on. Aidan and Nick had been friends with Zane since grade school.

"Big turnout," Del said. "The folks here?"

"Naw," Nick said. "Dad's got a commission and Mom's not feeling well."

Del remembered his conversation with Ceallach a few days before. "You think she's okay?" he asked.

Aidan frowned. "Why do you ask?"

Del told them about their father's visit. "He was worried."

"You mean he thought about someone other than himself?" Aidan asked bitterly. "Let's put a star on this day on the calendar."

Del wanted to chide his brother for being cynical, but he'd had the same thought himself.

Nick grimaced. "Yeah, you have a point. If Dad's noticing, it must be bad. I'll stop by and talk to her. Maybe getting the party together is too much for her. We can all help."

"Already offered," Aidan said. "She told me she was handling it."

"I'll make sure I go by, too," Del told them.

"That will make everything right," Aidan muttered.

"You're in a mood." Del stared at his brother. "What's your problem?"

"This isn't the time," Nick said, his voice calm. "Both of you, stop it. Zane's getting married. Zip it."

Del nodded. His brother had a point. Whatever Aidan's issue was, Del wasn't going to get into it now. He turned and walked toward the big tent in the backyard.

Inside, the catering staff was setting up for dinner. There were dozens of round tables. Crystal and silverware gleamed in the lights strung across the ceiling. The sweet smell of flowers mingled with the faint smoky scent of a smoldering grill.

He crossed the tent and went out the other side to where chairs had been set up in the shade of a grove of trees. There were two sections on either side of a center aisle. Ribbons and flowers framed the area. A woman played a harp while guests found their seats.

Del saw Eddie and Gladys and headed their way. The irreverent old ladies were exactly what he needed to forget about Aidan and whatever bug he had up his ass. Del didn't want to fight—not today. Tomorrow they could take it up, but for now, a good guy was marrying a great girl. They should stop and celebrate that.

It didn't take long for the rest of the guests to take their seats. The music changed to something slow and romantic. Zane took his place by the minister, his brother, Chase, next to him.

Maya appeared at the back of the grove of trees. Del about fell out of his chair when he saw her. She'd joked about her dress and having to get all fancy, but he hadn't expected her to look like a goddess.

She'd put up her blond hair into some complicated swirl of curls and swoops. Her dress was pale blue, long and with a deep V. The top of it had a crisscrossy thing going on and seemed to hug every curve. He was torn between wanting her and needing to throw his suit jacket over her shoulders so no one else could see her.

She walked slowly, a small bouquet of flowers in her hand. As she passed him, he caught sight of the dress from behind. It was cut low with straps that made an X and these drape things down the side. He was sure it was stylish and he liked how it looked on her but mostly what he was thinking was there was no way she was wearing a bra.

It was the wrong thing to fixate on during a wedding. Only a sleaze dog would be imagining taking that dress off her as the bride came down the aisle. Del half expected lightning to strike, and when it didn't, he knew he was damned lucky.

The ceremony passed in a blur of vows and the exchange of rings. Del kept his attention on Maya, who was obviously moved by the sight of her friend marrying Zane. After the bride and groom were pronounced husband and wife, they hugged Maya and Chase before walking down the center aisle together.

"That was so beautiful," Eddie said, clutching Del's arm. "They're a beautiful couple."

"Who are going to have sex tonight," Gladys added from Del's other side.

"They're having sex every night," Eddie responded with a cackle. "If you had Zane in your bed, you'd be doing it all the time, too."

"Good point."

Del extracted himself from the septuagenarians. "And that's my cue to excuse myself. Ladies, it's been a pleasure."

Eddie pouted. "We're old. No one wants to do it with us anymore. The least you can do is let us talk about it."

Del held up both hands in a gesture of surrender. "I'm not stopping you at all. I encourage you to talk about it."

Gladys grinned. "Just not with you here?"

"You're too much for me."

"Chicken."

"Absolutely."

He kissed them both on the cheek, then went to find Maya.

She was with the rest of the wedding party. They were taking pictures. He stood by the trees and watched the posing. In the background, a guy with a video camera recorded everything.

Del wandered closer and thought about the composition of the shot. The eye line looked good. There would be an establishing shot—probably a picture of the wedding invitation, or the veil or something to show the viewers were about to watch a wedding video.

He turned his attention back to Maya, who was laughing at something Zane said. Why hadn't she married? She was beautiful, talented, funny, easy to be with. He was surprised some guy hadn't snapped her up.

She turned from Zane and saw him. Her smile widened, as if she was happy to see him. Something hit him hard in the gut. Wanting, he acknowledged, but there was something else. A deeper sensation he was in no mood to analyze. Instead, he stayed where he was and watched them take the rest of the pictures.

When they were done, Maya walked toward him. She had trouble on the uneven ground and when she reached him, she grabbed his arm, then stepped out of her heels.

"These do not work on grass," she said with a laugh. "In case you had any transvestite tendencies."

"Not so far."

He took the bouquet from her and dropped it to the ground, then put his hands on her hips and drew her against him.

They were in relative privacy in the grove of trees. People were all around them, but no one was that close. The music had started, and judging by the scent of steaks filling the air, the barbecue was going. Which meant the guests would be moving toward the tent. *Better for him*, he thought as he lowered his head and kissed her.

Maya raised her chin and met him more than halfway. Her lips were soft and yielding, clinging to his. She wrapped her arms around his neck.

He settled his mouth more firmly on hers. She tasted of mint and champagne, and her lips parted before he asked. He moved his tongue against hers, feeling the heat, the electricity. They'd always been good together, he thought hazily. Well matched. Time away from each other hadn't changed that.

Wanting poured through him. Blood rushed to his groin with a predictable result. He moved his hands from her hips to her rear, sliding across the slick material of her dress. She nestled closer, relaxing into him, as if trusting him with all she was.

In the distance a bell rang. It was an insistent sound. She sighed against his mouth.

"They're calling us to dinner."

"You hungry?"

She chuckled. "Yes, and exactly the way you mean. But there's a head table and we're both at it. Someone's bound to notice two empty spots."

"Damn."

She stared into his eyes. "My thoughts exactly." Her mouth turned up. "It's the dress, isn't it? I knew it would make you hot."

He touched her cheek. "It's not the dress."

Her pupils dilated. "You say the sweetest things."

He kissed her lightly, then dropped to one knee and collected her ridiculous heels. "You want to go barefoot?" he asked.

"It seems like the best plan."

He grabbed the flowers and rose. She took the bouquet. He held her shoes in one hand and rested the other on the small of her back.

"Shall we?"

DINNER PASSED IN a blur. Despite the steaks done to perfection and the delicious side dishes, Maya didn't eat much. She was too aware of Del sitting next to her. Every now and then he would touch her. A brush of his fingers against her bare arm. His thigh pressing against hers.

She and Chase had written a toast together. She joined the teen to give it, then stood with Del as Zane and Phoebe stepped into the center of the room for the first dance. Once the chorus began, the DJ invited everyone to join them.

Del surprised her by pulling her into his arms.

They swayed together, the other guests around them fading to the background.

She liked being in his arms, she thought. Maybe it was the lingering effects of the kiss or the champagne she'd been drinking, but all of this felt good. Right.

They moved easily together. When the song ended, they were by the back of the tent, so slipping outside was simple. Without discussing a destination, they walked toward the barn. Halfway there, Del pulled her against him again, but this time he didn't have dancing in mind.

She stepped into his embrace and leaned into his kiss. His mouth was warm as it claimed hers. She swept her tongue against his. Their kiss deepened.

Her breasts nestled against his chest, as if seeking comfort. The night was cool, the stars bright. She felt the prickly softness of the grass beneath her bare feet. Del was the only solid object in a world that started to spin. She hung on, letting need blend with memories. She knew how they'd been so long ago. What would they be like together now?

She wanted to find out. She wanted to know it was just as good. She tilted her hips forward and let her belly come in contact with the hardness of his erection. All that for her? Talk about getting lucky.

A burst of soft laughter came from the other side of the barn. She jumped. Del drew back a little, but kept his arms around her.

"Seems like we're not the only ones thinking a little privacy would be a good thing," he murmured, his voice low and husky.

She moved her hands from his shoulders to his wrists. "Follow me," she said, taking his hand in hers.

She led him out of the barn to the back door of the main house. A few lights had been left on, but most of the rooms were dark. She took the back stairs, remembering exactly how many steps until they reached the main landing, then drawing him down the hallway to her high school bedroom.

Her windows faced away from the tent. Even so, she made sure the curtains were pulled before she turned on the table lamp. Del stood next to one of the two beds, his gaze intense.

Desire tightened the lines of his face. He looked like a man who wanted a woman. Lucky for her, that woman was her.

They stared at each other for several seconds. She thought he might ask if she was sure or wanted to have some other bit of conversation. Instead, he crossed to her and reached for the zipper on the side of her dress and drew it down.

She raised her eyebrows. "How did you know where that was?"

"I've been studying your dress all night."

"A man with a plan."

"I have more than a plan."

He pulled down the straps of her dress. The entire gown slid to the floor and pooled at her feet. Underneath she had on a thong and nothing else.

The room was silent except for the sound of his sharp intake of air. His muscles went tense and she watched as his already-large erection flexed.

"Where's Chase's room?"

The question had her blinking. "Ah, across the hall, two doors down."

Del was moving before she'd finished speaking. When he was gone, she hesitated, not sure what to do. Fortunately he was back less than twenty seconds later, a box of condoms in his hand.

She grinned. "Like I said, a man with a plan."

It was the last thing she said for quite a while.

There was the sigh when he crossed to her and cupped her breasts in his large hands as he kissed her. The little moan when he broke the kiss so he could bend over and lick her nipples. The gasp when he swept her up in his arms and lowered her onto one of the beds.

It was the same bed they'd made love in ten years ago, she thought hazily. The bed where she'd lost her virginity that weekend Zane had taken Chase to some science competition.

Everything was different now, she thought, watching Del kick off his shoes. They were both older. Neither of them frightened, inexperienced teenagers. His shirt and trousers hit the floor, then his socks and briefs followed. She got a quick glimpse of his erection as he slid onto the bed and pulled her close.

He shifted her onto her back and kissed her. His tongue pursued and she allowed herself to be delightfully caught. They enjoyed the age-old dance of soon-to-be lovers, exploring, touching, feeling, but with the added benefit of having been there before.

When he lowered his head to take her nipple in

his mouth, she knew how it was going to feel. Anticipation sharpened the sensation. As he sucked, need spiraled to her belly, then lower, causing her to swell and dampen. He moved between her breasts, back and forth, taking his time, as if they had nowhere else to be.

She wanted him, wanted this, wanted what would happen when he entered her. But she also needed time to stretch until this moment went on without ending. She didn't want to think about tomorrow or even later. There was just now.

She pushed on his shoulder, urging him to lie back, then leaned over him, so she could decide what happened next. Undeterred, Del cupped her breasts as she explored his shoulders, his chest. She ran her fingers down his belly and captured his penis in her right hand.

"You're playing with fire," he teased.

"Is that what we're calling it?"

He grinned. "You keep doing that, you can call it anything you'd like."

She paused to put a condom on him, then he moved his hands to her hips and urged her to straddle him. She braced herself with her hands on either side of his broad shoulders. He moved his hand between her legs and rested his thumb against the very heart of her. Then he began to stroke her swollen, hungry center.

He circled, slowly at first, before increasing the speed. She tried to stay in her head, to not get lost in what he was doing. But it was impossible. Everything felt too good. Need spiraled, taking her closer and closer to her ultimate destination. She wasn't ready and tried to hold back. If only…

She made the mistake of sinking down. Just a little but it was enough. His erection filled her and she was lost. Lost in the feeling of being stretched in the best way possible. Lost in the easy way they fit together and how good it was when she raised and then lowered herself again.

His touch on her clit never changed. He kept pace with her growing desire and up-and-down movements. His breathing matched hers. Their thighs tensed.

She moved a little faster, wondering if it could be better, then had to gasp as fiery pleasure shot through her. It was going to be too much, she thought frantically. Too good, too soon. She wasn't ready. She needed this to last longer.

Her head warred with the rest of her body and quickly lost the battle. Soon she couldn't think, couldn't do anything but raise and lower herself, moving closer and closer to the pinnacle of her release. *Faster*, she thought, feeling that familiar promise barely out of reach. She was almost there.

Up and down, his thumb in place, rubbing in time with his thrusts. The end was inevitable. The only questions was—

"Del!"

She gasped his name as her climax rocketed through her. Every cell in her body cried out as she came. His free hand clamped onto her hip and held her in place as he thrust in deep, and she lost herself.

When they had both finished, he pulled her close and held her.

"Maya."

Her name was a breath. An exhale. The sound cut through her, opening her until she was completely bare to him in every way possible. With that vulnerability came a truth so sharp it finished the job of separating her from the facade she'd been hiding behind for the past ten years.

The reason she hadn't fallen for anyone else, the reason she'd never found love, was because she couldn't. Del had claimed her heart and to the best of her knowledge he'd never given it back.

She was, after all this time, still in love with him.

CHAPTER ELEVEN

THE NEXT MORNING, Maya avoided looking at herself in the bathroom mirror. While it made putting on makeup somewhat complicated, she was terrified of what she would see in her eyes. She tried to tell herself it wasn't as if there was a reader board proclaiming in bright letters "I'm in love with Del." At least she hoped there wasn't. In the end, the need to apply mascara defeated self-preservation. She sucked in a breath and stared at her reflection.

Except for looking a little tired, no doubt due to not getting home until after two in the morning and then being unable to sleep, she seemed to be the same. There was no telltale expression of guilt or confusion. No newly formed *I love Del*–shaped birthmark. She'd escaped unscathed.

At least on the outside.

The inside was a totally different matter. To be honest, she had no idea what had happened. Or when. She couldn't believe she'd been in love with Del for the past ten years and hadn't known. That was impossible to imagine. She'd been happy. Living her life. Having a career. Surely she would have noticed ongoing unrequited love. Which meant what? That lingering feelings had just…lingered? That Del sparks had been smoldering this whole time, waiting to be brought to life?

Too many questions and not enough answers, she told herself as she collected her bag and headed out of the house. She paused to water her geraniums, then walked briskly to Brew-haha. Coffee was the obvious first step. Then maybe a thorough list or two would help her clear her mind.

She was in love with Del. The thought repeated itself in time with her steps. They'd made love in her old bed, and it had happened.

Okay, she was pretty sure the act of doing it hadn't caused her to fall for him. The sex had been great, but without magical powers. But the intimacy had caused the revelation. Even more confusing was what to do now.

She told herself she didn't have to do anything. She could continue with her regularly scheduled life and pretend nothing was different. Under the right circumstances, denial was perfectly healthy. Actually that made the most sense. Del was only going to be in town for a few more weeks. When he was gone, she would revisit what had happened and figure it out. But until then, she was going to stick her head in the sand and make like an ostrich.

Twenty minutes later, she had taken the first sip of life-giving coffee. She was still deciding what to do next when she saw Elaine walking Sophie toward the park.

Maya waved at her friend, then hurried toward her.

"You're up early," she said, hugging her. "How are you feeling?"

Elaine smiled at her. "The same as I was when you called me yesterday morning to check on me. Good. Tired, but getting through."

Maya bent down to greet Sophie. The beagle wiggled to get close for pats, her happy tail wagging.

"We decided a walk would be good for us," Elaine said. "Want to join us?"

"I'd love to."

They started for Pyrite Park, Sophie in the lead. The sweet dog stopped to sniff regularly.

"We missed you at the wedding yesterday," Maya said.

"I know. I was actually feeling okay, so I could have gone. But when I got the invitation, I just wasn't sure. Tell me everything."

Maya immediately flashed on being in bed with Del, his body over hers. The sensation of skin on skin was so intense, so real, for a second she thought she was back in time.

She quickly pushed the thoughts away. Although Elaine was her friend, she was also Del's mother. There was no way they were having *that* conversation. Talk about TMI.

"Phoebe was beautiful." Maya pulled out her smartphone and pushed a couple of buttons. "I took a few pictures before the wedding."

Elaine looked at them. "She looks wonderful. So happy. Good for them."

"I agree. Zane was nervous, which was great fun. They're a sweet couple."

Elaine linked arms with her. "When are you going to find a nice young man and settle down?"

"I have no idea. I'm open to meeting someone."

Which had been true until last night, Maya thought, wondering if maybe she could get a timing pass on the lie.

"Any sparks with Del?"

If Maya had been swallowing at that moment, she would have choked. "You're my friend. I love you, but no. We're not talking about me getting together with your son."

"Why not? Don't you think he's wonderful?"

Maya relaxed. Now she could be honest. "I do. And he's leaving and I'm not."

Which was easier than admitting that while he'd seemed to enjoy himself last night, when he'd dropped her off at her place, he hadn't said a word about them getting together again. Not romantically, anyway. Obviously they would see each other at work.

"Del does love to travel," Elaine agreed with a sigh, and pointed to a bench. "Let's sit there."

Once they'd taken their seats, Elaine unfastened Sophie's leash. The beagle immediately began exploring the area, without going too far.

Elaine watched her. "I worry about Del being alone. He's not the type to settle down, but he needs someone."

"Not everyone wants to be paired up."

"Del does. He doesn't talk about it, but he wants

to be married. He's a lot like me. Connections are important to him." She looked at Maya. "You might like to travel."

Maya allowed herself a three-second fantasy of seeing the world with Del, then pushed it firmly out of her consciousness. "No matchmaking. Del and I are working together. That's all."

Except for the sex. But she wasn't going to mention that.

"Fine. I won't push. I'll daydream, but I won't push."

"Thank you for that."

Maya SPENT THE rest of Sunday worrying about Monday morning. She didn't sleep well for a second night and was running out of concealer tricks to hide the fact. Her stomach was a mess, her brain swirling, and by the time Del strolled into the studio, she was ready to run screaming into the night. Or morning, as it were.

"Hey," he said cheerfully when he saw her. "How was the rest of your weekend?"

"Good," she said cautiously, searching for hidden meaning in the words. Only there didn't seem to be any.

"I'm glad. We're really interviewing an elephant and a pony?" he asked, sitting in the visitor chair by her desk. "Did I read that right?"

"Priscilla and Reno are a unique love story. They won't actually be talking. We'll interview Heidi Stryker, their owner."

"I don't know. I suspect an elephant has a lot to say."

"Because they never forget?" she asked.

"That's the rumor."

He grinned at her as though nothing had happened between them. Which, she realized, both relieved and devastated, was probably how he saw things. They'd hooked up for one night and now they were working together again. The evening had been nice, but without emotional significance. *Oh, to be able to compartmentalize like a man*, she thought. How did they do it? Was it a brain function thing or a hormone thing or the evolutionary equivalent of dumb luck? He was male and got to put their night together in perspective. She was a female and the act of their making love forced her to admit she was in love with him. How was that fair?

Not that there was going to be an answer, she told herself. Therefore, the smartest course of action was to move on.

"You ready?" she asked. "We should collect our gear."

Del nodded and they stood. Before she could walk out of her office, he gently touched her arm.

"About Saturday," he began, his voice concerned. "I had a great time. Better than I remember, which is saying something, because what I remember was pretty damned good."

Tension eased as she was able to breathe again. "Me, too," she murmured.

"You okay?"

That made her smile. Because a woman would approach the whole conversation differently. With an explanation of what might have happened, what did happen and what could have happened but hadn't. That would be followed by a detailed analysis of everyone's feelings.

"I'm okay," she said, not sure it was true, but willing to fake it until it was.

"Good."

He released her arm and she headed toward the studio to pick up her camera. On the way she realized she'd been telling the truth. She was okay. In love, but still okay.

BY NOON THEY were done with their interview. Maya had a meeting at City Hall, so dropped Del off in town. He was about to head home for some lunch when he spotted Aidan walking toward Brew-haha. His brother looked a little pale, considering the time of day and season. Del turned toward him.

"Hungover?" he asked as he approached.

Aidan sighed. "Yeah. There was a blonde and there was tequila. I'm not sure which was more deadly."

"Maybe it was the combination."

They walked into the shop and got in line. Aidan went first and ordered a large black coffee. Del got a latte. While he and his brother had both had the same outcome of their weekend, for Del it had only mellowed him.

He'd been telling the truth when he'd spoken with Maya earlier. Being together had been better than he'd remembered. They'd always had chemistry, and that hadn't changed. But now there was an added element. Maybe experience, maybe maturity. Either way, he'd spent all of Sunday with a stupid grin on his face. It had been a long time since he'd felt the need to grin after sex, and he planned on enjoying the feeling for as long as possible.

He waited for his latte, then joined Aidan outside. His brother sat at a table covered by a patio umbrella, carefully out of the sun. Del sat across from him.

"How much did you drink?"

"You don't want to know."

"I guess not."

He'd seen Aidan with a different woman every weekend. The man was into volume. Del considered asking why Aidan didn't want something more. After a while, the whole "all cats are gray in the dark" thing got old. There was more to life than getting laid. There was caring, connection. Maybe that was why being with Maya had been so good. They had a past and now they were friends who worked well together. He knew her, understood her. Genuinely liked her.

Making love under those circumstances was about as perfect as it got. If he had his way, they would be naked together right now. Because he still wanted her. Not that he was going to get his way. The rest of what they were doing was too important. But that didn't mean he couldn't think about it.

"What?" Aidan demanded, his voice a growl. "You have a stupid grin on your face."

Del chuckled. "I'm a happy guy."

"Go to hell."

Del ignored that. "How's business?"

"Good. Busy."

"You've done a great job growing the company, Aidan. You should be proud of yourself."

"Like I had a choice."

Del put down his coffee and pushed back his chair. "Okay," he said, knowing they'd been moving toward this moment from the second he'd gotten back to town. "You win. We'll do it, right here, right now. I'll give you a free first punch."

Aidan's bleary-eyed stare sharpened. "What are you talking about?"

"Settling it. You've wanted to have it out with me since you saw me. So let's do it." Del allowed himself a slight smile. "I'll go easy on you because of the hangover."

Aidan shook his head. "I'm not fighting you."

"Why not? You're pissed. Let's deal."

Aidan put down his coffee. "I'm pissed? Is that what you call it? Fine. I'm pissed. I'm pissed and angry that you betrayed me, you selfish bastard. You took off. I was eighteen years old and you didn't even bother to give me a heads-up. You disappeared, leaving me to take care of everything. I didn't have a choice. You took that away from me."

"I know. I'm sorry."

Aidan glared at him. "That's not good enough."

"That's all I've got. An apology. I can't go back and change the past. To be honest, I don't know if I would. I couldn't stay, Aidan. Not after what happened. At first I was running from Maya, but then I figured out I wasn't cut out for a life in Fool's Gold. I never would have made it."

He drew in a breath. "But how I did it was wrong. I should have talked to you. I should have explained what was going on. And I should have checked on you. I was wrong about all of that. I handled the situation very badly. I hope, with time, you'll be able to accept my apology."

His brother leaned back in his chair. "I will if you'll stop talking," he grumbled.

"Hurting your head?"

"You have no idea." Aidan rubbed his temples, then turned to Del. "You were a total shit."

"Agreed."

"I'm doing better with the business than you ever could."

"I won't argue."

"Did I mention you're a shit?"

"Yup."

"Fine." Aidan's mouth turned up. "Want to hear something crazy?"

"Sure."

"I like running the business. The way it's growing, the new tours. They're fun. I like the tourists. I have great people working for me. I didn't plan on this being my life's work, but now that I'm stuck, it's turned out to be the best thing that ever happened to me."

Del stared at him. "What? Then why have you been acting like such a dick?"

"To mess with you. You dumped everything on me without asking. That was cold, bro."

Del swore under his breath. "You're twisted, but I respect that." He raised his to-go cup. "To you, little brother. You done good."

Aidan did the same. "You haven't done bad yourself. You sold your business for a lot of money."

"How do you know?"

"I read a couple of business blogs. The sale was mentioned."

"Thanks. I told Dad about it."

Aidan snorted. "The old man wouldn't care. You could cure cancer and he'd yawn. It's how he is."

"Tell me about it."

"What are you going to do now?"

Del thought about the videos he wanted to produce. The way they would enlighten and educate kids around the world. *Talk about a lofty and self-important description*, he thought.

"I'm not sure. I'm still mulling things over. I have ideas, but nothing firm."

"You're not sticking around here."

"You asking or telling?"

"Telling," Aidan said with a grin. "You said it yourself. You're not cut out for Fool's Gold. You'll be leaving soon enough."

Del knew his brother was right. He would leave, because that was what he did. But this time, like the first time, he would regret leaving Maya. They were a good team.

For a second he wondered what it would be like if

she came with him. If she wanted what he wanted. Only how could they live in such close quarters without starting something they shouldn't? If he was with her that much, was he at risk of falling for her again?

While he could understand why she'd acted the way she had, all those years ago, the truth was, she hadn't been honest. Never once had she hinted there was a problem. Could he trust her to be honest now? To say there was something wrong and then work through it with him? Or would she simply cut and run?

Maybe he was a fool, but he was looking for a partner. Someone who would have his back. With Maya, he couldn't be sure.

"Good luck with whatever you decide," Aidan told him. "I'll admit that I don't get it. Don't you want to wake up in the same bed now and then?"

"I'm home enough. I like traveling around, seeing what's going on in other places. People are interesting. Besides, who are you not to understand? You don't want to be with the same woman more than a few days before moving on."

"You're right. We both have commitment issues. Just in different ways. Send me a postcard this time," Aidan told him.

"Promise."

When he and Aidan parted, Del knew that the rift had been mended. His brother was his friend again.

He started home, then changed his mind and walked by Maya's place. Sure enough, her new flowers had turned a sickly yellow and were drooping. He didn't know if she was overfeeding or overwatering. Either way, she was killing innocent plants.

He went by his place and got his truck, then drove to Plants for the Planet and bought replacements. With luck, he would get them in the ground and the dead ones gone before she noticed.

ELAINE'S TEMPORARY APARTMENT was small but cozy. It was a studio with a comfortable daybed. There was a ning alcove, a tiny kitchen that had all the basics a small bathroom.

It's perfect for what I need," Elaine said, stretched out on the couch, Sophie at her side. "When the princess here needs to do her thing, I can take her down to the small garden out back."

Elaine motioned to the kitchen. "I have snacks and tea. So it's working out."

"It's a good setup," Maya admitted. "I'm impressed you've managed to keep it a secret."

Elaine smiled. "I told the landlord it was a menopause thing. After that he didn't want to know."

Maya smiled. "How are you feeling?"

"Okay. Tired." Sophie rolled onto her back and Elaine rubbed the dog's belly. "This one keeps me company. She's always been more my dog rather than the family dog, but since I've started treatment, she hasn't left my side."

"She knows something is up."

Maya studied her friend. Elaine had dark circles under her eyes. She looked tired. And thinner. "Are you losing weight?"

Elaine raised one shoulder. "Maybe a little. It's hard to eat. I don't feel nauseous, exactly, but I don't feel great, either. It's difficult to explain."

"Can I tempt you with dinner at your favorite restaurant?" Maya asked, worried about how Elaine was going to get through the next few weeks of radiation. "You name the place."

"You're sweet, but I'm fine. I have my treatments, then I come here for a few hours. Mostly I nap. Then Sophie and I go home."

Maya tried to hold in the words, but they refuse to be suppressed. "You have to tell them."

"I really don't."

"They'd want to know. They will want to know. Ceallach already suspects something is up. It's going to come out. You'll mention something or your doctor will call. You're dealing with breast cancer. Your husband and sons want to be there for you."

Elaine's smile was both sad and knowing. "They couldn't handle it. Ceallach is in the middle of a big commission. I can't risk distracting him, so I told him it was a menopause thing, too. Who knew the change would come in so handy? As for my sons… I don't want anyone to worry."

"They would want to know. To help."

"There's nothing they can do. You and Sophie are all the support I need."

Maya wasn't sure that was true. She was also worried about what was going to happen when Del found out the truth. Because he would. They all would. While she could honestly say she was doing what her friend had asked, she couldn't shake the sense of being in the wrong. At least where he was concerned. Del would want to know, and she suspected the rest of the Mitchell men would share his feelings.

"You're not giving them enough credit," she said firmly. "Trust in how much they love you."

"I don't doubt their feelings, but I know their limitations. I suppose it's my fault. At least with the boys. I wasn't a very good mother."

Maya couldn't believe it. She'd had a horrible mother, and by any comparison, Elaine had been extraordinary. "What are you talking about? You were a fantastic mother. You took care of them, loved them, supported them. They're all lucky to have you as their mom."

Elaine smiled. "You're very sweet, but you're giving me too much credit. I didn't protect my sons from their father the way I should have. He's a brilliant man, but difficult. There were times when I took his side instead of theirs."

"You made choices. I'm sure some of them weren't what you'd do now, but no one is perfect. You're not giving yourself enough credit." Maya wondered if that came from feeling run-down from the treatment. "They adore you. Even more important, they're happy, kind, successful men you can be proud of. Don't you dare forget that."

Elaine smiled. "You're very good to me."

"And you're good to me. You're my friend and I love you."

"I love you, too. Don't tell the boys, but I always

wanted a daughter. I was so happy when you started dating Del and we became friends. I appreciate that you never cut those ties."

"You're family," Maya told her. "There were a lot of times that the only thing that got me through was wondering how you would handle a situation. I wanted to be strong like you."

Elaine drew her eyebrows together. "Strong? I'm not."

"You are. You just don't see it."

CHAPTER TWELVE

"YOU'RE BEING VERY MYSTERIOUS," Maya teased as she walked into Del's temporary office.

He'd texted her earlier and asked her to meet at the studio. All he'd said was that it was important, he hadn't given any other clues.

He stood by his desk. There was a stack of DVD cases next to him. She was about to joke that if he was volunteering his butt for Eddie and Gladys's show, she was going to lose all respect for him, when she realized he wasn't smiling. He didn't look upset, exactly, but he was obviously not playing.

"What?" she asked, hoping whatever it was, he didn't have a medical issue. She wasn't sure she had one more secret in her. Not when she was struggling to keep Elaine's.

"It's no big deal."

"You have big-deal face," she said.

His tense expression relaxed. "No one has big-deal face."

"You do, and it's a little strange with the sexy stubble."

Crap, she thought. Double crap. Had she said sexy? It wasn't her fault. The man looked good in jeans and a worn shirt. The three-days' growth only added to his appeal. Hmm, the last time they'd kissed he'd been clean shaven for the wedding. Would it feel different now?

She decided it would, but wasn't sure if it would be a good scratchy way or a bad scratchy way.

"Sexy?" he asked, raising one eyebrow.

She pointed to the stack of DVDs. "Explain."

He looked from her to the discs and back. "We've talked about doing that project," he began. "You know, a day in the life kind of thing."

"Right." She studied the DVDs. "Did you start it already?"

"Not exactly. These are videos I've done. Interviews with a lot of people—many of them children. I'm on-screen some, talking about where I am and what's happening there economically or politically."

She looked at him. "You want me to watch them?"

"No, I want to know if you can fix them." He shoved his hands in his front pockets. "I know what I see in my head, but I can't make it happen on the screen. After working with you, I'm sure I totally screwed up the settings. The eye line's going to be all wrong."

She'd seen his raw footage from their shoots. "You're probably missing establishing shots, and there might be issues with the audio."

"Thanks for that vote of support."

"You're not a professional. You do a good job with the training you have."

"You're right. Sorry. I don't mean to be defensive. It's just this project… It's important to me." He pulled his hands free and tapped the stack. "These are what I put together. I have the raw footage on my computer. I know the mistakes I made filming can't be corrected, but if you could maybe take what I did and work your editing magic."

"Of course."

"I'd pay you," he added.

She waved off the comment. "No way. I'm happy to help. I'll need to go through what you have. It's going to take a while, but I'd love to do whatever I can to make the material how you want it to be."

He was still touching the DVDs. "No one's seen these," he told her. "No one. I wanted you to know that."

Maya appreciated the information, even though she wasn't sure what to do with it. Del was trusting her with something important to him. That made her feel all quivery inside. Of course, it didn't take much to get herself worked up when it came to him.

For a second she wished things had been different. Back when they'd both been younger. But she'd been too scared, and there was no way he could have understood what was in her head. *Wrong place, wrong time*, she thought. But right guy. Funny how it had taken her ten years to figure out he was the one. Funny and maybe a little sad. Because he was leaving and she was staying. Even more significant, he hadn't hinted he had any strong feelings for her beyond friendship and sexual attraction.

"I will take good care of your footage," she promised. "Let me copy it onto my computer so I can work on it." She wrinkled her nose. "And I won't keep a copy of it lying around. Eddie or Gladys will find it for sure, and God knows what they'll do with it."

"You're still pissed about the kiss?"

"Not pissed, exactly."

"Then what?"

"It went viral. That's strange."

He dropped his arms to his side and winked at her. "I'm a good kisser."

"Oh, please. You think you're the reason the video went viral? What about me?"

"Riding my coattails."

She put her hands on her hips. "In your dreams, mister. You're lucky I kissed you at all."

"Am I?"

"You are."

She waited for the humorous comeback. Instead, Del circled the desk, put his hands on her waist and drew her against him.

"Maybe we should just see about that," he murmured right before his mouth claimed hers.

On a purely intellectual basis, she didn't think it was a good idea to kiss in the office. People could walk in, it was disrespectful to the workplace. There were other reasons, Maya was sure, but wow, was it hard to think of them. Or be the least bit indignant. Not when his skin was so warm and his lips were so tempting.

She parted her lips without even thinking about it. He swept his tongue inside. They tangled and teased.

She thought about shifting closer, about pressing her body against his. She thought about the desk and how the height seemed just so perfect for what would naturally happen next.

She put her hands on his shoulders, then slid her palms up and down his arms. *More warmth*, she thought dreamily. Muscles and man all for the taking.

Desire burned hot and bright deep inside of her. It radiated out, spiraling through her with every stroke of his tongue. When he moved his hands from her waist to her rear, she knew she was lost. Totally and completely lost. On the heels of that admission came the thought that she had no idea where they might find a condom.

He squeezed the curves of her butt. She arched against him and her belly pressed against his erection. The proof of his arousal made her shudder. Del had always been her greatest weakness, she thought. The man thrilled her.

He moved his hands up her sides, toward her breasts. Anticipation hummed through her. Somewhere in the distance her phone chirped insistently.

She ignored the noise, only to realize that it wasn't any of her normal ringtones. Nor was it her text notification sound. A second chirping joined the first. She drew back.

"What is that?" Del asked.

Without him kissing her, she could think. "The emergency notification system," she said as she lunged for her cell. "We have a message."

"The what?"

Maya ignored the question and grabbed her phone. The message flashed.

Missing child. Report to the HERO offices asap.

She grabbed his hand and pulled him along as she headed for her office to grab her bag. "Mayor Marsha made us both sign up for emergency notifications, remember? We're volunteer searchers."

Del looked at his phone. "A kid? Where do we go?"

"It's not far."

THE HELP EMERGENCY Response Operations or HERO offices were as close as Maya promised. Del and Maya arrived along with several other people. They parked at the far end of the lot, then hurried toward the main building.

Inside they found what could have passed for a war room. There were large computer screens showing different parts of the area surrounding the town along with huge maps on the wall. Kipling Gilmore, a tall, blond-haired man, stood in the center of the activity. He was calm and obviously in charge.

"We have a missing girl," he was saying. "Shep?"

A muscled man with dark red hair and piercing green eyes stood next to Kipling. *Jesse Shepard*, Del thought, remembering meeting him at The Man Cave a week or so ago. He had joined the search-and-rescue program less than a month ago.

Shep read from a tablet. "Alyssa Paige, age eleven." He gave them her height and weight. "She and her family were out for a picnic, so she's not dressed to be out for the night, people. She also doesn't have food or water with her and she has limited wilderness experience."

Near the windows, a woman in her thirties began to cry. The man at her side put an arm around her. Next to them, a boy maybe thirteen or fourteen, wiped away tears. He looked scared and guilty. Del would guess Alyssa was his sister, and he had been the one with her when she'd been lost.

"I'll send the info about where she was last seen to your tablets," Shep continued. "Jacob's told us as much as he can."

The teen flinched as his name was spoken and everyone turned to look at him. Del instinctively started toward the boy.

As he approached, he heard Kipling speaking on his cell phone. "Yeah, Cassidy went to get her horses. She won't be back for a couple of days."

Del looked at Shep. "Can you give me a minute?" he asked, nodding at the teen.

"Sure," Shep said.

Del turned to Jacob. "Hey," he said in a low voice.

Jacob hung his head. "I didn't do it on purpose."

"No one thinks you did anything wrong," Del assured him.

"They do. My parents tell me I'm not responsible enough." Jacob looked at him. "She's my sister. I love her."

"I know you do. Look, I'm the oldest of five brothers. Believe me, I know what it's like. You're told to watch them and you do, but they're as fast as squirrels. You turn around for a second, and bam, one of them is in trouble. Only you get the blame."

Jacob sniffed, then nodded. "I know." The boy's dark eyes were red from tears. "I was texting with a friend."

"Sure. It's boring out there, right?"

"Yeah. Alyssa said she saw a baby bunny. She wanted to pet it. I told her to leave it alone, and when I looked up again, she was gone."

Tears filled his eyes again. "I called her name and ran after her, but I couldn't find her."

"How long were you looking?"

"About an hour."

"By your phone or it felt like an hour?"

Jacob flushed. "It felt like an hour."

"Great." He put his hand on the teen's shoulder. "You did great. Let me give the information to Shep, and then we'll go find your sister."

Del shared what Jacob had told him. Shep input the information to the program while Kipling passed out equipment to the various search teams.

"You know how to use this?" he asked Del.

"Sure."

Maya moved next to him. "Seriously? You're familiar with this?"

"You don't go exploring in remote parts of the world without some kind of tracking equipment. Not if you want to be found."

"I thought the point was not to be found."

"It is, unless someone gets hurt."

She looked at the map on the wall. "Or gets lost. Are we going to find her?"

"We're not going to stop looking until we do."

He and Maya joined a group of people from town. He saw that several firefighters and deputies had their own groups. The guys from the bodyguard school were also out searching. The program might only be a few months old, but it was growing. Kipling knew what he was doing.

He and Maya were joined by Angel, along with Dakota and Finn Andersson. Finn had a satellite phone with him in case the decision was made to call in a helicopter to help with the search.

"We expect to find her before that's necessary," Kipling said. "Good luck."

The volunteers drove out in a caravan, with Shep leading the way. Kipling stayed behind to man the command center. The family's outing had started at one of the campgrounds closer to town, where the trails were well marked.

"If she went after a rabbit, she could be anywhere," Maya said.

When everyone was ready, Shep gave them last-minute instructions, then they headed out.

They walked in groups of six, spread out and moving forward in the same direction. At regular intervals, they called Alyssa's name. Del kept track of their progress on the screen of his tablet, and had them make adjustments as they were directed by the search program.

Maya kept up easily. She scanned the area and

when it was her turn, yelled for the girl. The afternoon was hot, but she didn't complain about the temperature.

She got the job done, Del thought as they continued to search. She stepped in and did what had to be done. Hyacinth had been willing to work hard for what she wanted, but if the results in question were about someone else, she wasn't likely to participate. She didn't believe in putting herself out for other people.

It had taken him a while to recognize that about her. Once he'd figured out what she was thinking, he'd wondered if it was the result of being successful or simply a personality trait. Not that the answer mattered. Although she had claimed to love him, she wasn't willing to change to make him happy. Not when she wanted things a different way. Her way.

Maya was more of a "how can we both get what we want" kind of person. There wasn't the same level of drama or stress. She was easy to talk to. He respected her. Their night together had been amazing.

He glanced at her and wondered about the odds of a second go-round. His only hesitation in asking was that he knew Maya wasn't one to give herself without the promise of some kind of relationship. And while the two of them were friends, he wasn't sure that was enough.

There was also the fact that he was leaving and she was staying. Which meant whatever they started would never go anywhere.

For a second he allowed himself to think it could be more. That she would want to leave Fool's Gold with him and see the world. That they could continue their partnership in other ways. But could he trust her to be a true partner, to give it to him straight, even when she thought he wouldn't like what she had to say?

Before he could take the next mental step, his tablet started flashing and beeping. He looked at it and saw the message.

"She's been found," he yelled. "Alyssa's been found."

Thirty minutes later, they were back at the HERO offices. Alyssa had been reunited with her family and the volunteers had turned in their equipment. He and Maya walked back toward his truck.

"I'm glad they found her," Maya said.

"But?"

She shrugged. "That was oddly unsatisfying. I guess I wanted to be in thick of things. I know we helped, but it was kind of a letdown."

"Since when did you want to be where the action was?"

She laughed. "I don't know. I guess you're having an influence on me. Next thing you know I'll be taking off to remote corners of the globe." She wrinkled her nose. "Not that there can be corners on the globe, but you know what I mean."

"I do."

Come with me.

The words came from somewhere deep inside. He toyed with the idea of saying them, but changed his mind. He'd asked Maya to be with him once and she'd said no. As far as he could tell, there was no reason for her to say yes now.

MAYA MET MADELINE outside of Paper Moon. "Shelby texted me that she and Destiny are already there."

Madeline laughed. "You don't think they'll start having fun without us, do you?"

"I hope not."

The women linked arms and headed toward their destination.

Rather than meet for lunch, several of them had decided to enjoy a girls' night out. While each of them had been to The Man Cave before, they'd never been as a group.

"Think we'll shock the guys when we stroll in?" Maya asked.

Madeline wrinkled her nose. "I wish, but no. Now, if we walked in topless, they'd take notice."

Maya laughed. "You have an adventurous streak I didn't know about."

"I'm a lot of cheap talk," Madeline admitted. "The truth is, I'm pretty traditional at heart. I want to fall in love, settle down, get married and have some kids. You know, normal but not exciting. What about you?"

I want to see the world. The thought came out of nowhere and surprised Maya. See the world? Since when? Sure, she had her scrapbook, but it had been years since she'd added to it. She'd never been all that interested in the world beyond getting into network news. And she'd left that dream behind when she moved to Fool's Gold.

It was Del's pictures, she thought wistfully, remembering the slide show they'd shown the Saplings. So many interesting and beautiful places. She wanted to see them all.

"It wasn't supposed to be a hard question," Madeline told her.

"What? Oh, sorry. I got lost in something else. I want to be in love with someone who loves me back," she said.

"But not home and hearth?"

"That would be nice, but it isn't a requirement." It had been once, she reminded herself. Until a few weeks ago. Was she figuring out a truth about herself, or was being in love with Del messing with her head? Hard to be sure.

They walked into The Man Cave. There was a life-size statue of a caveman right by the entrance. Several tourists were taking selfies with the statue.

Maya and Madeline walked past them and looked for their friends. They found Shelby and Destiny sitting at a table. Jo was with them.

"Scoping out the competition?" Maya asked with a laugh as they approached.

"No, this is pure fun for me. Will has something going on with a friend of his. So here I am." She looked around. "It's nice. A good vibe."

"Wait until the live entertainment," Shelby said, smiling at her sister-in-law Destiny. "It's going to be amazing."

Destiny sipped her glass of water. "You're very loyal. I'm nervous. Being nervous isn't a good thing."

"You'll be fine," Jo said. "And if you're not, who are we to judge?"

A reasonable sentiment, Maya thought, not sure it would help Destiny's obvious case of jitters. The venue might be a local bar and the event simply karaoke night, but Maya knew it was more than that for Destiny.

She and her sister had recently signed a record deal with a Nashville label and were set to head to the studio in a few weeks. So she wasn't simply a small-town girl out on a girls' night.

Madeline grabbed Maya's arm. "OMG. I can't breathe! I can't breathe."

Maya turned to see her friend gesturing frantically with her free hand. Shelby looked up and grinned.

"Well, look at that."

Maya turned and saw Shep of the search-and-rescue team had walked into The Man Cave with none other than Jonny Blaze.

The action superstar didn't do anything other than accompany a friend to the bar. Even so, conversation momentarily dipped as everyone turned to stare. Most immediately went back to what they'd been doing before. A few tourists pulled out cameras.

"Nice-looking man," Jo said, her voice very matter-of-fact. "Nothing as good as my Will, but still. Broad shoulders."

Destiny nodded slowly. "He's taller than I expected."

"A lot of muscle," Shelby added.

Maya smiled. "I like his eyes."

"What is wrong with all of you?" Madeline asked, her voice low and breathy. "It's Jonny Blaze. You can't separate him into parts. He's… He's…"

"You should go say hi," Maya teased.

Madeline glared at her. "I should not. Speak to him? Are you crazy?"

"Why not?" Destiny asked. "He's just a person."

"There's no *just*. Don't say just." Madeline looked away, and then immediately swung her head back. "I can't breathe."

"If you can talk, you can breathe," Jo told her. "What's the big deal? Maybe he'd like to meet a local girl. You're single, he's single."

Madeline put her hands on the table, then rested her head on them. "Kill. Me. Now."

Maya patted her friend on the back. "You don't want to die before you've slept with him, do you?" she asked teasingly. "Isn't there a song about heaven only being a kiss away?"

Madeline straightened. "Ha, ha. Very funny. I get it. Totally. I'm basing my reaction to him on his looks, how he is in his movies and nothing real. But you know what? I'm okay with that. It's fun. The reason I don't want to meet him is that he might be a jerk. That would spoil everything."

Shelby grinned. "You're adorable when you go for logic."

"You are." Maya hugged her. "For what it's worth, Phoebe says Jonny's actually a very nice man. You sure you don't want to go say hi?"

"I'm sure. Why on earth do I feel this way when I'm around him?" Madeline asked.

"It's the movie-star thing," Shelby told her. "The power in the tribe. We want to be close to the most powerful tribe member. It means survival. At least it did, you know, back when we still lived in caves. Whoever was the best hunter or soldier got the best lodgings and most food. That meant not dying when…" Her voice trailed off. "What?"

Maya saw they were all staring at Shelby. "You sort of morphed into someone else just then."

"I know. I sounded so smart." Shelby grinned. "Felicia comes into the bakery and we talk. She's always interesting. We talked about Jonny Blaze a couple of weeks ago. She finds celebrity fascinating. Not because she cares about them but because of how other people react to them. So she told me about tribes."

"Gotta love Felicia," Jo said as their server came up and took their drink orders.

Except for Destiny, they all ordered the special. A martini made with ginger, coconut and a hint of lemon. Maya had a feeling it would go down very easily, which made her glad she was walking home.

After they'd placed their orders, conversation shifted to things happening around town. No one could believe how fast summer had flown by.

"Have you seen the changing leaves up in the mountains?" Destiny asked. "The year is going to be over before we know it." She turned to Maya. "You and Del would look adorable kissing against a background of red-and-orange leaves," she joked. "Any more kissing videos planned?"

Maya laughed. "No. We're holding out for the movie release."

Everyone chuckled. Jo mentioned the upcoming Fall Festival, and Shelby talked about orders at the bakery for Thanksgiving. Maya listened, but in the back of her mind she kept seeing herself kissing Del. They'd looked good together. Right. Funny how she'd never realized her feelings for him before. Maybe the love had become such a part of her, she'd been unable to see it for what it was.

She glanced around at the bar. It was crowded, but in a friendly way. Conversation was pleasant. No one was too drunk or too loud. Jonny Blaze sat at a table with a group of guys, acting like everyone else.

It was the town, she thought. Fool's Gold had a way of sucking people in and changing them for the better. Making them who they were meant to be. Maya was grateful she'd come back.

Back, she thought as their drinks arrived. Back, not home. Because the restlessness she'd been feeling hadn't gone away. If anything, it was growing inside of her.

She was going to have to figure out the cause, she told herself. And then an antidote. Or at the very least a way to mitigate the need. Because wandering the world wasn't in her future. She was going to settle down here. She could only hope settling down wasn't the same as settling.

CHAPTER THIRTEEN

MAYA MOVED THE cursor quickly across the screen, clicked the left button on the mouse and watched the footage merge seamlessly together. She hit Play, and together she and Del watched the eight seconds become seventeen.

"Add that shot with Priscilla against the sun," Del suggested. "You know the one?"

"Where she fills the screen." Maya was already clicking through what they had. She found the clip and added it to the segment, then hit Play again.

"Nice." He leaned back in his chair. "These are getting better and better."

As he spoke, he put his arm around her. She was pretty sure the gesture was meant to be friendly. Team-like, even. But just sitting close to him was enough to make her aware of his body right next to hers. She liked being around him, even though he was a big distraction.

"We're getting into our work rhythm," she said, looking for another clip and adding it. When she hit Play, the camera moved from the elephant to pan across the ranch where Annabelle, a local librarian, stood by her husband. They were only talking, and standing far enough away to practically be background. But there was something about their differences in height, the way he stood protectively close to her, not to mention the sexy angle of his cowboy hat, that added a spark to the otherwise-traditional landscape shot.

"Damn, we're good," he breathed, then laughed. "Mostly you."

"I disagree. Without you dazzling the camera, we couldn't connect the shots. Okay, we need twenty-seven more seconds. It's going to be hard to pick what we want to use. Everything is really good."

The door to the office opened and two men in suits walked in. They were both in their late forties or early fifties. One was short and balding, the other a little taller. Maya knew she'd never seen either of them before.

"Maya Farlow?" the shorter of the two men asked.

Maya nodded slowly, half expecting him to pull out a law enforcement badge and utter the spine-chilling phrase, "I'm going to have to ask you to come with me, ma'am."

The two men looked at each other, then back at her. The taller one smiled broadly. "I'm Ernesto. This is my business partner, Robert. We're in big trouble and we need some help. Can we bother you for a minute?"

"Of course," she said, not sure what they could want with her.

Del rose and got two chairs. The men sat by the table.

"We own the Lucky Lady Casino," Ernesto said.

"We've planned an advertising campaign. We're about to film a series of national commercials. Robert and I wrote the commercials with an ad agency and we're shooting this week."

His partner nodded. "We have the equipment rented, the actors, hair and makeup people, the costumes and perfect weather. The team hired to do the actual filming just told us they weren't going to show up. We're stuck. Can you help?"

Maya processed the information. "You want me to produce your commercials?"

Ernesto nodded. "Direct, create, produce. Whatever you want to call it. We have storyboards and a script. Everything you need."

It was both intriguing and crazy, she thought. "How did you know to come to me?"

"We didn't. We went to Mayor Marsha. She showed us some of your work." Robert turned to Del. "We understand you work with Maya, and we want to hire you, too. She said you were a team."

Just then Maya's cell phone rang. She would have ignored it except she had a feeling she knew who was calling.

"Hello?"

"It's Mayor Marsha, Maya. Are they there?"

"Uh-huh."

The mayor laughed. "I know it's a lot to take in, but they're a local business and we do help out our own. I spoke to the city council and we're going to release you for a week. That should be enough time, don't you think?"

If she worked twenty-hour days, Maya thought. Still, a national commercial was a big deal. To have that on her résumé would be something.

"Oh, and tell them we want copies of their B-roll. They're going to ask you to get shots of the town and the area. We should be able to put those to good use in our videos, don't you think?"

"I'll make it a condition," Maya murmured, more than a little impressed that the mayor knew what B-roll was.

"Good luck."

"Thank you." She hung up and looked at the men. "That was Mayor Marsha. When would you want us to start?"

The men exchanged a glance.

"Today," Roberto said. "Now."

Maya nodded. "Give me a second. Del?"

They stood and walked into the hall. Maya led the way to a second, empty office and went inside. When he followed, she shut the door.

He grinned at her. "Are you excited? That's so great. They want you, Maya."

"I've never done a commercial," she admitted, her head spinning. She felt light-headed and shaky, but in a good way. Possibilities crowded her brain. "I don't know what I'm doing."

"You have great instincts. You can do this."

"I want to," she admitted. "It would be great." She told him about Mayor Marsha wanting access to the B-roll.

"You should get a copy of the footage for your résumé, or whatever you call it."

"You're right." She bit her lower lip. "I'm terrified. Can do you do this with me?" Because she would feel better with him along.

"Are you kidding? It's a chance to work with you. Think of what I'll learn. I'm in."

She stared into his eyes. Loving Del was easy, she thought. Especially at moments like this. He wasn't insulted they hadn't come to him instead of her. His ego wasn't bruised because he knew he was good at what he did. His self-confidence meant he wasn't threatened by her. *A rare trait*, she thought. At least from what she'd seen in her career.

"We only have a week," she warned him. "It's going to be long days. I'm guessing their advertising agency will hire someone to do the editing. If they do, we won't have control over the final product."

He put his hands on her shoulders. "What does your gut say?"

"Jump."

He lightly kissed her. "What was that line from *Titanic*? If you jump, I jump?"

She laughed. "All right, Mr. King of the World. We're about to take a really big leap."

FORTY-EIGHT HOURS OF preproduction wasn't nearly enough, Maya thought, telling herself to breathe. The temporary offices for the commercial production were housed in a large conference room in the Lucky Lady Hotel. She had three computers, a giant screen, the rented equipment, a list of people hired for the shoot and ordering privileges with room service. The latter would be great if she wasn't so nervous that she couldn't eat.

Ernesto walked her through the storyboards for the three commercials they would be shooting. Three commercials in five days. Impossible, but she was going to make it happen. The alternative was telling them no—forcing them to rehire all the equipment, production people and actors. No way that was going to happen.

Editing would take another couple of weeks, but that wasn't her problem. Right now she had to get organized to take advantage of the best hours to shoot outdoors. The indoor shots could be done in the middle of the day and throughout the night.

Del hurried over with several printouts. "Weather," he said, handing her pages. "Cloudy tomorrow."

If they'd been alone, she would have kissed him. Because clouds were her friend. Everyone wanted the magic shot. Blue skies or a perfect sunset. Great for B-roll, but when it came to shooting actors, clouds dispersed light. Clouds allowed her more control over her own light and when it came to making the shot look amazing, light ruled.

She returned her attention to the storyboard. "You're missing the call to action."

Robert and Ernesto looked at each other, then back at her. "Excuse me?"

"The call to action." She lowered her voice to sound like an announcer. *"Call now and reserve the time of your life.*" She returned her voice to normal. "Whatever it's going to be. You want whoever is watching to do something, right? Not just think, hey, great commercial. You need to show the phone number, the website, offer a discount. Close the sale. Technically, we refer to that as a call to action."

"She's right," Ernesto said. He stared at the storyboard. "They're all missing a call to action."

"We'll fix that," Robert told her quickly. "Can you still get this done on time?"

"Sure. The call to action will be added during editing. Just be thinking about what you want your message to be."

The men nodded and left. She and Del returned to the storyboards. Each scene would require setup, filming and then breakdown of the equipment. Time of day was essential for outdoor shots. She'd already prepared a list of B-roll shots she wanted. Once they broke down the storyboard, she could do a detailed schedule, basically hour by hour, for the next five days.

She'd already gone over the equipment. It was good enough to make her both envious and weak at the knees. *Just the lighting*, she thought, wishing her Fool's Gold budget allowed for the extra lights. On the commercial, they would use 3-point lighting, with the primary outdoor shots being filmed in the morning, preferably on a cloudy day.

She had an assortment of lenses for the cameras, tripods, not to mention designated hair and makeup people, along with a wardrobe person. *Just like the real thing*, she thought humorously, thinking how she and Del had made do when filming their stuff.

The commercial would be more complicated. They would be shot in high resolution. She'd already confirmed the commercials would be shown only in the States, which meant NTSC rather than PAL. It had taken five minutes of explaining so Ernesto and Robert understood the difference between formatting for the United States—in NTSC—and formatting for Europe.

"I want to sort through the various shots," she said. "What we're going to shoot when. With the clouds forecast for tomorrow morning, we'll get some great outdoor footage. Can you look up sunrise time tomorrow? And I'll need the twilight information."

Del raised his eyebrows. "*Twilight* as in Team Edward and Team Jacob?"

She laughed. "No. Not the movie. How do you know about them?"

"I'm a man of many sides."

"So I've heard. I need to know what time the morning and evening twilights are. Astronomical, nautical and civil. They'll be earlier than actual sunrise and later than actual sunset."

"Because it's all about the light?"

"You know it."

THE NEXT MORNING Del tried to figure out a way to work "astronomical twilight" into a sentence, but didn't think anyone would actually care. Still, the information was interesting. Astronomical twilight was at five twenty-three, when the sun was eighteen degrees below the horizon. It was the moment when the sky first turned light. Civil twilight was when objects became visible to the naked eye. Today that was at six twenty-five. The actual sunrise would occur at six fifty-one.

In terms of the commercial, it meant a 4:00 a.m. start time for the team, with actors ready and in place by six for blocking and walk-throughs.

Controlled chaos didn't begin to describe what was happening on set. Equipment had to be placed and then checked. He and Maya had already blocked out the scene, frame by frame.

She worked quickly and efficiently. There was no attitude, no demanding. She gave her best and it was obvious she expected the same from everyone else. Her style was quiet and controlled, with a confidence that allowed everyone else around her to relax.

He was the only one who knew she'd been too nervous to sleep the night before. He'd seen her shaking when no one else had, but he wasn't going to tell. He admired the hell out of her. Maya had talent, and the ability to make it work. As they'd discussed, she'd jumped and he was right there with her.

The actors appeared—six men and women in their twenties and thirties. They would play happy, romantic couples having a wonderful time at the casino. Later in the day, they would be filming a family of four having fun together by the pool.

He and Maya talked to the actors. He walked them through the actions, demonstrating where their marks were and the pacing of the flow. Maya watched it all through the lens of the camera, nodding as he explained.

"We're fighting the clock," she said loudly. "Let's start from the top. Couple number one, take your place."

Del used the stopwatch function on his phone to time the action. The couple did as he'd directed, with the second couple following quickly behind. They ran through it twice more. Del watched closely.

After the third time, he walked over to Maya. "Are you seeing what I'm seeing?" he asked. "Her dress." He pointed to the actress in a red cocktail dress. "When she turns to the left, the skirt does something funny."

Maya gave him a quick smile. "Good eye. It's distracting. If she turned to the right, we'd get better flow with how they're moving. Let's try it."

They made the change and did another walk-through. Maya did a sound check with her audio guy, then called for everyone to get ready.

Del knew the drill. The slate would show the shot name and take number. Quiet was called for on set. Audio went first, then the cameras rolled. The actors got their cue and the filming began.

He watched the action, but he was also keeping tabs on Maya. She ran the show. He was comfortable with that, but he also wanted her to know that she wasn't in this alone. He would be there if she needed him. As a side benefit, he was learning the equivalent of a master's class from her. Information he could use when he started his video series. No more amateur mistakes for him.

"Hi. I'm Cindy. I'm one of the hair and makeup people." The woman who had walked up to him was about twenty-five, with gold-blond hair and big green eyes. A tight T-shirt stretched over impressive breasts.

"Del."

"I know. I asked about you." She smiled. "Want to get some breakfast?"

The invitation was clear. She leaned toward him as she spoke. Her smile was easy, and when she finished with her question she put her hand on his arm. Del took a step back.

"Thanks, but I'm with her." He nodded toward Maya.

Cindy shrugged. "You sure?"

"Yeah, I'm sure."

BY THE END of the shoot, Maya knew two things for sure. That she'd never been so exhausted in her whole life, and that together she and Del had created magic. She'd only viewed the raw footage, but she liked what she'd seen.

The actual editing would be handled elsewhere. Still, she had copies of all she'd shot and later would get the finished commercials for her portfolio. In theory, she would never need them. She already had a job she liked. She wasn't looking to make a change. But it was good to have options.

She parked by her office. Del had wanted to drive her home, but she had a few things she needed to check before she could return to her small house and crawl into bed. She hadn't slept more than four hours for a week. She was so tired she was punchy, but it had been worth it.

She was proud of what she'd done. There'd been a challenge and she'd pulled it off. Del had been a big part of that. He'd stood by her the whole time. He'd offered great suggestions, had provided a buffer when one of the actors got a little full of himself and had ignored the blatantly sexual invitations of several cast members, not to mention from the crew.

Watching some big-busted sex kitten make eyes at him hadn't been fun—especially knowing how great a night with him could be. But he'd refused them all. From what she could tell, he hadn't been tempted. Not that he owed her anything. It wasn't as if she'd ever told him how she felt.

She walked to the rear door of the office and opened it. "I love you, Del," she said aloud, then giggled. There was a conversation changer, she thought. Would he back out of the room slowly or run for the hills? Because she was pretty sure he wasn't going to be happy with the news.

Del liked her—she was sure of that. They worked well together. But love? He was interested in his next project, not forever. While she wanted...

Her brain was foggy, her thoughts unclear. Sleep beckoned. Just as soon as she sent off a few emails, she promised herself. She would sleep for two days and wake up refreshed. It was a plan. A good plan. She—

"There you are."

Maya jumped and screamed as two small figures appeared in front of her. It took a second for her eyes to focus in the dimly lit hallway. Eddie and Gladys hovered.

"It's two in the morning," she said. "What are you doing here?"

"We could ask you the same question," Eddie said. "You're young. You should be home having wild sex with Del."

Gladys sighed. "I'll bet he's hung like a—"

Maya instinctively covered her ears. "Stop," she pleaded. "I've been working around the clock for a week. I'm in a weakened condition. I plead for mercy."

Eddie and Gladys looked at each other, then back at her.

"Just this once," Eddie said. "But we want something in return."

Oh, no. Were they going to ask for a picture of Del's butt? Because she wasn't sure she could get them that. And even if she could, she wasn't sure she wanted to. While she was a big believer in freedom of speech, she didn't think the founding fathers had the naked butt of the man she loved in mind when they'd penned that amendment.

"We want to talk to you about our show," Gladys told her.

Eddie nodded. "It's not what we want it to be. Not the content. That's perfect. It's the production value. We'd like it to be higher."

Maya's sleep-deprived brain scrambled to keep

up. "Did you search online to find that phrase?" she asked.

The two old ladies nodded. "We did and we think people would enjoy our show more if it looked better. We want help."

"Now?" she asked weakly, pretty sure she was beyond rallying.

"No. We want you at your best." Eddie smiled. "We want you to hold a class. Like Sam Ridge did to help small businesses with their finances. It wasn't that interesting a topic, but the man does know how to fill out a suit." She sighed, then looked at Maya. "We want a class about how to film our show. You can teach us about lights and camera positions and how to pan."

"Like in the movies," Gladys added.

Maya wasn't sure if she meant she wanted the show to look as if it were shot like a movie or that she wanted to make the movements they do in movies when they're pretending to film a show. Then she decided it didn't matter.

"You're on," she told them. "Although one of you will have to remind me of this conversation. I'm pretty sure it's all going to be a blur."

"We will," Gladys promised, then winked at her friend. "This means Del is also in a weakened condition. Think we could sneak into his place and have our way with him?"

Maya gave a strangled laugh and decided at that moment, her emails could wait. Anything she sent out tonight—or this morning, seeing as it was well after midnight—wouldn't make sense, anyway.

"I love you both," she told them with a yawn. "If you can catch him, go for it. He's totally hot." She hugged the old women. "The class will be fun. I promise."

"We'll hold you to that," Eddie told her, then touched her cheek. "All right, young lady. You go get some sleep."

"I will. Thanks." She started for the door, then turned back. "About Del…"

Gladys waved her hand. "Not to worry. We're only teasing about him. He's like a son to us. Which is very sad, but there we are."

Eddie nodded. "Don't tell anyone, but we're a lot more talk than action."

A relief, Maya thought. She waved. "Your secret is safe with me."

CHAPTER FOURTEEN

Two DAYS AFTER the commercial shoot wrapped, Dcl and Maya were ready to get back to their town project. He watched her add segments together, then compare the finished product to a previous version.

"It works better the other way," he told her. "With Priscilla and Reno in the middle. Ending with an elephant and a pony is fun, but the tone is off. To quote you, you're not asking for the sale."

"The call to action," she said, her attention on the screen.

"Yeah. That. It's missing."

She wrinkled her nose. "It's annoying when you're right."

He leaned back in his chair. "I don't know. I kind of like it."

"You would." She sighed, then glanced to the screen in front of him. "Can you play them for me, back to back?"

He used the mouse to start the first video, then followed it with the second. Partway through, Maya stood and leaned over him. *To get a better look*, he told himself. Not to be closer to him, although that was a happy by-product.

She was still tired. He could tell by the way she carried herself. But she was getting caught up on rest. Her feistiness had returned. Their week of work had been as long and hard as she had promised, but still interesting as hell. He'd learned a ton, most of which he could apply to his new project. He would do a better job this time around. Not as good as Maya, but better than he'd been doing.

"Priscilla in the middle," Maya said. "You're right." She returned to her seat and made a few notes. "I should have seen that."

"You can't be right about everything."

"Why not?"

He chuckled. "Because I said so."

"Well, then. It must be true." She smiled at him. "That was a good time."

He knew she was referring to the commercial shoot. "Yeah. Imagine what it must be like to have a crew like that all the time."

"It would be a killer budget. For what you want to do, it's not necessary. Frankly, that much production would get in the way. The kids can learn to ignore one person with a camera, but all those other people milling around?" She shook her head. "It would drive the story. By the time they started to ignore it, you'd have to be moving on."

She angled her chair toward his. "So not the people, but I could sure get into the equipment. I have lens envy."

"Just the lenses, not the camera?"

"Cameras are easy. It's the lenses that kill you.

Have you thought about applying for a grant? There must be several that you could qualify for. I've heard that writing grant proposals is a pain, but it could be worth it."

"Something to think about," he told her. In truth he didn't need grant money. He'd sold his company for enough that he could afford to buy Maya any lens she wanted. A whole set, even. But he didn't say that because he wouldn't be buying them for her. He would be buying them for himself, or a camera guy, if he took one along.

Come with me. The words were there, just a breath away. All he had to do was say them. Make the offer. They could travel the world together.

Would she do it? Leave everything she'd ever known behind to travel with him? He had his doubts. Maya had always been more interested in the sensible choice. She hadn't been willing to gamble on him before—when he'd had a stable kind of life to offer her. Why would she be willing to risk it all on him now? And even if she said she was, could he trust her to tell the truth? To follow through?

"You could talk to Mayor Marsha," she said.

It took him a second to realize she was still talking about the grants.

"She seems to have all the answers," he said.

"Not all of them." She sighed. "Did you know someone in town gave me a scholarship and I can't find out who? I'm sure Mayor Marsha knows, but she's not telling."

"Why do you want to know?"

"Mostly to thank them. It was a full ride. They paid for everything. I couldn't have gone to college without it."

Del put his hand over hers and squeezed her fingers. "That's not true. You would have found another way. You were determined."

"I'm not so sure." She looked at him, then away. "I didn't grow up here, like you did. My mom wasn't exactly supportive. She used to tell me how much better her life would have been if I hadn't been around."

"You know she's wrong about that. She was unhappy and taking it out on you."

"Yeah, I know, but believing it in my head and believing it in my heart are two different things. She always said I wouldn't ever amount to anything. That I was a screwup and useless. The thing I was best at was making her unhappy and disappointing her. So when I say I don't know if I would have gotten through college on my own, I mean it. If I'd had to work two jobs, plus go to class... What if I'd heard her words in my head? What if I'd stopped believing in myself?"

"You didn't."

"Because I didn't have to. So it's not just about the money. Whoever gave me that scholarship allowed me to succeed, despite my past."

She pulled her hand free and turned toward him. "When I was little, I used to read all those stories about white knights coming to the rescue. I knew early on that no one was going to rescue me. That I had to rescue myself. I don't know if that's a good lesson or a bad one, but I haven't been able to let it go."

"It's what makes you strong."

"Maybe. And being strong is important. I get that. But kids also need hope. Understanding that is one of the reasons I'm so interested in your project. Kids need to know that it's okay to want a decent future and believe it's possible. They need to see what else is out there. Moving here allowed me to believe, for the first time ever, that I just might be able to go to college. To have a better life. Teachers were there for me. Being smart and doing well in school was actually rewarded."

She paused, then gave him a slightly embarrassed smile. "Sorry. I didn't mean to go off like that."

"Don't apologize. I don't share your experience, but I appreciate that you went through it. I grew up here. I always had a place, not to mention expectations."

"Ah, yes. The Mitchell family. Be an artist or take care of those who are creative."

"We have two functions in life. There's no middle ground."

She studied him. "Did you find middle ground by leaving?"

"Yeah, thanks to you."

"No, you found it on your own. I was simply the kick in the pants you needed to break free. And as my motives were completely selfish, not to mention ridiculously immature, I won't take credit at all."

"You weren't immature," he told her. "You were

scared. How could you have trusted me? There'd never been anyone you could trust. Love was just a word."

"If that's true, why did it hurt so much to lose you?"

Her tone was light when she asked the question, but he sensed they were treading into dangerous territory. He and Maya had already had their chance. Their time.

Despite the tension in the room, he forced himself to lean back and speak casually. He chuckled. "You had to miss me, Maya. Come on. I'm a catch."

As he'd hoped, she relaxed, and then laughed. "You're not all that."

"Then you're looking at me wrong."

They both returned their attention to the computer screens. She pointed out a shadow in a few of the frames and he went to check for other versions of that day's shooting. The moment was lost.

He told himself it was for the best. That whatever they might have had with each other, it had been over years ago. This was different. Two adults with a common goal. After his father's birthday party and the summer was over, he would leave. Without Maya.

AT THE END of her workday, Maya checked her calendar, then got in her car and headed out of town. Zane and Phoebe had been due back from their honeymoon the previous evening. Technically it might be too soon for visitors, but she had a strong need to see her brother.

Strange how quickly she'd gotten used to living close to Zane. For years she'd dissed him, behind his back and to his face. They'd argued about Chase, had assumed the other couldn't possibly understand and generally acted more like enemies than family.

But they hadn't been able to let go. Whatever tenuous bond connected them, it couldn't be broken. Not completely. And when Zane had needed her over the summer to help with Chase, she'd been there.

Those couple of weeks on the cattle drive had changed everything. She knew some of it was him falling in love. There were those who would say he'd been healed by the love of a good woman. Maya knew the metamorphosis had come from the opposite place. It wasn't being loved that had softened the hard edges around Zane's heart—it was loving Phoebe.

He was a changed man. Whereas before she would never have thought to run to him for comfort, today she drove directly to the ranch and bypassed the house in favor of his office.

He was exactly where she would expect to find him at the end of a workday. At his computer, scowling. She smiled as she entered the room.

"Welcome home."

He looked up at her, then rose and walked toward her. "Maya," he said, before pulling her into a bear hug.

She went willingly, gratefully. Zane was a rock. Sometimes he was an annoying rock, but he was steadfast and dependable. Something she hadn't appreciated enough when she was sixteen and sure his only goal in life was to make sure she and Chase were unhappy.

"Hey, you," she said as she stepped back. "How was your honeymoon? And as I ask, remember you're my brother. Don't gross me out with too many details."

"It was great." He motioned for her to take a seat. "I'm sure Phoebe will give you the particulars."

"Too many of them," she grumbled, but without much energy. "I keep having to remind her that hearing her gush about you isn't the same as when she talked about other guys. There's an ick factor."

"If she wants to talk, let her talk."

"Oh, sure. Take her side."

"I can't help it."

Zane settled back in his chair. He was relaxed in a way she'd never seen before. *Love*, she thought, trying not to be bitter that the woman he'd fallen for had loved him back. No such luck for Maya. While she was pretty sure Del wouldn't say no to having her in his bed, he didn't seem to have any sense of urgency in the "I want more" department. Not that she'd shared her feelings, either, but that wasn't the point.

"What's happening with you?" he asked.

She started to tell him about the commercial, but instead found herself saying, "Did you know that Phoebe was missing her mom at the wedding?"

"She told me. She missed having her around, asking for her advice." His tone gentled. "Not all mothers are bad, Maya."

"I know. I'm friends with Elaine and she's got five kids. Some mothers are great."

"Most are. You got a bad one. I'm sorry. I wish I could go back in time and make it better."

"If you could, you should probably use your power for something more significant than my past. You could stop a war or save someone's life."

"You're worth saving. She was wrong about you." His gaze was steady. "You know that, right? That every day you're proving her wrong?"

Because Zane had heard the fights. The angry accusations of how Maya had ruined her mother's life. Whatever had gone wrong, Maya had been to blame.

"What brought this on?" he asked.

"I don't know. I've been thinking about my past. The scholarship. Not knowing who helped me is kind of a drag."

"If that person wanted you to know, he or she would tell you."

"Logic. You know I hate that."

"You and Phoebe both. Not that I'm surprised. You're alike in other ways."

Maya straightened. "What are you talking about? Phoebe and I are nothing alike." Her friend was sweet and giving. Maya was career obsessed and sometimes pretty bitchy. "I'm difficult and stubborn. Phoebe's great."

"You are, too. You both lead with your heart. Look how you were always worried about Chase."

"Yeah, but I was mean to you."

"You had something to tell me. I should have listened."

"This is just plain creepy."

He chuckled. "I'm simply pointing out there's a reason the two of you are friends. You have a lot in common. It's part of why I love you both." He winked. "In very different ways."

"Thank you for clearing that up. Because otherwise, ick."

Zane didn't smile. "You understand that I love you."

"Yes. You've said it. Why are you repeating it?"

"Because I'm not sure you see yourself as lovable."

Maya felt her mouth drop open. Were her flaws so obvious that everyone saw them? And if they were, what was wrong with her?

Or maybe she was looking at the situation from entirely the wrong perspective. Maybe she should embrace being lovable. Open herself up to the possibility. Stop being defined by hurtful words uttered by a woman who had never known how to be happy.

"I love you, too," she told her brother. "Now I'm going to go see my best friend and hear intimate details about your honeymoon. Be afraid. Be very afraid."

"Not a chance. Any reports you get are going to bother you a lot more than me."

She sighed. "I really hate it when you're right."

"I know you do."

MAYA FOUND PHOEBE in the kitchen. She was pouring brownie batter into a pan. The scent of butter and chocolate drifted to her, making her stomach growl. Maya sighed, knowing the smells would only get better—or worse, depending on her perspective—when the pan was put in the oven.

"Hi," she said with a smile. "Welcome back."

Phoebe put down the bowl and hugged her friend. "Hi, yourself. Did I know you were coming by?"

"Not unless you've turned psychic. How was your honeymoon?" Maya held up a hand. "Remember, I'm asking in the most general of terms."

Phoebe giggled, then returned to pouring the brownie batter into the pan. "Amazing. Fantastic. Wonderful. I highly recommend honeymoons to everyone. Especially with a wonderful man like Zane. We had perfect weather and the food was delicious. I think I gained five pounds and I don't even care." She sighed blissfully.

Phoebe had always been pretty, Maya thought, but today there was something about her. A glow. *From being in love*, she thought wistfully, *and having that love returned.* A couple of weeks of hot sex probably didn't hurt, either. Wasn't sex supposed to be good for the skin?

"I'm glad you had a good time."

"Me, too." Phoebe popped the brownies in the oven, then leaned against the counter. "Can you stay a bit?"

"I can."

Phoebe pulled a pitcher of iced tea out of the refrigerator and poured them each a glass, then they sat at the table by the island. "What happened while I was gone?" she asked. "Anything exciting?"

Maya thought about the commercial shoot, her upcoming class mostly for Eddie and Gladys, the subtle but inescapable restlessness she didn't want to acknowledge and knew there was a lot from which she could choose. So it made no sense for her to blurt out, "I'm in love with Del."

Phoebe's mouth dropped open. "You're what? When? I was only gone a couple of weeks. How could I miss that? Start at the beginning and tell me everything."

"There's not much to tell," Maya admitted. "It was at the reception." She hesitated a second, then told her friend what had happened that night. "After that, I just knew."

"OMG, seriously? You had sex with Del at my wedding?"

"Technically, it was after and we were in my old room, so it wasn't *at* the wedding."

"But still. You had sex on my wedding night before me!" Phoebe laughed. "You go, girl." Her humor faded. "Are you okay? Have you told him? What did he say? Are you going to tell him? How do you think he feels about you? Does anyone else know?" She paused. "You can talk now."

"Gee, thanks." Maya considered the list of questions. "I don't know how I feel. No, I haven't told him. Yes, I am scared. Very scared. I blew it the first time. Why would Del trust me now?"

"So he doesn't know how you feel?"

"No. I haven't said anything. I don't know what to say." Maya shifted in her chair. "We have to work together. I don't want things to be awkward. We're in a good place. Saying something would mess that up."

"Maybe in the best way possible. What if he's in love with you?"

"Then *he* can say something." Maya drew in a breath. "I dumped him before and I was cruel about it. He has every right to hate me or punish me and he's only been nice. While I appreciate that, I can't help thinking he would never trust me again. It's too soon. It's just…"

"You're scared."

"More like terrified."

There it was. The truth. Nothing to be proud of, but real, she thought.

Phoebe's expression was kind. "What do you want?"

"I don't know. Del isn't the type to stick around. I just got back. I'm settled."

"You don't sound settled."

"I'm confused. I love being back. The town is fantastic. I have everything I should want."

"Don't talk to me about *shoulds*," Phoebe said firmly. "I let them run my life for way too long. What does your heart tell you?"

That she loved Del and wanted to be with him. That seeing the world appealed to her. That she wanted to be a part of a project that meant something more than celebrity gossip and cable access butt contests.

"I don't know," she lied. Because she was afraid. Afraid of asking and being rejected. But if she didn't ask, didn't she risk losing out altogether? Wasn't it better to put it out there, to go for it?

"Maybe it's time to find out," her friend told her, speaking more truth than she could possibly know.

DEL PULLED UP in front of his parents' house. His mother had texted him, telling him she needed to see him as soon as possible. Normally a request like that wouldn't have bothered him, but he remembered his father's concerns about Elaine, so had hurried right over.

Over the past couple of weeks, he'd stopped by twice. His mom had seemed like her normal self. A little tired, but she'd claimed she wasn't sleeping well. Something about "the change." A topic he hadn't been comfortable discussing. Now he wondered what was suddenly so urgent.

As soon as he stopped the engine, Sophie bounded out of the house. The beagle ran toward him, her soft ears flopping in the early afternoon. She greeted him with a doggie grin and wagging tail.

"Hey, girl," Del said, crouching on the ground and petting her. She wiggled close to get as many rubs as she could. He obliged until he saw his mother step onto the wide porch.

Elaine looked pale and tired. There were shadows under her eyes and a slump to her shoulders. Alarmed, he went to her.

"Mom?"

Before he could say anything else, she started to cry.

"I can't do it," she said, tears spilling down her cheeks. "It's too much. All of it. The party, your father. I just heard from Ronan and Mathias, and they're both coming. Their rooms aren't ready, the house is a mess and I'm so tired. I can't do it."

Del wasn't used to seeing his mother as anything but an even-tempered, calm, capable woman. He'd only ever seen her cry a handful of times and that was nearly always over his father. He would have sworn that when it came to easy stuff like throwing a party, she was unflappable.

He walked up onto the porch and drew her into his arms. "Whatever it is, I'm here. We'll deal. You don't have to do this alone."

She sagged against him. He was shocked by how thin she felt. How frail. He'd dismissed his father's concerns, but now knew he should have listened. Something was going on.

He led her to the bench by the front door and waited until she sat. He settled next to her, then had to make room for Sophie, who jumped between them. The beagle stared at him as if to say *"Finally. I've been worried about Mom."*

"Tell me what's up." He kept his tone as calm and caring as possible.

She wiped her eyes. "Nothing. I'm tired. I have a virus or something. I haven't been sleeping." She faked a smile. "I'm fine."

"Mom, you're not fine. You don't let stuff like this

bother you. There has to be something." He braced himself to hear something that would make him uncomfortable, then forced himself to ask, "Is it Dad?"

"Your father? No. He's exactly as he's always been." She tried another smile. This one worked a little better. "You should ignore me."

He put his arm around her and kissed her cheek. "That's not going to happen. Mom, are you sure there isn't anything wrong?"

"Yes. Like I said, I had a summer virus. It happens. I'm still recovering, but I'm getting my strength back. It's just the party."

He rose and pulled her to her feet. "Come on. We'll get this thing managed. Then you'll feel better."

They walked through the house to the big kitchen. There he found a pad of paper. When they were both seated at the stools by the island, he looked at her.

"What's the party going to be like? Big? Small?"

She gave a soft laugh. "It's your father, Del, and he's turning sixty next week."

Del nodded. "Big, then. Half the town and everyone he's ever met?"

"Pretty much."

"Great. How much is planned?"

She went over the details. There was already a caterer, along with a bar service. The out-of-town guests had been invited and they all had reservations at various hotels around town. The twins would be driving home in a couple of days.

Ceallach's assistant was handling the various art

pieces that would be flown in to be displayed. The press would be there.

"You didn't want to have it somewhere else?" Del asked. "Like the resort or the convention center?"

"Your father wants his party here. We'll have tents in case of bad weather. I just have to get the house cleaned and prepared for the twins. Also, we'll be having a family dinner." The tremor returned to her voice.

He touched her arm. "Mom, listen. I'll get in a cleaning service to take care of the house. As for the family dinner, let's get it catered. That way you can spend more time with the twins and less time cooking. You know they love the food at Angelo's. I'll order from there and pick it up."

"I don't know. I should be cooking."

"No, you shouldn't."

"Let me think about it." She seemed to be fighting tears. "I have a guest list in the bedroom. Let me go get that."

He waited until she'd left, Sophie at her heels, then pulled out his cell and dialed.

"Hey," he said when Maya answered. "Are you free? Something's going on with my mom and I need your help."

He couldn't deny the relief he felt at the sound of her voice when she said, "I'll be right there."

CHAPTER FIFTEEN

"You should have called me," Maya said firmly from the chair by Elaine's bed. "I told you I want to be here for you."

"I know. I would have. I just kind of lost it and turned to Del. I have no idea why."

Because he was back in town, Maya thought. Because he'd always been there for his mom, taking care of things when she couldn't. Looking after his brothers, the family business. Being responsible.

Elaine relaxed on the bed, Sophie stretched out next to her. She stroked the beagle and looked at Maya.

"I didn't mean to worry anyone."

"I think Del was more freaked than worried." Maya had come as soon as she'd gotten his call. Together she and Elaine had reassured him that his mother would be fine after a nap.

Now she drew in a breath. "Elaine, you *have* to tell them. This isn't right. I don't like keeping this secret. I mean it. I love you, but this is wrong."

Tears filled Elaine's eyes. "Maya, please. I can't. Not a week before Ceallach's birthday. Don't make me. After the party, we'll talk. I promise."

Meaning she and Elaine would talk. Not that Elaine would tell her family. Maya didn't understand. Ceallach and her sons loved her. Sure the news would be upsetting, but they would rally around her. Give her support. That was a good thing. Being fussed over had a way of raising a person's spirits.

"Has it occurred to you that part of the reason you're feeling so overwhelmed is how much you're having to do on your own?" she asked. "Not just the party, but Elaine, you're dealing with breast cancer. You're getting radiation. You have to tell them."

"I will. Later. Help me get through the party. You have to understand why that's important."

Honest to God, she didn't understand, but there was no point in going there. "I love you," she told her friend. "How can I help?"

AN HOUR LATER, Maya and Del went over the to-do list.

"She has most of the party organized," he said. "I've got a cleaning service coming in tomorrow. How did you get her to agree to have the family dinner catered?"

Maya thought back to conversation with Elaine and the other woman's stubborn refusal to share something as important as her diagnosis and treatment with her family. "She owes me."

"I'm glad." Del made a few more notes. "Dellina has confirmed everything else. The tents, the food. The twins will be here in a few days and then we'll be in party mode."

Maya flipped through the guest list. Excluding

those coming locally, most were names she didn't recognize. Notes after some of them helped. *Minister of Culture, France,* had a way of clarifying who someone was.

"Your dad's a big deal," she murmured, noting a former United States vice president on the list and a couple of big-time actors. *Not Jonny Blaze,* she thought with a smile. Madeline would be disappointed.

"Always has been."

She looked at Del. "What?"

"I didn't know how big the party was. There are five hundred people on the guest list. Mom shouldn't have tried to handle this on her own."

"Dellina helped." Although she knew that wasn't what he meant.

"She never said anything. I know he didn't lift a finger. It's always been like that. She takes care of them. That's the marriage they have."

She put her hand on his arm. "She loves him. There's no regret. It might not be what you'd want or what I'd want, but it works for them."

"I can't figure out why." He turned to her. "I used to ask her why she stayed."

"She told you it was because he was her world."

"How'd you know?"

"She's my friend and her love for her husband isn't a big secret. You look at your dad and you see how he disappointed you. How cruel he's been. She doesn't see that. Not in the same way. It works for them."

"I guess." He leaned over and kissed her. "Did I ask you to the family dinner?"

"No. It's for family."

"I want you with me. Is that okay?"

"Sure."

The evening would be highly charged and difficult, but she didn't care. Time with Del was precious. Summer was drawing to a close. The changing leaves coloring the mountains moved a little lower every week. Soon fall would arrive. Del had said he was staying for the summer. With his father's party over, there wouldn't be anything to hold him here. Certainly not her.

"I'm going to change the subject," she said.

He leaned in and kissed her. "Want to tell me how much you want me?"

"With every breath, but this is about your project."

He straightened. "Shoot."

"You could get some feedback. School started this week. Talk to the local drama teacher at the high school about speaking with his or her class. You could show them one of the videos and then get their thoughts. What worked, what didn't and why. I'm sure the teacher would be pleased for them to see real-world application of the arts and you'd get information."

He stared at her. "Damn, you're good."

She smiled. "So I've been told."

"Seriously good. That's brilliant."

She shrugged. "I'm a good team player."

"The best."

He kissed her again, then slid off the stool. "I'm going to go find out who the instructor is and contact the school right now."

He was out of the room before he finished talking. Maya appreciated his enthusiasm, even as she wished he wanted to talk about that team thing a little more. As in the two of them working together. Permanently.

NEARLY A WEEK LATER, Maya watched the Mitchell family men standing together. There was no doubt Ceallach was the father of his five children, she thought humorously. Talk about a powerful gene pool.

All five sons were tall, with dark hair and eyes. Del and Aidan looked a little more like Elaine, while the younger three favored their father. Each of them was strong, muscled and annoyingly handsome. Not a loser in the bunch. She might be a little biased, but she was confident that Del was the best looking of them.

Elaine joined the family. She looked so much more delicate than her boys. Maya refused to think about the illness she was battling on her own. This was a night to enjoy good company. Not to worry about her friend.

Sophie was in doggie heaven, going from brother to brother to get pats and treats. In addition to ordering dinner, Del had instructed Angelo's to send over appetizers. There were trays of bruschetta, a couple of dips with crispy focaccia bread, stuffed mushrooms and mini mozzarella with tomatoes and basil on a toothpick. Wine flowed freely and Maya noticed that by the third bottle, conversation was a lot louder.

"Do you like it there?" Elaine asked, sounding doubtful.

Mathias and Ronan stood by their mother. "Happily, Inc. is a great town. A little like Fool's Gold, but with a different vibe."

"You're still working in glass?" Ceallach demanded. "You must work in glass. The rest of it, any idiot can draw or paint. A three-year-old can paint. But to create something from fire, that's talent."

The twins exchanged a look. "Dad, we saw that article about you in *Time* magazine," Mathias said. "Nice coverage."

"The reporter mostly got it right," the older man admitted grudgingly. "They don't always."

"That must be frustrating," Nick said. "Remember the guy from the *New York Times* a few years ago?"

"Idiot," Ceallach bellowed, then proceeded to list every way the reporter had failed him.

Del moved next to her. "You're seeing it, too," he murmured directly in her ear.

The feel of his breath against her skin made it difficult to concentrate, but she did her best to focus and process the words. "That they're deflecting him every time he asks what they're doing? Yeah, I noticed. Nick's part of it." She studied the middle brother. "Do you think it's a plan?"

"Absolutely."

She turned back to Del and found him standing deliciously close. If they'd been alone, she would have leaned in to press her mouth to his. Only they weren't. Worse, they were surrounded by his family.

"Why do you think they don't want to talk about what they're doing?" she asked, then sighed. "Never mind. I know the answer." Ceallach. He had a way of sucking the joy out of a room.

She wondered if it was really because he was brilliant or was he simply taking advantage of everyone around him. She knew Nick had a lot of talent, yet he managed to be a pretty decent guy. The twins were rumored to be just as brilliant as their dad, and although she didn't know them well, they seemed okay. Maybe it was a generational thing.

"After dinner we'll all go to the studio," Ceallach was saying. "You can see what I've been doing."

"We'd love that, Dad," Mathias said. "There's no one like you."

Ceallach puffed out his chest in pride. "This I know."

SOMETIME AFTER ELEVEN, Del stepped out onto the porch. The night was clear and cool and he could smell smoke from the fireplace.

Maya had ducked out an hour before. He couldn't blame her for leaving. He would have done the same if he could have. Talk had turned to art and stayed there for much of the meal. Now Mom had gone to bed while Ceallach, Nick and the twins argued style, technique or whatever it was they could talk about for days.

He sat on the bench and stretched out his legs in front of him. A few minutes later, Aidan joined him.

"Tired of hearing about process?" he asked.

His brother grimaced. "That and being ignored."
Aidan sat in one of the chairs. "They give me a pain
in my ass sometimes. It's as if nothing else matters."

"Nothing else does. To them, anyway. You know
that."

Aidan stared up at the sky. "They'll be at it for
hours."

"Luckily we both have somewhere else to sleep."
Del knew he should head home, and he would. But
for now, this was good. "How's business?" he asked.

"Busy. Labor Day freaks people out. They realize
summer's nearly over, so we get a lot of last-minute
bookings for weekend tours. Some people deliberately take time off in September because it's less
crowded and the weather is usually still good. So
we're slammed."

"Does it ever slow down?"

"Some. October and November have less going on.
Once it starts to snow, we're running ski weekends,
back country trips, that kind of thing."

Del nodded. "Makes sense. You've really grown
the company. You should be proud of yourself."

Aidan looked at him. "I am. Thanks. It was difficult at first. I didn't know what the hell I was doing.
But I've made it my own. There's nothing I'd rather
be doing."

"I appreciate you saying that."

"I'll bet you do. Now you don't have to feel guilty."

"It's going to give me a lot of free time."

Aidan grinned. "I'm not sure that's a good thing."

"At least I spend my days off pursuing something worthwhile."

Aidan's grin turned into a chuckle. "So do I. Just with a different outcome."

"All your outcomes are the same."

"Jealous?"

"Nope." Del thought about all the women he'd seen his brother with. What they had in common was they were female. Otherwise, Aidan didn't seem to have a type. "Don't you ever want more than variety?"

"Hell, no. Why would I? Every time, it's a new day. A new woman. I have my fun and we all move on. Why complicate life with a relationship?"

"Because it's nice to have someone who has your back. It's nice to belong."

"So speaks the man who travels the world. Where do you belong?"

An interesting question. He thought of Maya, wanting to say he belonged with her. Only he didn't. Working together wasn't the same as being romantically involved. He wanted to be with her in the most intimate ways possible. But that was different. It had to be. Trusting her again wasn't possible.

"I'm still figuring that out," he admitted. "Which is a great way to try to distract me from what we were talking about."

"Saying it didn't work?" Aidan asked with a chuckle. "I'll try harder next time." His humor faded. "I'm okay. I like how I live my life. I keep all my risks related to work. There's nothing dangerous about what I do with women. It's never serious and I never get stuck."

"Sometimes being stuck isn't a bad thing."

"Believe that if you want. I won't."

"Don't you worry that going from woman to woman means never connecting with any of them? What if one of them falls for you? Unlikely, but it could happen."

Aidan grinned. "I'm clear with the rules. They know going in it's just for the weekend or the week. Nothing long-term. I don't want more. Don't need it, don't have time for it. If they push, we're done."

"Doesn't that make you an asshole?"

"Maybe, but a lucky one."

"One day it's all going to crash in on you," Del said, knowing his brother wouldn't heed his warning.

"Never gonna happen." Aidan sounded confident. "I know exactly what I'm doing."

Del hoped he was being honest with himself. Because if he wasn't, things could go bad, and fast.

DEL STAYED ANOTHER half hour, but his father and brothers didn't seem inclined to discuss anything but art. When he called out that he was leaving, they barely paused from their heated conversation about blending colors in nontraditional mediums. Whatever that meant. Aidan had gone home fifteen minutes before, so Del left them and made his way to his truck.

It was late. If he checked on his smartphone he could figure out how much time had passed since the astronomical twilight. Not that it mattered, but the thought of it made him smile.

He started the truck and headed toward the lake. At the light, he made a left turn, telling himself he wasn't going to stop. He was just going to drive by.

When he got to Maya's street, he slowed. Most of the houses were dark. It was still and quiet, with only a bit of moonlight filtering between the leaves of the trees. As he approached her house he saw the lights were on.

He pulled into her driveway and waited. Seconds later, her front door opened and she stood in the doorway. They stared at each other for a couple of heartbeats before he gave in to the inevitable.

There were a thousand reasons to walk away, but the need to be with her, to touch her and be touched was more powerful than any of them. He'd loved her once. Maybe that kind of intensity left a mark on a man. One that couldn't be erased by time and distance.

Maybe it was just who she was, or who he was when he was around her. Maybe the draw couldn't be explained. It simply was one of those strange laws of the universe.

He turned off the ignition and got out, then walked toward her. She stepped back into the house. He followed her inside and carefully closed the door behind himself.

She stood barefoot in a T-shirt and yoga pants. She'd washed off her makeup and her hair was long and loose. She looked as she had when he'd first met

her. Young and sweet and sexy. He'd wanted her
then—more than he'd ever wanted anyone else. That
hadn't changed. He still wanted her. The difference
was, now he knew exactly what to do to please them
both. And he could last longer than fifteen seconds.

"Hey," he murmured, reaching for her.

"Hey, yourself."

She stepped into his embrace. Their arms came
around each other. She was soft and smelled good.
Even better, she fit. The right height, the right curves.
When he was around her, he wanted her. He supposed
in some ways he had always wanted her.

He lowered his head and kissed her. She met him
more than halfway, her lips already parted. There
was no way he could resist that, resist her. He eased
his tongue inside her mouth and felt the familiar heat
slam into him.

She wrapped her arms around him, squirming to
get closer. He tilted his head so he could deepen the
kiss. At the same time he ran his hands up and down
her back.

She was the perfect combination of curves and
softness. He dug his fingers into her butt, bringing
her lower body up against his. He was already hard
and ready. She pressed her pelvis against his erection, arousing him until thinking became difficult
and there was only wanting.

He drew back so he could kiss his way along her
jawline, then nibbled on her earlobe. He pressed his
lips to the sensitive skin on the side of her neck. At
the same time he reached for the hem of her T-shirt

and pulled it over her head. By the time he was tossing it away, she was already undoing her bra.

The fabric fell away. He cupped her breasts in his hands, feeling the weight of them, the softness of her skin. He didn't get it. Men had skin and women had skin, but hers was a thousand times softer than his.

He shifted his fingers to her tight nipples. As he brushed his thumbs across the tips, her breath caught and her head fell back.

He wanted more of that, he thought as he lowered his head and captured her left nipple in his mouth. He wanted her gasping and panting, calling out. He wanted her naked and shuddering her release.

He remembered when they'd been together so many summers ago. They'd been so young. Inexperienced teenagers with more love than sense.

Hunger had burned hot and bright, and as they'd made out in the front seat of his car, he'd come in his jeans. He hadn't said anything and she hadn't realized. The darkness had concealed the telltale damp spot.

Later, when he'd finally seen her bare breasts, he'd had the same reaction. Touching them had been worse. He'd finally confessed, and she'd been nothing but fascinated by his body and how she affected him.

They'd progressed quickly from there, moving from the front seat to the backseat. Together they'd discovered what made her quiver. They'd found her clitoris together and learned what she liked. She'd learned how to stroke him to climax. Days later she'd gone down on him. A first for both of them.

The first time he'd come in her mouth, he'd thought he would die from the pleasure of it. He'd returned the favor and she'd screamed out her release. It had been weeks before they'd moved on. Weeks until they'd taken each other's virginity.

He remembered everything about that night. How she'd carefully lowered herself onto his erection, sliding down until he'd filled her. She'd already pleased him once, so he'd been able to hang on for all of thirty seconds before exploding inside of her.

They'd practiced together, finding the right rhythm. They'd mastered the art of bringing her right to the edge, then having him thrust so they came together. They'd made love in her bed out at the ranch, whispering their love, kissing deeply through their releases so there wasn't any sound.

Those old memories crowded up against current need. Del released her breasts and dropped to his knees. He pulled down her yoga pants and bikini panties in one quick tug. She'd barely stepped out of them when he gently parted her and pressed his mouth against the very heart of her.

Memories returned. Of how she liked an open-mouthed kiss first. Soft, all lips. Then a light flick of his tongue—more teasing than passionate. He played until he felt tension start to tighten her muscles, until her breathing quickened. Only then did he settle down to a steady rhythm of moving his tongue against her clit. She grabbed the small entryway table behind her and hung on.

"Don't stop," she begged.

Time fell away and he was that kid again. He would swear he could hear music from the car radio and feel the slick leather of the backseat. They'd had their favorite positions—ways to make a cramped space workable. Now there was a whole house for them to play in. Assuming he could pause long enough to leave the foyer.

Only he wasn't going to do anything but keep on pleasing her. How could he resist when she began to whimper? One of Maya's best qualities was there was no doubt about what was working for her. All the signs were there. He moved a little faster and she trembled. He sucked deeply and she groaned.

He continued to hold her open. Under his palms he felt the first telltale quivers of muscles preparing for her release. Her breathing quickened. She was so close and he was in control.

He slowed, just a little. He circled her with the very tip of his tongue, then flicked across the swollen nub. She gasped again. Behind her, the table shook against the wall.

"Del."

Pleasure laced with anticipation in her voice. *Need*, he thought with satisfaction. He pressed his mouth against her clit and sucked. At the same time he pushed two fingers inside of her, then withdrew them before pushing in again. Her body contracted. He began to move his tongue against her, faster and faster until she cried out her release.

He felt her orgasm from the inside out. She tightened around his fingers, drawing him in deeper. He

moved his tongue steadily, drawing out her pleasure.
She moved her hips, grinding against him, taking
it all. Her sharp, high-pitched cries brought him to
the edge.

Just a few more seconds, he told himself. That was
all he had to hang on.

When the last shudders had faded, he started to
stand. She surprised him by kneeling down next to
him and undoing his jeans. He decided this was a
good time to let her have her way with him and didn't
protest when she jerked down the fabric, along with
his boxers. His erection sprang free.

She pushed him onto his back. He lay on her entry
carpet, mostly dressed, his dick sticking straight up.
Maya straddled him, and he reached into the pocket
of his nearby jeans for a condom.

She was flushed, naked and smiling that self-
satisfied smile that made a man feel as if he'd conquered the world. He didn't get long to enjoy the
feeling. As soon as she lowered herself onto him,
he had other things on his mind. Like how tight and
slick and warm she was. How he filled her. Of the
aftershock that had them both groaning.

She reached for his hand and placed it between
her thighs.

"Rub me."

He was happy to oblige. She was still swollen and
wet. He began to move his thumb against her. Then
fumbled the movement as she reached her arms up to
hold her hair on top of her head. Maybe under other

circumstances, it wasn't a big deal, but somehow that simple movement exposed her whole body to him.

She began to move.

Del didn't know what to look at first. Her closed eyes and parted lips. Her bouncing breasts. Her spread legs and his thumb stroking her. It was live, sexy and he was feeling it all. Her riding him, up and down, up and down. The pressure building at the base of his dick, her thighs tightening as she got closer to coming again.

The muscles inside clamped around him. She began to move faster. She lowered her arms to her sides, but kept her head back. Her breasts kept time with their movements. He swore—this was the hottest show ever and he was going to ruin it all by coming. But damn, how was he supposed to hold on?

The change in her breathing caught his attention. He knew she was close. He forced himself to pay attention to how he touched her, doing it just how she liked. Her eyes opened and he watched her get closer and closer. When she was just a heartbeat away, he let go of his control and shoved all the way in.

They came together, gazes locked. She cried out, then massaged him with her body as he released himself in her. The world faded to just the two of them. Time shifted and bent, and he saw the kid he'd been with the girl she used to be.

She sagged down and he caught her. After pulling her against him, he hung on until they could both breathe again. Breathe, but not let go.

CHAPTER SIXTEEN

MAYA TOLD HERSELF that throwing up in front of her class would not make a good first impression. Still, she couldn't help the case of nerves that had her hyperventilating as she drove to City Hall, where she would teach her first class in one of the community rooms.

She'd spent the past three nights coming up with her lesson plan. Del had helped and she thought she had a pretty decent handle on what she wanted to talk about. But she'd never actually taught a class before and wasn't sure what to expect. She supposed in a perfect world, no one would show up. That might hurt her feelings in the short-term, but at least then she wouldn't have to worry about screwing up.

She walked into the room and found there were already about a dozen people there, including Eddie and Gladys. Del, who had offered to be her assistant, was setting up equipment.

Eddie hurried over. "We told all our friends about your class. Everyone is very excited. Oh, and we told Del he has to work shirtless."

Maya laughed. "What did he say?"

"He refused, but we're still working on him. It's not fair that you keep him all to yourself."

"I'll mention that."

She crossed to the front of the room. Del had unpacked several cameras and lenses, along with a second case with lights and tripods.

"Eddie wants you shirtless," she told him.

"She said something about that."

"I said I'd put in a good word for her."

He raised his eyebrows. "Really?"

She tried not to smile. "Eddie has a point. I mean you're a pretty hot guy and I've been hogging you all to myself. That's hardly fair."

"So now you're going to pimp me out?"

"Just a little. You know, above the waist."

Humor brightened his dark eyes. "A side of you I never would have guessed."

"Is that a no?"

"It is, and later, I'm going to have to punish you."

She giggled. "In your dreams, big guy."

"Promise?" He leaned close. "By the way, we have confirmation from the high school."

"You heard from the drama teacher?"

"I did and she's excited about the project. She said her students are happy to give us as much feedback as we want. So I'm going to need your help with the questionnaire."

"Of course. We can work on that tonight."

One corner of his mouth turned up. "Don't think for a second I've forgotten about your punishment."

"Never."

She turned back to the class and realized that the ridiculous exchange had taken care of her nerves. At least the ones that made her want to barf. Now she was a little apprehensive, but in a good way.

She waited until one minute past the hour, then welcomed everyone to the class.

"Tonight we're going to talk about how to create a visually appealing video. Once you have conquered the technology so that your shots are in focus and well lit, there's a lot you can do to make them more interesting."

She paused, half expecting Eddie or Gladys to make a crack about naked butts, but both women were busy taking notes. The sight of them scribbling away made her oddly happy. *This town*, she thought ruefully. Just when she thought there weren't any more surprises, she found herself playing teacher and liking it.

As HIS MOTHER had promised, Del thought, Ceallach Mitchell's birthday was celebrated in style. The weather had cooperated, no doubt willed by his stubborn father. The sun was shining, the temperature warm enough that the sides of the tents could be rolled up, allowing the hundreds of guests to move easily through to all parts of the venue.

There were magnificent pieces of his father's work on display. Several slide shows highlighted other pieces of his work. Music played through speakers and waitstaff circulated with appetizers and champagne. There were foreign dignitaries, friends from town, other artists and plenty of reporters. Ceallach Mitchell was a big deal. Del sometimes forgot that, but today was a good day to be reminded.

"Mom owes us," Aidan grumbled, snagging a glass of champagne from a passing tray. "Why did we have to get dressed up? We just did that for Zane's wedding."

"I don't think one counts against the other."

"It should."

Not that it mattered. Elaine had been clear on the dress code. Given how much work the party had been to organize, he wasn't going to argue. On the bright side, the party meant Maya was dressed in some fitted dress with a low neckline. Talk about a great view. The dark red material looked soft. He planned to find out if that was true later. When he took her home.

They weren't living together, but he hadn't left her place since the evening of the family dinner. They made love over and over again, hanging on to each other as if they never wanted to let go. He wondered how much of the intensity was them and how much of it was knowing their time together was limited.

"Nice party."

Del turned and saw his brother Mathias approaching. He was the more outgoing of the twins. Funny and charming, he always had a woman or five hanging on him. He and Aidan shared a love of variety, although Del was pretty sure Aidan would win the volume challenge.

"If you like this sort of thing," Aidan grumbled. "What's with the suits?"

Mathias chuckled. "Let it go. Mom will kill you if you loosen that tie."

"Why aren't you uncomfortable?"

"I look damn good in a suit," Mathias pointed out. "Besides, I do this sort of thing all the time at the gallery. Charm the patrons. They want to see the artist, touch our magic." He winked. "Trust me, letting them touch brings out the checkbooks."

"While Ronan is in the back working?"

Mathias shrugged. "You know he's the dark, brooding one. He'd rather be alone with his art than meeting our clients."

Del believed that. Ronan was the twin who kept to himself. He supposed the differences could be explained by the brothers being fraternal twins. No more connected than he and Aidan or Nick. Just as well. If they'd been identical twins, they would have been even more trouble.

"Ever wonder how Mom got through it all?" Del asked.

Mathias's humor disappeared as his gaze sharpened. He went completely still. "What are you talking about?"

"The five of us, so close in age. We were terrors. Was there a single piece of furniture we didn't destroy? I'm amazed we didn't set the house on fire."

"Oh, that." Mathias relaxed. "She was a patient woman. Of course, she had to be to put up with Dad."

"How's he taking the news you're not moving back?"

Mathias sipped his champagne. "I think he's relieved. He doesn't want the competition."

"That's harsh."

"Maybe, but it's true. If Ronan and I were here, Dad couldn't ignore the attention we get from the press. The sons of the great Ceallach Mitchell take the art world by storm. With us far away, he can pretend it's not happening."

"There's no storm," Del teased. "Maybe a lonely cloud, but it'll pass."

"Jealous much?"

"Not at all. I couldn't take the pressure of having to keep up." Art had never been his thing. He didn't have the talent or the interest. Although he supposed his desire to make his videos could probably be traced to his father. Not that Ceallach would see what he did as anything worthwhile.

Maya strolled up to them. She moved close to Mathias and kissed his cheek in greeting.

"So many handsome Mitchell men. Whatever is a girl to do?"

Mathias grinned. "It's overwhelming."

She pretended to fan herself, then linked arms with Del. "I'm sticking with this old guy. He's more my speed."

Del frowned. "I'm searching for a compliment buried in there."

"There isn't one, bro. Let it go." Mathias turned to Maya. "I heard you're doing commercials these days."

"It was a onetime thing, but very fun. How are you

doing? Happily, Inc.? Is that the name of the town for real?"

"Yeah. It's got a great history. Back in the 1880s, a couple of stagecoaches of women were heading to gold rush country to find husbands. The stagecoaches broke down outside of our little town and the women were stuck. By the time new parts arrived, they'd all fallen in love with local guys. They decided to stay and lived happily ever after. One of their sons suggested the name change and it's been Happily ever since. Then in the 1950s, they changed it to Happily, Inc. No idea why."

"I love it," Maya told him. "I've heard it's beautiful. Desert, but with mountains. Aren't there rumors of some kind of mystical convergence? Like in Sedona?"

"We have the crazies," Mathias said easily. "And we like them. Lots of weddings." He winked. "It's a destination wedding town so if you ever get tired of Fool's Gold, come see us. You'll make a killing with your skills."

"You're sweet to offer. I'll let you know."

Mathias excused himself and moved away. Del looked at Maya.

"I thought you were settled here in Fool's Gold."

"I am. Mostly." She stepped away from him, then shifted to face him. "I'm wrestling with my future." Her gaze skittered away from him. "It's kind of your fault. All your talk of your world travels is making me restless."

He was surprised and pleased at the same time. "What are you going to do?"

"I have no idea. Nothing for now. When I didn't get the network job, I knew I had to make a change. Now I want to think about what's next. In the meantime, I like what I'm doing here." She smiled. "Maybe you'll hire me to do your editing."

"I'd like that." He would like her with him more, but wasn't sure about asking. He'd never considered it before because he'd assumed Maya wanted to stay in Fool's Gold. But if she didn't, they had options. Options he would have to consider.

His mother hurried toward him.

"Ceallach is ready to make his speech," she said. "We have to round up all the guests." She sighed. "He's having a wonderful time. This is everything he wanted."

Maya touched Elaine's arm. "How are you feeling?"

"Wonderful. Ceallach deserves to be celebrated. I'm so thrilled to have been a small part of this."

Del started to point out that his mother was the reason there was a party, but Maya shook her head. He wasn't surprised she could read him—she'd always been good at that.

"Come on," she told Elaine. "I'll walk you to the microphone and you can call everyone in."

"Thank you."

"I'll round up the stragglers," Del promised.

He watched them walk away. Maya seemed protective of his mother, which he appreciated. He started guiding guests toward the front tent, where there was a stage set up. Aidan joined him. When the five hundred people were facing the stage, Ceallach appeared.

His father was a handsome man, Del thought. Aging gracefully. Probably more than the old man deserved. At least Del knew he came from a strong gene pool.

As his father began talking about his life and his work, Del thought about how things had been so many years ago. When he'd been a kid and his father had been so disappointed by his lack of artistic ability.

Del had keenly felt his father's dissatisfaction. He'd cried himself to sleep hundreds of times, had prayed to wake up with some small ability to draw or paint or sculpt. Eventually he'd decided he didn't care anymore. He would find success in other ways— just not in his father's eyes.

Perhaps that was what growing up was about. Being proud of himself. Finding peace with his past while moving into his future.

Maya stood beside the stage. She looked at him and smiled.

Wanting kicked him in the gut. Wanting and maybe something more. But was he willing to take another chance on her? She wasn't Hyacinth, but that didn't mean he shouldn't remember the lesson learned there. To walk that road again would be trouble.

He thought about his father, how everyone was here to celebrate a man who had made his family's life hell for decades. Del remembered the old couple they'd interviewed in the woods. The ones who were still in love after years and years together. He would guess nearly no one attending his father's party had heard about them or would take the time to know them.

Who was to be more admired? Ceallach or the old couple? Who did he want to be like? There were lessons to be learned from both, and if he were smart, he would be careful to learn the right ones.

DEL HAD SEEN Maya's nerves before her class and now it was his turn to experience some of his own. While her students had been adults, he was facing a room full of fifteen- to eighteen-year-olds. He thought to himself that Eddie and Gladys were a bit less intimidating.

He'd watched Maya's presentation and had enjoyed her breezy, friendly style. While he'd always enjoyed talking to kids, the ones he usually interacted with were younger. Although it wasn't the teens that had him on edge. It was what they were going to say. Not counting Maya, they were going to be his first audience for the videos he'd done, and he was asking them to be critical.

Whatever happened, he would get valuable information, he told himself. If his work was crap, he would start over. If it was salvageable, then he would save it. Maya's editing had already made a huge difference. If only he'd had her along to do the filming, he thought.

The high school classroom was large, with a wall of windows and plenty of space between the desks and the dry-erase boards up front. Open shelves along the back wall were filled with clear plastic bins labeled with things like hats, masks or poster paint.

Maya flipped through the stack of papers they'd brought with them. It had taken nearly two days, but they'd come up with the questionnaire. The format of their class was going to be simple. The students would watch different clips from various videos and answer the questionnaire, then participate in a question-and-answer session.

The drama teacher, a tall, thin woman in her thirties, introduced him and Maya and explained why they were there. When she had finished, he walked to the front of the class. Starting was always tough. He'd come up with various opening lines, then figured out one that accomplished what he wanted.

"How many of you can read?" he asked. "Show of hands."

The students glanced at each other, then at him. Slowly they all raised their hands.

He grinned at the teacher. "Good to know," he said with a chuckle. "Because in ancient Rome only about 2 percent of the population could read. Today there are over 774 million people over the age of fifteen who can't read. Fifty-two percent of them live in South and West Asia. Twenty-two percent of them live in sub-Saharan Africa. If you can't read, you can't know what's in an instruction manual or a textbook or understand the label on a bottle of medicine."

He paused. "Who here knows the country with the most college degrees?"

"The US," someone called out.

One of the female students rolled her eyes. "By percentage or actual numbers?"

"Good question. By percentage."

"Sweden," she said smugly. "Higher education is free there."

"I've heard that. Any other guesses?"

"Australia."

"China."

"America, dude. The answer is always America."

"Not this time," Del told him. "The answer is Russia. Fifty-four percent of their adult population has a college level degree."

"Whoa. No way," one of the guys in the back said.

"Way." Del settled on a corner of the instructor's desk. He was feeling more relaxed now. These students were older, but not all that different than those he usually talked to. The trick was to engage them.

"I'm here because I want to create a series of videos showing what life is like for kids living all over the world. What do you and they have in common? What's different and in what ways? You're going to watch clips from videos I made before I knew what I was doing. Then I want your feedback. The more honest, the better. What do you like? What don't you like? When did you start wishing you could be doing something else?"

A few students laughed at that.

One of the girls raised her hand. "Later, will you come back and show us what you've done with our feedback?"

"I promise."

MAYA HIT THE pause button on the computer. She waited while the students wrote down their comments. Del paced along the side of the room. She would guess he was trying not to look nervous, but she could see the tension in his body.

So far the feedback had been excellent. They'd prepared several short clips, varying the content but not the length. Some had him doing the voice-over, some had her. They'd added music, written notes and suggested questions for discussion. They were getting a lot of good information from the students. She had pages of notes and was sure Del had the same. The potential was there.

When the last student finished writing, Del walked to the front of the room.

"If you'll pass your papers forward, Maya and I will look them over later. But for now, let's talk about what you think."

"The videos were good," a guy said. "Interesting, you know. I didn't like the music."

"Me, either," one of the girls added. "It made it too... I don't know. Commercial, I guess. Just let us hear what's happening. Like the bells on the cows. That's better than music."

Several students nodded.

"The discussion questions were good," another girl said. "But you know that means teachers are going to use them to make us write an essay or something."

Del held up both hands. "I can't be responsible for that."

"The questions were good," someone else said.

"They're things for us to think about. We're lucky here, in Fool's Gold. We need to know this stuff."

Maya could see the value of that and made a note to talk to Del about some kind of study guide or teacher's guide. Suggested test questions or maybe even some book recommendations for further study. That might be helpful. Or could they come up with a companion book? One with facts and still pictures. Maybe transcripts of interviews. Because they would have way more film than they could ever use. The longer conversations could be summarized. Something to think about.

"What about the voice-over?" Del asked.

One of the girls wrinkled her nose. "You're really good on camera, Del, but it's better when Maya does the voice-over. I don't know why. You both sound okay."

"She's got the Mom voice," the guy next to her blurted. "But sexy." He flushed and squirmed in his seat.

Maya blinked in surprise. She had a sexy voice?

Del nodded. "My man, you have that exactly right. Maya's voice is appealing. How many think she did the better voice-over?"

Nearly everyone raised their hand.

The teacher stepped forward. "I agree, Del. Maya, you have a natural ability. There's a warmth in your tone. Maybe it's that teachers have been traditionally female so we respond to a woman's voice. I'm not sure. Also, getting back to the questions and discussion points, I would very much like a companion book. A series like this could send us in many directions. We can talk politics, history, world studies, even economics. Well done."

Maya recognized the wrap-up and glanced at the clock. She was shocked to see that nearly two hours had passed. The students would have to head to their next class. She scrambled to her feet.

Del thanked the students and they applauded. They were excused from class. When they were gone, Maya and Del spent a couple of minutes getting more feedback from the instructor, then collected their equipment and headed to the parking lot.

"That was so great," Del said when they walked outside. "The kids enjoyed the videos."

"I know. The questions they asked were so smart. I can't wait to go through their comments. We're going to get a ton of feedback."

They walked to his truck. He put the box with all the questionnaires behind his seat, then reached for her computer bag.

"I hadn't thought about high schools as a place for the videos," he admitted. "I wonder if we could take the same material and change the accompanying lesson plan to match the grades. So simpler questions for younger kids and so on."

"That would be easy. Also, depending on how much raw footage we had at any given point, we could edit the videos differently. Show a grittier version to older kids. We'll have to figure that out, but it's doable." She paused, nearly overwhelmed by possibilities.

"This is going to take some funding," she went on. "I know a couple of people who've been able to get grants. I want to get in touch with them to find out what's involved. You have to do this, Del. It's a wonderful project."

He hugged her. "You're a big part of it," he told her.

She wanted to be, she realized. His idea had become important to her. For so long she'd held back, sticking to what was safe. Going after the familiar, like the network job. What had been up with that? She didn't belong on-screen, and she didn't need to be loved by a faceless audience to feel special. She wasn't that scared little girl anymore. There was no worry about being rescued or even having to rescue herself. She was a successful, competent adult. She could take care of herself.

Coming back to Fool's Gold had allowed her to figure out what she really wanted. She wanted to be a part of Del's video project. She wanted to travel with him and love him and be loved by him.

He was the one. Maybe he always had been, maybe they'd had bad timing before. Whatever it was, she knew that it was time for her to tell him how she felt. But before she could do that, she had to come clean about a secret she'd been keeping. And that meant talking to Elaine first.

CHAPTER SEVENTEEN

"You've got a few crumbs right there," Maya said, pointing. Not that it made any difference. Sophie didn't much care about the telltale evidence of her recent foraging in the kitchen. She was more interested in stretching out in the sun and getting a nice tummy rub.

"It's a good thing your mom loves you so much," Maya continued, stroking the beagle. "Because you're kind of a scamp."

"She is," Elaine said fondly as she handed Maya a glass of lemonade.

Maya took it and studied her friend. Elaine still looked tired. There was a dullness to her skin and the darkness under her eyes had deepened.

"Only a couple more days of radiation, right?" she asked.

Elaine sat on the sofa and sighed. "Yes. I've been warned that it will take a while for the fatigue to go away. It didn't come on immediately, so I guess that's to be expected. Still, I'm looking forward to being my old self again."

Maya shifted so she was facing Elaine. "I need you to tell them."

Elaine's expression tightened. "We've been over this. It's my decision and I don't want to. You have to let it go."

"I can't. This is really important to me. I'm lying to Del every day. It's horrible."

"He'll survive and so will you."

Maya was surprised by her friend's harsh tone. She'd hoped Elaine would simply agree.

"It's not just that," she said quietly. "Things with Del have gotten complicated. He's..." Maya wasn't sure how to explain, then realized the truth was generally the right answer. "I've fallen in love with him and I can't tell him while I'm keeping your secret from him."

Elaine had been hinting how much she wanted Maya and Del to get together, and Maya was expecting a happy reaction. Smiles. Maybe laughter. She didn't think her friend would cover her face with her hands and start to cry.

"What?" Maya asked, moving next to her and hugging her. "Are you angry? I'm sorry if I upset you."

"You didn't. It's not that. I just don't have anything more in me. I'm so tired and I never meant to hurt anyone."

"You didn't. We're all fine."

Elaine straightened and sniffed. She wiped her face with her fingers. "You've been keeping this from him because of me. I'm sorry."

"It's okay." Maya studied her. "Are you sure you're all right? You haven't heard anything bad from the doctor, have you?"

"It's not that. Just everything seems like so much. Ceallach's birthday party, having all the boys back in town. It was wonderful to see them. I wish the twins would move back, but they seem to like where they are."

Maya eased back a little. "Kids leave home. Most parents want that to happen."

Elaine gave her a shaky smile. "I don't want them underfoot every day, but it would be nice to have them around more." She drew in a breath. "You're right. I need to tell them and I will. Ceallach's finishing a piece this week. He'll be done Friday. I'll call a family meeting on Saturday morning and tell them then. I promise."

Maya felt herself relaxing. "Thank you. I appreciate it. Once you've explained what you've been through and Del has had a chance to deal with it, I can talk to him about us." Assuming there *was* an us.

She knew he liked her, liked being with her. But how much of that was because she was convenient and how much of it was real? There was only one way to find out, she reminded herself. And that was to talk about her feelings and ask about his.

"You're really in love with him?" Elaine asked.

"I am. I don't know what's going to happen. He might not care at all."

"He cares. He's with you constantly."

"Some of that is because we're working together."

"Is it? I don't think so." Her smile faded. "They're going to be angry."

"They're going to be concerned. This is a big deal.

Even knowing you're okay now, they'll be worried about you. They're your family and they love you. What if Ceallach kept secrets from you?"

Elaine reached over and patted Sophie. "That would be difficult," she said.

Maya studied her. There was something in her voice, she thought. Something she couldn't quite explain. Then Elaine looked up, her eyes bright with humor.

"Give me until Saturday," she said with a laugh. "If I haven't told my family by then, you have my permission to rat me out."

Maya winced. "Could we call it something else?"

"We can call it anything you like." Elaine drew in a breath. "Seriously, I'll tell them Saturday morning. You'll see."

"THE SIZE OF the boat determines how many people at a time," Del said as he and Aidan strapped on their harnesses. "The bigger the boat, the more can go together."

"I'd need an experienced captain," Aidan said, his gaze on the vivid blue of Lake Tahoe.

They'd driven to the famous lake together for an afternoon of parasailing. Aidan was considering adding it to the activities his company offered. Lake Ciara was big enough for him to offer the sport and he'd invited Del along to help him with the research.

"Are there state regulations?" Del asked.

"I'll have to check. We're not on the ocean, so we don't deal with the coast guard. But I'm sure there are things for us to keep in mind." Aidan watched the crew guy hook up the cables that would keep them connected to the boat.

Del liked any sport that had him in the air. Parasailing offered an easy trip for those without any kind of training. Once you were in the harness, the boat, the wind and the parachute did all the work. All the rider had to do was sit back and enjoy the ride.

He and Aidan sat facing the front of the boat. The parachute billowed out behind them. It was big—nearly forty feet—to support their weight. Del didn't know the specifics about requirements, but he knew that the bigger the chute, the more it could handle, be it number of riders or strength of the wind.

"Weather wouldn't be a big issue," he said as the boat picked up speed. Seconds later they were slowly rising up in the air.

The boat seemed to get smaller and smaller. Sound faded as they were able to see more of the lake and mountains that surrounded it. Wind buffeted them and still they rose higher.

"This guy charges by how high we go, along with the length of the ride," Aidan said.

"How do you want to do it? The longer people are out, the more you pay in terms of fuel and employee time, not to mention wear and tear on the boat."

Aidan nodded. "But I don't want a complicated menu. Plus, I see us doing a lot of families. Maybe rides of diffcrent lengths of time."

They reached eight hundred feet. The boat moved across the lake, leaving a wake behind. The water itself was made up of dozens of shades of blue. *Maya would like it here*, Del thought, wishing she were with him. There were plenty of nice hotels in the area. They could get lost in one of them for a few days. Stay in bed, resurface from making love to grab a meal, maybe go hiking. His idea of a good time.

She was a complication he hadn't expected. When he'd first decided to come home for the summer, he'd been uncertain about what to do next. Having resources was a good thing, but more options meant more decisions. Now he was sure about what he wanted—or at least what he didn't want.

He didn't want to fund someone else's dream. He didn't want to invent something else. What had happened to him had just been one of those things. His passion lay elsewhere. In a few weeks, he would be ready to leave Fool's Gold. The question for him was, would he also be ready to leave Maya?

The boat turned in a wide circle. Aidan and Del followed along. As the ride came to a close, they were pulled in. For the last twenty feet, they hovered right above the water. The captain had offered to let them plunge into the chilly lake, but they'd declined.

"It would be great on hot days," Aidan yelled, the boat noise growing louder as they approached. "We could drop people into the lake. They'd love it."

"At least the kids would."

His brother laughed.

Del was grateful they were able to hang out like this. To talk without any misunderstandings between them. Aidan might not have been happy about having the business dumped on him, but he was obviously good at it.

"What's the verdict?" he asked when they were back in his truck.

"I gotta get me one of those." Aidan grinned. "It was fun. I'll get my captain's license or whatever it is I need, and hire a couple of guys with the right qualifications. It's going to be a great addition to what we already offer." His eyebrows rose. "Plus, pretty ladies in bikinis. Where's the bad?"

"You and your women."

"Jealous?"

"Nope. I'm not into volume."

Del would admit that Aidan's lifestyle might sound like nearly every guy's dream—endless sex and no commitment—but he couldn't get excited about it. He wanted something else. Something special. Someone special. As he drove back toward Fool's Gold, he had to wonder if he'd found her. Because there was a lot about Maya that he liked.

But what about the parts that worried him? Honesty was important to him. He'd grown up with secrets, and he was determined to make sure he didn't repeat that pattern in his own life. He told the truth and he expected it from the woman he loved. Ten years ago Maya had kept her worries and fears from him. She'd broken his heart and lied about the reasons.

They'd both been young. They'd both grown and changed. But was it enough? Could he trust her to be honest now? To not keep secrets? Because lying undermined every relationship, no matter the intentions. That he knew for sure.

"LEAN," MAYA SAID, motioning to the scarecrow. She studied the screen of her camera as Del leaned into the straw creature. He put his arm around it and smiled broadly.

"Perfect. Hold it…hold it."

Just when she was going to tell him to relax, he winked.

While the part of her that was wildly in love with him, desperate to tell him and hey, maybe looking for a little Del-flavored action, sighed at the gesture, her filmmaker brain recognized pure gold when she saw it. Talk about appealing.

"Got it," she told him and pressed the stop button, just as a toddler ran into the shot.

"Sorry," the mother called, racing after him.

"No worries," Maya assured her. "We're just playing here."

Del grabbed the young boy before he could make his way into the street. The mother took him gratefully. Her husband jogged over to relieve her.

It was the Thursday of the Fall Festival long weekend and downtown was crowded with tourists and residents alike—all wanting to participate in the various activities, shop at the stores and carts, and sample delicious seasonal dishes like Pumpkin Spice Latte Muffins and Roasted Tomato Soup with Cheddar Crostini. She and Del were shooting B-roll to edit into the town videos they were doing.

A lot of today's clips would be purely devoted to the season, but they would also get shots that were simply town based and could be used at any time of the year. Later in the week, they would be filming at The Christmas Attic to simulate the end of the year. Morgan over at Morgan's Books was going to decorate one of his windows to celebrate all things spring and Easter to help them out. Maya had gone over their footage a couple of days ago. Her best guess was they were within a week of wrapping up their project. While she would still have postproduction work to do, Del's part would be finished. Leaving him free to move on.

They hadn't talked about when that would happen. She knew why she was keeping quiet, but was less sure about him. She hoped that he was trying to figure out how to ask if she wanted to go with him. In her wildest dreams, she imagined him telling her he'd always been in love with her and...

She ran the video back and made sure it was there, clear and usable. She worked automatically, leaving her brain free to admit that even in her mind, she wasn't sure what happened after the hoped-for admission of love. Did he propose? Offer to show her the world? Or simply carry her off into the sunset?

Telling herself that not only was it a fantasy, but that even if it came true, she didn't have to write his lines for him didn't make her any more comfortable with the unknown. She knew her twisting stomach nerves came from the fact that there was a shoe waiting to drop. This one in the form of Elaine coming clean with her family. And when that happened, Del was going to find out that Maya had known about the cancer all along and hadn't told him. She had a feeling that conversation wasn't going to go very well.

If only she knew how he felt about her. Asking made sense, but she couldn't. Not until she could tell him how she felt, which she couldn't until she didn't have to lie to him.

And here she was, back where she'd first started.

Del walked over. "Why are you looking so serious? That was a great shot."

"You have no way of knowing that."

"I could see it in your eyes." He flashed her a grin. "I nailed it."

"Have I mentioned how your modesty is your best quality?"

He moved close and lowered his voice. "Is that what we're calling it these days?"

He leaned in as he spoke. His warm breath teased the side of her neck and made her shiver. Or maybe it was simply being near the man himself. Del had always had the power to get to her. Time and distance hadn't changed that fact.

She stared into his eyes and wondered if what they had was enough to survive what he was about to learn. Del had a lot of great qualities, but from what she could tell, forgiveness and understanding weren't two of them.

She returned her attention to the camera and played back what she'd filmed. He watched intently.

"Great shot," he told her. "The colors pop against

the backdrop. You can see enough of the mountain to get a real sense of place."

She nodded. "We have a lot of material. I'll want to do a few shots of the live nativity in December, but otherwise, we're nearly there."

His dark gaze settled on her face. "Does that mean you'll be going back to your desk job?"

"Sure. I have editing to do and cable access to worry about."

"How interesting is that?"

"It depends on who Eddie and Gladys talked into giving over their butt photos."

"Ever think about doing something—"

Two teenage girls approached. "Hey, Del. Hi, Maya. Filming for the town videos?"

Maya held in a sigh. Talk about bad timing. She turned to the teens and reminded herself that they'd been a big help with the questionnaire and discussion.

"We are," she said cheerfully. "Shooting B-roll. Do you know what that is?"

"Background stuff," one of the teens said. "For between the main action shots. It provides color and context."

"Good answer," Del told her. "What's up?"

The girls exchanged a look, then glanced at Del. "We've been talking about your project," the blonde said. "And we have some ideas."

Her brunette friend nodded vigorously. "Like going to a country where girls have to get married really young. You could follow the couple for a few years and see what happens. Also, what about careers? Here everybody talks about how we can be anything."

The blonde wrinkled her nose. "Which isn't exactly true. Trust me. No one wants me doing anything with the space program. We'd crash for sure. But if I was good at math—"

"Like me," her friend said with a smile.

"Yeah, like you, then I could do anything. Is it like that everywhere? Do all kids have opportunities? Or does it come down to what your parents do? If your dad's a farmer, you're going to be a farmer?"

Del listened intently. "I like this and I see what you're saying. How much is choice? How much is geography or financial means?"

"Uh-huh. And there are expectations. Like getting married and having kids. But at what age? If you're supposed to get married at eighteen, it's hard to go to college, right?"

Her friend nodded. "Plus, there are family rules. In my family, everyone goes to college. But if you're the first one to go, are you supported or expected to help pay the bills?"

"Nice," Del said. "You've given us a lot to think about. Thanks."

"You're welcome," the teens said together, then headed back to the festival.

"Good ideas," Maya told him. "Although it would make me sad to see a young girl have to get married."

"I agree, but it happens." Del looked around. "What about different cultural celebrations? It's been done a lot. Is there a fresh twist?"

"We could brainstorm that."

"I'd like that." He paused. "About what we were talking about before," he began, just as her cell phone rang.

Maya pulled it out and glanced at the screen. "Caller ID says City Hall, and as I work for the mayor, I need to take this one."

She pushed the talk button. "This is Maya."

"It's Bailey. Mayor Marsha needs you to go to the Lucky Lady Casino right away. Ernesto and Robert want to talk to you and Del."

"Did anyone say about what? Am I worried or happy?"

"I'm sorry, she didn't say. For what it's worth, she didn't seem the least bit upset."

Maya tried to find comfort in that. "Does she ever?"

"Sometimes."

"You're just saying that to make me feel better."

Bailey laughed. "A little, but I doubt anything is wrong."

"I guess we're going to find out."

DESPITE IT BEING a weekday, there was plenty of traffic on the highway leading to the hotel-casino. Del drove his truck onto the property, then found a parking space in the back lot. He and Maya walked toward the large building.

"Nervous?" he asked as they approached the glass doors leading into the casino.

"Yes. I want to say I'm not, but I am. I saw the raw footage for the commercials. We did a great job."

"Mostly you," he told her.

"Thanks. I hope there's not a technical problem."

She was too careful for it to be that, he thought. She'd had multiple cameras, had checked each shot, backed up the footage. If there was a mistake, it wasn't on her end.

Del liked that Maya was careful about her work. She took pride in what she did—something he could respect. Too many people were only interested in doing just enough to get by.

Once they were in the casino, they followed the signs that pointed them toward the hotel. In the lobby, the concierge directed them to the general offices where a receptionist led them to a small conference room.

Ernesto and Robert were waiting inside.

"Thank you for coming," Ernesto said with a smile as he rose and shook their hands.

Robert followed his business partner, then gestured for Del and Maya to take a seat.

The businessmen sat on the other side of the table.

"We've seen the rough cut of the first two commercials," Ernesto said, nodding as he spoke. "Very impressive. We've worked with several production companies before, and none of them have captured exactly what we were looking for nearly as well as you two did."

Robert leaned toward them. "We like what we saw very much. Ernesto and I have talked it over. We'd like to hire the two of you to handle all our publicity videos. We have twelve properties in all—two are in the United States and the rest are around the world. The shoots would likely take about eight weeks a year."

Del hadn't known what to expect from the hoteliers, but it hadn't been a job offer. Sure it was just part-time, but making commercials? Talk about an unexpected second act.

Ernesto explained about what would be required, then named a proposed salary offer that nearly made Del laugh out loud. He would guess it was about double what Maya was currently making with the city. Not bad for a few weeks' work.

He glanced at Maya and saw she was wide-eyed with obvious shock. She looked at him, as if asking what he thought. He nodded slightly. She turned back to their hosts.

"You've made a generous offer," she told the two men. "We'll need to talk about it."

"Of course. Let us know if you have any questions. We can work around your schedule by planning well in advance. This could be a profitable partnership for all of us."

CHAPTER EIGHTEEN

"I'M IN SHOCK," Maya said for the third time since they'd left the casino. "I can't believe it."

The offer was incredible. Not just the money, although that was spectacular, but all of it. The chance to work so creatively, to learn and grow. To see other parts of the world.

Del pulled up into her office parking lot, then turned to face her. "I had no idea they were so impressed with your work."

She opened the passenger door and got out. "*Our* work. They're hiring both of us."

"You're the talent," he told her, then stepped out and joined her.

"Behind the camera," she said with a laugh. "You dazzle in front." She grabbed his arm. "Del, this is incredible. Do you realize the opportunities this opens to us? With your name and my contacts..." She waved her free hand in the air. "I don't even know where to start."

There were a thousand things they could be exploring, she thought. More commercials. Shorts. Taking his ideas for the videos about the kids and running with them. Possibilities swirled, each brighter and more alluring than the last.

He stood in front of her, illuminated by the sun. Tall and handsome and exactly who she always wanted to be with.

"We should find out where the other casinos are," he told her. "Maybe we could piggyback trips. You know, film the commercials and then go locate a couple of schools. We would already know the area."

"I was thinking the same thing. Obviously we're not doing videos for every hotel every year. But that's okay. It means that in a couple of years, we'd be going back to the same location. We could follow up. See how the children we filmed before have grown and changed. Ask the same questions and get the new answers."

"We could also find a writer somewhere. Someone who does freelance work. Maybe hire him or her to write articles on what we're doing to drum up interest."

She nodded excitedly. "Or do companion articles. Supplement the videos. For teachers, like we talked about before. Sample discussion questions. With everything digital it's easy to change and update content." Maya pressed her hands together. "What about an online newsletter? We could talk about where we're going next. Students could subscribe. We could give kids in other countries a forum for talking to kids here."

There were a thousand possibilities, she thought happily. So many opportunities.

"You know," she said, "with the money we're getting from this, funding your project wouldn't be such a stretch. I wouldn't need much of mine and—"

She pressed her lips together as she realized what she'd said. "Not that you've said you want me involved or anything," she added, feeling awkward and uninvited.

Del grabbed her arms and pulled her close. "Maya, without you, there's no idea and there's certainly no job with the hotels." He released her and looked at her.

"I've been thinking about this a lot," he admitted. "About us. The way we work together. You understand what I want to do with my life."

Her breath caught as her body went still. Hope filled her. Hot and bright, it grew like a bubble and she nearly floated away.

"I hope you want the same thing," he continued. "We're good together. A great team."

"We are," she whispered, thinking that loving him was the best thing to ever happen to her.

"I have some money."

She blinked, not sure what he was talking about. "Okay," she said slowly. "That's nice."

He laughed. "I sold my company for a healthy profit. I have enough money to fund our project. Ever since I got back to Fool's Gold, I've been trying to figure out what's next for me. I've had offers, but none of them were right. This is right."

He touched her face. "I want us to form a partnership. Create a company. We'll do the commercials for Ernesto and Robert and go film our kids and create programs teachers can use in classrooms. We'll hire a writer or two and some production staff, but most of the work, the fun stuff, we'll do together."

He released her. "I know you just got back. That you're not going to want to leave right away. If you aren't sure, you could ask Mayor Marsha for a leave of absence, so you'd know you could return here. I hope you'll consider what I'm offering. The world is beautiful and I'd like to show it to you."

Disappointment had a flavor. It was bitter with an unexpectedly sharp aftertaste.

"You want us to work together," she said softly, needing to be sure she got it right. "To be business partners."

He nodded eagerly. "I bring the financial capital to the table, but you have the talent. We'd be in this fifty-fifty."

The "this" being their company.

He didn't love her. He didn't want to marry her or tell her he couldn't live without her or that he'd never forgotten her. There was no confession of undying devotion or a ring. Not even a hint of anything remotely personal. In his mind, they were friends, colleagues. Nothing more.

"It's a lot to think about," she murmured. "My head is spinning."

And her heart was breaking, but she wasn't about to share that with him.

"You need some time," he said. "I get it." The engaging smile returned. "We could be great together, Maya."

"I know."

They could. Just not the way he meant.

MAYA SOMEHOW GOT through the rest of her work-day. As soon as she could, she headed out of town. She was confused, hurt and scared. That meant she needed help and there were only a couple of people she trusted with that information.

She arrived at the Nicholson Ranch just before five. She'd already called Phoebe to let her know she would be stopping by. Her friend had insisted she stay for dinner and was waiting on the front porch when Maya pulled up.

For a second Maya just looked at her friend. Back in LA Phoebe had been the one not sure what to do with her life. While she'd loved selling real estate, she'd never been able to shake the feeling of it not being enough. Helping others find their dream home had been satisfying. And that sense of having done a good thing had allowed her to mask an uncomfort-able truth—that she never felt as if she deserved a place to belong, as well.

Falling for Zane had changed all that. Maya wasn't sure if it was loving the man or allowing him to love her that had caused the transformation. Either way, Phoebe was now a confident woman who knew she belonged. Whatever might be messed up in her own life, Maya knew she could take comfort in know-ing that two of the people she loved most were bliss-fully happy.

"Hey, you," Phoebe called as Maya got out of the

car. "I have a bottle of your favorite red wine already open and we're having pasta for dinner."

Maya hoped she didn't look as pathetically grateful as she felt. "Did I sound like I needed carbs when I called?" she asked. She stepped onto the porch.

Phoebe hugged her. "You kind of did."

"Then thanks for reading my mind."

They went inside.

Maya remembered the ranch house from when she and her mother had first moved here twelve years ago. The sheer size of the place had surprised her, as had the furnishings. She was used to plastic and hand-me-downs. Not big pieces made of wood. Not hand-carved tables and plush fabrics that were warm and comfortable.

In the few weeks Phoebe had been in residence, she'd started making changes. Several of the walls had been painted a pale yellow. The layout of the open family room had been shifted so the sofas faced each other, instead of the fireplace. Gone was the big TV on the wall and in its place were bright paintings.

Her presence was felt in small ways, too. Cut flowers stood in pretty vases and fashion magazines nestled with a livestock quarterly. Just being in the house made it easier to breathe, Maya thought. Whatever happened, she had family. Should she need rescuing, there would be a contingent, if not a village. She wasn't on her own.

Phoebe pointed to the sofa by the coffee table. A bottle of wine sat on a tray. There were two glasses along with a plate of cheese and crackers.

"Sit," she said. "I'll pour while you start talking. This is Del related. It has to be."

Maya accepted the glass of wine and waited until Phoebe settled on the sofa opposite. She took a sip of wine, then drew in a breath and wondered where to start. Maybe with the most painful truth.

"Del's not in love with me."

Phoebe grabbed a piece of cheese. "I don't believe that at all. He's crazy about you. I can see it when you're together. There's serious sparkage."

Despite everything, Maya laughed. "Sparkage? Because you're twelve?"

"Sometimes. Now what happened?"

"Remember the commercials he and I shot? For the Lucky Lady Casino?"

"Uh-huh."

Maya explained about the meeting with Ernesto and Robert and what they'd offered.

Phoebe waved her hands. "That's fantastic. Did you say yes? You have to say yes. I mean, I'll miss you desperately, but come on. You'd love doing that."

"I would," Maya admitted. "Of course I'm interested, but I was surprised. We both were."

"And?"

Maya put down her wine and tucked her legs under her. "I've told you about the children's series of videos Del and I have been talking about."

Phoebe nodded. "You'd be able to do those, too. It's perfect."

"That's what I thought. Del and I could do both. We'd work together..." She drew in a breath. "Actually, that's what he offered. A business partnership. He has money from selling his business. I bring the technical ability to the table. We work well together. Share a vision. It's all good."

Phoebe looked at her. "So what's the problem?"

"All he offered is a business partnership. I thought he'd say something else." Had hoped for words that would make her giddy. "He never once said anything about his feelings."

"Did you say anything about yours?"

"No."

"Well, then. He could be feeling exactly what you are and be keeping it a secret."

"Del's not like that." Maya would have told him the truth, only she couldn't. Not until he found out about Elaine. Saturday, she told herself. If Elaine didn't call her family meeting, Maya was going to be the one breaking the news. Just forty-eight more hours.

Only now she didn't know if she wanted to say anything. To what end?

"If he had any romantic thoughts, he would have said something," she insisted.

"You have no way of knowing that. You're talking business. You know how guys get. They compartmentalize. Work is work and everything else is different." Phoebe smiled at her. "I think you need to plan a romantic evening with Del and confess all. Tell him you're interested in the business thing, but you want it to be more. He's going to be so happy."

Maya wished she shared her friend's optimism. "I'm less sure about that. He'll probably be horrified and then run for the hills. I'll lose both him *and* the opportunity."

"Do you want one without the other?"

A question for which Maya didn't have an answer. She knew she wanted to travel with Del and film his videos. She also wanted to do the project for the hotels. But to only be business partners, friends—being around Del, but not a romantic part of his life. Did she want that?

"I don't want to be left behind," she admitted. "And I don't want him falling in love with anyone else." Talk about horrible. "I can't believe I went so long thinking I would never trust a man to be there for me. I've finally found the man I trust with my heart and he's not interested."

"Stop saying that," Phoebe told her. "You don't know how he feels because you won't talk about it."

Maya heard footsteps in the hallway, then Zane walked into the family room. He approached the back of the sofa, but stayed carefully out of reach.

"Still talking girl stuff?" he asked, stroking the back of Phoebe's neck.

Despite her confusion, Maya grinned. "Notice how he's poised to bolt in case he doesn't like the answer."

"I'm not big on the emotional side of things," he admitted. "It's a guy thing."

Phoebe leaned into his hand. "That's okay. You have other, sterling qualities. We're talking about Del and Maya. Do you want to voice an opinion?"

Maya was surprised when Zane looked at her and

said, "I support whatever you want. If he breaks your heart, I break him."

While not elegantly worded, she had to admit she appreciated the sentiment. "Thank you."

"You're welcome."

Phoebe patted the sofa next to her. "Come join us. We need the male point of view."

Maya expected her stepbrother to take off at a run, but he surprised her by circling the sofa and settling next to his wife. After putting his arm around Phoebe, he looked at Maya.

"Okay. Tell me what's going on."

She recapped the situation with Del, including the job offer, the videos they wanted to do and her feelings for Del.

"I think he's probably desperately in love with her," Phoebe added when Maya had finished. "But he's not going to mingle work and personal stuff."

"Possible," Zane said.

"But?" Maya knew there had to be more.

"Be honest. Not just with Del but with yourself. What do you want? Would you be happy to be just work partners? What happens if you don't say anything and it turns out he's not interested? You end up stuck in Nairobi, watching him fall in love with someone else."

He laced his fingers with Phoebe's, but kept his attention on Maya. "On the other hand, you could do the first commercial and see how it goes. Maybe your feelings for him aren't that strong and you'll discover he annoys you. Or you'll learn it's everything you want and you'll tell him then."

She frowned. "You do realize you're arguing for telling him and for not telling him."

"Just trying to be fair." He released Phoebe and shifted forward on the sofa. "The deal with the videos. You want that?"

"The ones for the kids? I do. I think it's a great project."

"Then if you decide to go into business with Del, let me know. I'll front you the money to buy in as an equal financial partner. I know you bring the talent, but in business, whoever has the money has the power. I don't want you to have to worry about that with Del."

He was still talking, but Maya stopped listening. Tears filled her eyes. She stood and crossed to him. Zane rose and pulled her close, then kissed the top of her head.

"I thought it would make you happy," he murmured.

"It does."

She felt Phoebe join them in a group hug and let the love wash over her. Whatever happened with Del, she had this, she thought. People who cared. She wasn't that kid trying to survive anymore. She was thriving.

She sniffed, then straightened. "Thank you," she whispered. "Both of you."

"Of course," Phoebe said, squeezing her hand.

"We're family. We're here for you, Maya. No matter what."

Maya nodded, then returned to her seat and sipped her wine. She asked about the ranch and conversation shifted away from her and her confusion about Del.

As she listened to Phoebe and Del talk and laughed at their stories, she wondered why it had taken her so long to figure out the truth. Why had she needed to come home to Fool's Gold only to realize it was time for her to leave?

DEL FELT THE excitement humming through him. He was back at his cabin, but he couldn't settle. He paced, he made notes on his laptop, then paced some more. There were a thousand things to organize, he thought eagerly. Details to be worked out.

He and Maya had to come to terms with Robert and Ernesto. Once that was done, they could start making other plans. His gut told him their first shoots should be in China. The country was huge and growing. Everything it did had an impact. To document that, to share it with kids back here, could help them better understand their future.

A lofty goal, he thought, chuckling to himself. But why not? With Maya as his business partner, anything was possible.

He returned to the kitchen table and his laptop, prepared to attack more lists, when his cell rang. He picked it up and saw his father's name on the call display.

For a second, Del hesitated. He wasn't in the mood

for one of Ceallach's rants about Nick and how he was wasting his talent. Because there was no way the old man was calling to talk about Del. Still, his father rarely phoned. He pushed the talk button.

"Hey, Dad."

"It's your mother."

Del stood. "What do you mean?"

Ceallach's voice shook as he spoke. "She's gone."

"You're not making any sense. How can she be gone?"

"She's not at the house. I came in from work and she wasn't here. I finished my commission today. We always celebrate. She had a big dinner planned. I couldn't find a note or anything, so I drove into town."

Del didn't like the sound of any of this. "What happened?"

"I've found her car, but no one has seen her. I've been calling her cell and she doesn't answer. I've spent the last three hours going from store to store, and she's nowhere. Not shopping, not having dinner." His father's normally strong voice broke. "I don't know what to do."

Del glanced at the clock on the stove. It was nearly eight in the evening. Not unusually late for anyone to be out, but they weren't talking about anyone.

"Does she have friends in town?" he asked.

"How would I know? She's never out in the evening. Never. She sees her friends during the day. She's home at night. With me." Ceallach cleared his throat.

"She's gone. Left. I should have known this would happen eventually."

Del was already walking toward his truck. He wasn't as upset as his father, but he would admit to some worry. His mother was a creature of habit. Taking care of her husband was the most important part of her day. She would never deliberately worry Ceallach. So where was she?

"Mom didn't leave you, Dad. She wouldn't. She loves you. Something else is going on. Have you talked to the police?"

"And say what? It's been three hours. They're not going to care. They'll assume she's fine. They'll tell me they can't do anything for twenty-four hours. Not unless I suspect foul play. She's left me. I know it. I'll never work again."

"Dammit, Dad, this isn't about you. For once, get your head out of your ass and think about someone else. Who are Mom's friends? Have you talked to them? Maybe she had a girls' night out thing and you forgot."

"She wouldn't do that."

"It makes more sense than her leaving you." Del started his truck and waited until the phone switched over to Bluetooth. "Dad, Mom loves you. She's not going to leave."

"There are things you don't know. Truths in a marriage." Ceallach groaned. "I should have seen this coming."

"You're not helping, Dad," Del said loudly. "Where are you?"

"By Jo's Bar."

"Give me five minutes. I'll meet you there."

"I'm calling your brothers."

"Good idea."

He hung up, then phoned Maya. It took her several rings to answer.

"Del? What's up?"

"Where are you?"

"With Phoebe. Why?"

He explained what had happened. "I know my dad is overreacting," he told her. "There's a logical explanation for whatever is going on. She's somewhere. I thought you might have some ideas."

What he'd really been hoping was that Maya was *with* his mother. Now that he knew she wasn't, he was willing to admit to some small measure of worry.

"Has he tried calling her?" Maya asked, her voice tight. "Your dad. Did he call her?"

"He says she's not answering. Maya, what aren't you telling me?"

"I might have an idea of where she is. Meet me by Morgan's Books in twenty minutes."

She hung up before he could ask her anything else, and he knew that five minutes after she left the ranch, she would enter a dead space in cell coverage. There was nothing to do but wait for her to show up.

He drove into town. During the short trip, he tried his mother's cell several times. It rang and rang before sending his call to voice mail. Once in town, he easily found his father. For once Ceallach looked old.

Tired. There was a stoop to his shoulders and something that looked a lot like fear in his eyes.

Three years ago Ceallach had survived a mild heart attack. Del had spent a couple of days at the hospital, then helping his mother get his father settled. Back then, Ceallach had been full of bluster, despite the *episode*, barking orders and insisting he would make a full recovery. He hadn't looked scared. In fact, until tonight, Del had never seen his father afraid of anything.

"We have to find her," the older man said as Del approached. "I don't care what she's done, I just need her back. She keeps my life going. Without her…"

Del told himself there was love buried in there somewhere, but it sure wasn't easy to find. He wanted to point out that if his father took a little extra time to appreciate his wife, they might not be having this conversation right now.

"Maya's on her way back from her brother's ranch," he said instead. "She has some ideas on where to find Mom."

Ceallach stared at him. "Who?"

"Maya? I dated her ten years ago. She's the reason I left Fool's Gold. She and Mom have stayed friends all this time."

"Have I met her?"

Del swore. "Dad, if you're right and Mom's left you, you have no one else to blame."

"Tell me something I don't know," his father growled, and turned away from him.

"Then why don't you do something? Act like a

normal person once in a while. Bring her flowers. Tell her you love her."

Ceallach swung back to face him. "You think I don't love her? She is everything to me. She's the reason I breathe. Without her I could never create a single piece. She knows that. She knows that better than anyone. She protects me, takes care of me. She allows my work to happen."

Del glared at his father. "Then why would she leave you?"

Aidan's SUV pulled up beside them. Ceallach hurried toward the vehicle. Nick jumped out of the passenger side.

"Where's Mom?"

Del knew the moment was gone and he would never hear his father's answer. There was a reason the old man had jumped right to Elaine leaving.

Aidan joined his brother. "What do you mean she's missing? Mom doesn't just walk out on her family. Did you two have a fight? What did you do to her?"

Ceallach glared at the three of them for a second, then dropped his gaze and inhaled slowly. "I don't know what happened. Nothing out of the ordinary. I've been busy. Working. She's always home and now she's not."

As much as Del wanted to join Aidan in blaming their father, he knew that line of questioning wouldn't help anyone.

"Maya's on her way in from the ranch," he said. "We're meeting her at Morgan's Books. Let's get there and wait for her. She knows Mom. I think she has an idea of where she went."

"If she doesn't, we're calling the police," Aidan said grimly. "And the search-and-rescue team. We're going to find her tonight."

Cheap talk, Del thought, understanding his brother's frustration. But willing something to happen didn't matter a damn.

They walked the short distance to the bookstore. About three minutes after they arrived, Maya pulled up. She got out of her car and approached them.

"You still haven't found her?" she asked Del.

"No, and we've been calling her cell. She's not answering."

Maya looked more resigned than upset. Del put his hand on her shoulder.

"What do you know?" he asked.

"I have a good idea where she is. Come on."

Before he could ask what she was talking about, she started walking. She circled the building to the side, then opened a door leading to a staircase.

Del glanced at the mailboxes on the wall, the open entryway. There were apartments above the retail businesses on the street. Small places that were often summer rentals. Why would his mother be here? Unease tugged at him as he followed Maya up the stairs.

When they reached the second floor, Maya led the way to a door at the end of the hall. She knocked once, then used a key to let herself in.

Del followed, along with his brothers and father. He didn't know what they were thinking, but he could only stand in the middle of a small studio apartment and wonder what the hell was going on.

There were two large windows overlooking the park, a small kitchenette, a TV and a door leading to what he would guess was the bathroom. His mother lay asleep on a daybed, Sophie stretched out next to her. There were fresh flowers in a vase, a couple of his father's smaller pieces of glass on the table by the bed and jazz softly playing from an ancient clock radio.

Maya knelt by his mother and gently shook her shoulder. "Elaine, honey, you have to wake up."

His mother stirred, then opened her eyes. "Did I over—" She looked past Maya and saw the four of them, staring at her. Her mouth formed an O.

"Mom!" Nick hurried to her side. "What's going on? We were so worried. Dad said you were missing and you weren't answering your cell."

"I'm sorry," Maya murmured. "They were frantic. I didn't know what to do. I tried to call from the car, but you didn't pick up."

Elaine swung her legs to the floor and blinked several times. "My cell phone should be in my bag. Unless it fell out in the car. I'm sorry. I didn't mean to sleep so long. You were looking for me?"

Ceallach took a single step toward her. "I thought you'd gone."

"Where would I go?"

Maya rose and moved toward the window. Del watched her, wondering what she knew that the rest of them didn't. Maya didn't look relieved, nor had she been concerned before. Worry began to bend toward anger.

"Mom, is this your apartment?" he asked, his voice too loud for the small space. "And how did Maya know about it?"

Maya paled, but didn't speak. His mother twisted her hands together.

"This isn't how I wanted to tell you all. I was going to explain everything in the morning. When you boys came over for breakfast."

"This apartment is why you invited us over?" Nick asked. "Mom, what's going on?"

She drew in a breath and gave them a smile. "Everything is fine. You're not to worry." She turned to her husband. "A few months ago I was diagnosed with breast cancer. I had a lumpectomy and then radiation. My doctor told me that if I had to get breast cancer, this is the one to have."

Del saw his brothers' expressions of shock and had a feeling he looked just as stunned. Thoughts crowded his brain, stupid factoids and snippets from news stories. Cancer? His mother?

"After I healed, I started on radiation. I've been getting treatments every day for a few weeks. I'm fine, but it makes me tired. I didn't want to worry anyone." She smiled at Ceallach. "You had your big commission and this would have been a distraction."

She looked at her sons. "You're all so busy with your lives. So I kept it to myself and I got this place so I could rest in the afternoon without having to explain what was wrong. And if I'd remembered to set the alarm, I would have been awake on time and no one would have known until I told you in the morning. I'm sorry I worried you."

Del got that his mother apologizing was wrong on every possible level, but he couldn't seem to speak. He was still dealing with the news. Cancer? His mother had cancer.

Involuntarily, he looked at Maya. She was watching his mom but not speaking. Then all the pieces clicked into place.

Maya was his mother's friend. Maya had known about the apartment. Maya had known a lot of things.

"You knew," he said, his voice low. "You knew about this and didn't tell me."

Betrayal slammed into him with the force of a tornado. She'd worked with him, laughed with him, made love with him, all the while knowing his mother was sick, possibly dying, and she hadn't said a word. She'd lied. Every single day, for weeks. He'd been right not to trust. He could never trust her.

"Del," she began, but he shook his head and pointed to the door.

"This is a family matter. You need to get the hell out."

CHAPTER NINETEEN

"YOU HAVE CANCER and you didn't tell me?"

Del wasn't sure if his father meant the words as a question or a statement, but as it was the fifth time he was saying them, he wasn't sure it mattered anymore. Everyone had left the mystery apartment and returned to the family home. As expected, his mother's cell phone had been on the front seat of her car. He couldn't begin to comprehend how different everything would have been if the stupid thing hadn't fallen out of her purse.

Now his mother sat in a chair in the living room, Sophie stretched out next to her. The beagle watched them all with a combination of worry and defiance, as if prepared to take on all comers. Sophie might love the whole family, but Elaine was her person. Ceallach paced, and Del and his brothers claimed the sofa and one of the chairs.

It was dark outside. Lamps illuminated the room, but not the shadows beyond.

"I didn't want you to worry," Elaine said stubbornly.

"That's no excuse."

"Mom, we had the right to know," Aidan told her.

"Did you? It was my illness, not yours. There's nothing you could have done."

"We could have been there for you."

Which Maya had been, Del thought bitterly. No doubt she'd been at her friend's side the whole time. He didn't get it. How could she have kept that a secret from him? He'd trusted her. Hell, he'd wanted a future with her. They'd been planning to work together. He'd thought they'd shared a dream.

He should have known, he told himself. She'd lied to him once—of course she would do it again.

"I'm not going to accept blame in any of this," his mother said firmly. "It was my decision to make. This family runs on secrets and this is simply one more of them. I had cancer, I've had treatment and I'm fine. Tired, but fine."

Del remembered how she'd looked when he'd first come back to town. She'd been pale and drawn, he remembered. He'd asked her about it and she'd claimed it was nothing more than "the change." But it hadn't been menopause at all—it had been cancer.

"Mom," Nick said, "I don't get why you wouldn't tell us. We love you. We would have been there for you."

"You couldn't have handled it. Not any of you." She turned to Del. "You barely come home every other year. What are you running from?" She spun to Aidan. "There's a reason you can't date a girl longer than three days. What is it?" Nick came next. "You're hiding what matters most to you because you want to spite your father. That's mature."

Her gaze swung to Ceallach. "You're worst of all. You care about your art. After all these years, I know the rules. Don't distract the master. Maybe I flatter myself, but I assumed you finding out I had cancer might serve as a distraction. So I didn't say anything. Now you know. Does it honest to God make a difference?"

The room fell silent. Del figured they were all dealing with the uncomfortable truths she'd exposed.

Ceallach spoke first. "I thought you'd left me."

His mother sighed. "Now why would I do that? I love you. I always have."

"I'm not an easy man." His voice was gruff. "I thought maybe you'd found one who was."

Elaine's eyebrows rose, as did her voice. "You thought I was having an affair?"

Ceallach sighed. "Yes. To pay me back for mine."

Del swung his head to stare at his father. Nick and Aidan did the same. Their mother sprang to her feet.

"Don't you dare tell them."

"It's time, my love. They have to know." Ceallach looked at each of them. "Nearly thirty years ago, I had a mistress."

Del hadn't thought he could feel the same level of shock again, but here it was—hitting him like a two-by-four. He glanced at his mother, who had returned to her chair. She watched her husband with a combination of frustration and affection.

"The relationship didn't last," Ceallach was saying. "I came to my senses and returned to my wonderful wife. But a few months later, we heard from the woman. There'd been a child. Ronan and Mathias aren't twins. Ronan is the result of my affair."

Nick swore. Aidan started to stand, then sank back on the couch. Del managed to speak.

"Ronan isn't yours?" he asked his mother.

"Of course he's mine, in every way but one." She pressed her lips together. "I can't believe you told them like that. We'd agreed no one ever needed to know." She squared her shoulders. "When that woman told us she was pregnant, she said she wanted to give up the baby. We couldn't have that. I was already pregnant with Mathias, so it made sense to take in Ronan, too. He was born only a few weeks after Mathias. You three were so young. We told you that he had to stay in the hospital awhile, and that was that."

Del had no memory of any of that. He'd been all of three or four, so the lack of detail made sense, but shit.

Nick and Aidan looked as shocked as he felt. How could they just now be learning all this?

"You never thought to tell us?" Del asked, even as he knew the answer.

His mother's expression was stern. "Ronan is your brother in every way that matters. We didn't want you treating him differently."

"What about his birth mother?" Aidan asked. "Is she still alive?"

"Sadly, no," Ceallach murmured.

Del involuntarily winced even as his mother turned on her husband.

"Sadly? What does that mean? You miss her?"

"Elaine, you know that's not true. What Candy and I had all those years ago was nothing."

"Candy?" Nick murmured. "Her name was Candy?"

Del shook his head. The other woman's name was the least of what was going on. In the past hour he'd learned that his mother had been dealing with breast cancer, the woman he trusted and was hoping to work with around the world had once again lied to him, his father had had an affair that had resulted in a child and that child had been passed off as their mother's son.

"Do they know?" he asked. "Ronan and Mathias. Did you tell them?"

"Of course not," Elaine said.

"Yes," Ceallach answered at the same time.

Elaine glared at him. "You told them?"

"After my heart attack. I thought I was dying. They were with me at the hospital and I told them."

"Without letting me know? Three years of—" Her lips formed a straight line. "That's why they left town, isn't it? Because you told them."

Del wanted to say that of course his younger brothers had left because of the lie, but didn't think that would be helpful. Aidan glanced at him and nodded, as if he, too, was thinking the same thing. That kind of a lie would be unforgivable. No wonder they'd taken off. There was nothing left for them here. Nothing they could count on.

He wished he'd known. He would have gone to see them. Not that he could have helped, but he could have let them know... What? That they were still family? Ronan and Mathias had returned for Ceallach's sixtieth birthday and not hinted that anything was different. Everyone in this family was blind, he thought.

"Is there anything else?" he asked.

His mother turned to her other two sons. "Not that I'm aware of. Unless one of you has something you want to share."

Nick and Aidan both shook their heads.

"Good," Del said as he came to his feet. "Mom, I'm sorry about what you've gone through. I wish I'd known. I could have helped."

"I know you would have, but it was my disease to fight. There wasn't much for you to do."

He could have done what Maya had done, he thought bitterly. He could have listened, could have driven her to her appointments, helped her when she was tired. Suddenly her emotional meltdown about the party made sense. She'd been dealing with more than was fair.

He crossed to her and pulled her to her feet, then held her close.

"If you need anything, you have to call me."

"I will," she promised.

"Why don't I believe you?"

She gave him a smile, then stepped back. "I'll walk you to the door."

He followed her to the front of the house. Sophie stuck close as if sensing the person she loved most of all needed protecting.

"You're angry," his mother said quietly.

"Not at you."

"It should be me. I'm the one who didn't want you to know." She touched his arm. "Maya didn't like keeping my secret, but she did it because I asked her to. She was a good friend, Del. Don't punish her for that."

"She knew and she didn't tell me."

"I know. That's on me."

"She was the one to keep the secret." Maya had been with him every damn day for the whole summer. There were a hundred times when she could have come clean, and she'd never hinted. Not once.

"She cares about you," his mother told him.

"Not enough for it to matter."

MAYA HEARD FROM Elaine the next morning, but the news wasn't encouraging.

"He's upset," her friend said. "Give him time. I told him it wasn't your fault. I'll talk to him again later."

Maya had a feeling that talking to Del wasn't going to help. From his perspective, she'd lied to him. She'd kept a significant secret about someone he loved very much. She'd known the truth for weeks.

Now, alone in her office, she wondered how long it was going to take to be able to breathe without missing him. Without the sense of loss that accompanied her like a shadow. Knowing that she'd wanted to tell him what was happening with his mother wouldn't count, she thought sadly. As for her loving him—there was no way he was going to care about that now.

She wondered if he would get in touch with Ernesto and Robert or if he wanted her to. She honestly didn't know what she was going to say to them. While the job offer had been incredible, it wasn't as if she could take it on her own. They'd wanted to hire a team.

She checked her email, then reviewed her schedule for the day. She had a good life here, she told herself. Family. Friends. People who cared about her. It wasn't loving Del, but it was more than she'd had in Los Angeles. In time she would forget her plans with Del. She wouldn't think about all the places they were going to see together.

When it came to loving him, she had a bad feeling that was going to be with her always. She'd never fallen out of love with him, and they'd been apart ten years. The difference was, before she hadn't known. She'd been able to go on with her life without being aware her heart was forever in the possession of someone who didn't want it.

Close to noon, Eddie and Gladys walked into her office.

"Do you have a minute?" Eddie asked as they took the plastic chairs on the other side of her desk. "We have to talk."

"Don't say it like that," Gladys told her. "You'll scare the poor girl." Gladys gave her a bright smile. "We love our show."

That made Maya smile. "I suspect everyone already knows that. Your enthusiasm is both obvious and contagious."

"Except for the butt segments," Eddie said. "We're

still getting some flak for those. Marsha needs to get a sense of humor, if you ask me."

"Or maybe you shouldn't show so many naked butts."

"As if that's going to happen." Gladys winked. "It's our highest rated segment. But that's not why we're here."

"I'm almost afraid to ask the reason," Maya admitted. Silently, though, she was happy for the interruption. It was impossible to feel sorry for herself while in the company of these two.

"We heard what happened with Del and his family," Eddie said, her voice low. "Breast cancer. Poor thing."

While part of her brain assumed Eddie was referring to Elaine, the rest of her was trying to figure out how they knew.

"Word is spreading quickly," Gladys said. "Now that it's out. Ceallach ran into Morgan this morning, and while I love Morgan, he's something of a talker. It sounds like they got it all and got it early, so that's good."

Eddie pressed her hands against her chest. "I know I worry about my girls, but what can you do but get them checked? Elaine was very brave and you were a good friend."

"Not everyone sees it that way," Maya murmured.

"Some people are buttheads. He'll come around. She needed you and you were there. That's what counts."

Maya knew that Eddie was right. And when she

was curled up in pain from missing Del, she would tell herself the same thing. While she regretted the outcome and she'd thought her friend had been wrong to keep the information from her family, she didn't regret what she'd done. And if the situation were to happen again, she would do exactly the same thing. She would be a friend.

Gladys smiled at her. "We want to thank you for your help with our show. We've used everything you taught us in class and it's made a big difference."

"I'm glad you're happy with the results."

Eddie nodded. "We are. You know, we've always admired you, Maya. Even when you were a teenager, you understood that making something of your life was up to you. Your mother wasn't the nicest person, but you didn't let that stop you. You worked hard in school and applied yourself."

The unexpected compliment had Maya fighting tears. "Thank you for saying that," she said softly, not sure how they knew so much about her. But then this was Fool's Gold, and information had a way of getting out.

"We knew you were destined for greatness," Gladys added.

"Then you must be disappointed. Here I am, back where I started."

The two old ladies exchanged a glance, then returned their attention to her.

"Don't be silly," Eddie said. "You were in television. That was really something. We liked seeing your name in the credits every night when we watched your TV show online. And now you'll be taking off with Del to travel the world."

"I won't. He and I aren't exactly speaking right now."

"Pshaw." Gladys shook her head. "He'll come around. They always do. Then you'll go see the world. Take lots of pictures and send them to us. We'll love seeing what you're doing."

She raised her hand toward her friend. "High five for a job well done?"

"You bet." Eddie raised her hand and they slapped palms.

Maya looked between them. She felt as if an important truth was sitting right in front of her, only she couldn't quite grasp it.

"What are you talking about?" she asked.

"You," Eddie told her. "We're proud of you, child."

Gladys chuckled. "You still don't get it, do you? You've been asking around about your college scholarship. It was us. We're the ones who put you through school."

Maya was sure her mouth dropped open, but she couldn't seem to care. "You?" Her mind had trouble grasping the information. "The two of you?"

"Slick, huh?" Eddie asked. "We've been doing stuff like this for years. Our husbands left us well-off and we both have family money. We're not going to spend it on silly things like cars or clothes, so why not?"

Maya scrambled to her feet and circled the desk.

She hugged them both, as tightly as she could, before remembering they had elderly bones.

"Thank you," she whispered. "Thank you so much. You have no idea how much that scholarship meant to me."

Gladys touched her cheek. "We know, and we're proud of you, Maya. We want you to be happy. Pay it forward or whatever it is you young people say today."

"I will."

Eddie smiled at her. "Don't worry about Del. I've known him all his life. He'll figure out what's what. And if he doesn't, I'll smack him with my purse."

Maya hugged them again. They'd believed in her back when she hadn't been able to begin to believe in herself. Whatever happened, she would keep moving forward. If not for herself, then for the two old ladies who had seen promise in her when she wasn't sure there had been very much.

DEL HAD LOST count of the beers he'd had, but what with being able to walk back to the cabin, knew it didn't matter. Nick was sprawled next to him on the sofa, while Aidan had claimed his big recliner.

The evening together hadn't been planned, but somehow they'd all ended up here, at Aidan's place. They'd talked about football, the chances of an early snow and whether or not they should get in a camping trip together before it got too cold. But they hadn't addressed the real reason they were drinking beer together.

Del figured he was the oldest, so it was up to him. "The twins didn't tell either of you?"

Calling Ronan and Mathias "the twins" was no longer applicable, but they'd been that for as long as he could remember. Changing now seemed impossible. He wondered how they thought of themselves.

"Never said a word," Aidan told him. "I didn't know either of them were capable of keeping any kind of secret, let alone one this big."

"Damned straight," Nick muttered. "Secrets. Hell of a way to live." He looked up. "No. They didn't tell me. Didn't even hint when they were home for Dad's birthday."

"How'd they do that?" Aidan asked.

Del had the same question. Sure, they'd had three years to work through what they'd learned, but to not share it with their brothers. *Talk about a twisted family dynamic*, Del thought grimly.

"At least we know why they moved," Nick said. "They wanted to get away from Dad."

"Mom, too," Del added. "She kept the truth from them, too." Ronan would have been wrestling with his identity, while Mathias would have lost half of how he'd defined himself. They'd always been the twins. Two parts of a whole.

"Wonder what else they're keeping from us." Aidan sipped his beer. "Could be a million things."

"It's not like they're going to tell us," Nick said. "Too many secrets."

Del thought of his brother's artwork, hidden in the forest. Not that he was going to mention it. There was enough to deal with. He didn't want to be fighting with his brothers. Not today.

Aidan looked at him. "You're being an ass about Maya. In case you didn't know."

So much for not fighting, Del thought. "No one cares what you think."

"I have to agree with Aidan," Nick said. "Come on. She was helping Mom."

"She lied to all of us."

"She kept something from us."

"That our mother has cancer." Del glared at both of them. "That's unforgivable."

"Only if you decide to make it unforgivable," Nick told him. "It was Mom's decision to tell us or not. I don't agree with what she did, but that was all her. Maya was doing a good thing. She kept a promise."

Del stood up and walked into the kitchen. He finished his beer and grabbed another from the refrigerator.

"You can run, but you can't hide," Aidan called from the living room. "She's good for you, bro. She's smart and sexy and for reasons neither of us can figure out, she wants to be with you. You've got a good thing. Don't screw it up by being a jerk."

Del returned to the living room, but didn't take his seat. "I'm not the bad guy. I trusted her and she lied to me. I knew better. She'd already done it once. She lied about being scared and she lied when she broke up with me. Nothing's changed."

"If that's what you learned from what happened with Maya, then you don't deserve her. Go on. Make your movies by yourself. Because you shouldn't bother trying to make it work with another person. One way or another, they'll screw up and then what? You'll have to get rid of them. It must be a bitch being the only perfect person in the room."

"You wouldn't understand," Del said, putting down the beer and heading for the door.

"We do understand," Aidan told him. "You're looking for a guarantee. Life isn't that tidy. Shit happens and you deal. At the end of the day, the question is, can you trust the person you love to have your back? That's what always went wrong with Dad. We knew that the art came first. Always. I don't know how Mom reconciles that, but she chose to marry him and she's going to stay with him. It just is. But with Maya—she had Mom's back. Considering what she'd had to deal with, married to Dad, I'm glad someone was there for her."

"We could have been there for her," Del pointed out.

"She didn't want us. She wanted Maya. And Maya didn't let her down. That should count for a lot. If you're too stupid to see that means Maya would have your back, too, then walk out of here. I'm not going to stop you."

Del looked at the door, then back at his brothers. Nick raised a shoulder.

"He's got a point. I'm as surprised as you, but even a blind squirrel finds an acorn every now and then."

"You know I could take you," Aidan said conversationally.

"In your dreams."

Del grabbed his beer and returned to the sofa. "You two give me a pain in my ass."

"I know." Aidan grinned. "Gotta love family."

CHAPTER TWENTY

MAYA HAD HEARD all about the infamous Fool's Gold breakup parties, but she'd never been to one herself. Her only regret was that her first time attending one was because Del had broken her heart. She had a feeling she would have enjoyed the night a lot more if it hadn't been for her benefit.

Her small living room was crowded with women, and loud with the sound of a blender making drinks. All her friends were there. Phoebe, of course, Madeline, Shelby and several other women from town. Jo was handling the drinks. On the food front, everyone had shown up with some kind of sugary or salty snack. There were chips and nuts, brownies, cookies, chocolate and gallons of ice cream. Maya hadn't yet started eating, but her pants already felt tight. There was going to be some serious working out in her future. After she recovered from the hangover she planned to have in the morning.

Sophie, who was staying with her for a few days, was in beagle heaven, going from guest to guest. Maya wasn't sure which the happy dog was enjoying more—all the attention, or the crumbs that fell on the floor.

"You doing okay?" Phoebe asked, passing her a margarita.

"Sure."

"Okay, silly question." Her sister-in-law hugged her. "I'm just so mad at Del."

"Men are stupid," Destiny Gilmore called from across the room. "Difficult, emotional and annoying."

"Including Kipling?" Shelby asked.

Destiny sighed as she touched her growing pregnant belly. "No. Not Kipling. He's kind of sweet."

"You're not helping," Phoebe told her.

Destiny wrinkled her nose. "Sorry. Men are idiots."

Maya managed a smile. She appreciated the evening of being coddled. The past couple of days had been long and lonely. She'd had a lot of time to think about what had happened and where she was going from here. None of it had been easy.

She understood why Del felt betrayed. She wasn't sure she could even blame him for how he'd reacted. If she'd been in his position, she would have been as angry.

Madeline walked over and sat next to her on the sofa. "I'm sorry," she said. "How are you holding up? How is Elaine?"

Word of the other woman's cancer diagnosis and treatment had spread quickly through town.

"She stopped by the office this morning," Maya said, and put her arm around Sophie. The pretty girl snuggled close, then sniffed the carpet. "She feels awful about all of this. I keep telling her that she doesn't have anything to apologize for. She had enough to deal with."

Phoebe and Madeline exchanged a look.

"What?" Maya asked. "Don't you get on Elaine."

"We won't," Phoebe promised. "You're sweet to defend her. It's just if she hadn't asked you to keep the information private in the first place, you and Del would still be together."

"Maybe," Maya said. "But something would have happened to piss him off or make him feel he couldn't trust me. Del's looking for a reason not to get involved." Sadly, knowing that was great, but it didn't take away the emptiness in her heart.

Shelby joined them. "I talked to Elaine this morning. She said that she and Ceallach are going away for a few days. Just the two of them."

Her friend had stopped by to tell Maya the same thing and to ask if Sophie could stay for a couple of days. Maya was pleased for her. Elaine deserved a vacation. Elaine had also offered to talk to Del again, but Maya had refused. There was no need. Del would either figure out why she'd done what she'd done or he wouldn't. Telling him over and over again wasn't going to help either of them.

"It's so interesting about Ronan and Mathias," Madeline said. "That they're half brothers. I knew them all through school and I never would have guessed." She tilted her head. "Okay, maybe *interesting* is the wrong word."

Maya smiled at her. "We know what you mean. They always seemed like twins."

"I've been thinking about that," Destiny said. "Do we act the way we act because of how we are or because of what we're told?"

"Feeling a song coming on?" Shelby asked, her voice teasing.

"Maybe. You never know. Life inspires me."

"Would being half siblings change things?" Shelby asked. "Kipling and I are technically half brother and sister, but I can't imagine feeling closer to him."

Maya was an only child and didn't have a frame of reference. Being Zane's stepsister had always made her happy. Even though they hadn't always gotten along, he'd been like an anchor. Something she could depend on.

"Starr and I are half sisters," Destiny said slowly. "You and Kipling."

"Chase and Zane," Phoebe added. "They share a father."

Maya wondered what differences would have occurred in her life if she'd had a sibling. Someone with whom to share the journey. The blame from her mother would have been split between them, she thought. At least she could hope it would have been. Maybe hearing how someone else ruined her mother's life would have made her realize sooner that she wasn't actually to blame. That would have changed her relationship with Del.

If only, she thought sadly. If only she'd been able to tell him the truth all those years ago. If only she'd been able to say she was scared instead of dumping him by telling him he was too boring. So many regrets.

As for what had happened with his mother, she still didn't have an answer. If Del couldn't understand why she'd kept her friend's secret, then he was the wrong guy for her. But saying that didn't much help her fall out of love with him. If only it could.

Madeline raised her own margarita. "As a sign of love and friendship, Maya, I offer you Jonny Blaze."

Nearly everyone laughed and there were a few hoots.

"I didn't know he was yours to give," Jo said from the kitchen. "Does he know?"

"I suspect somewhere in his soul he senses we're destined to be together," Madeline said primly. "He's resisting, but that only makes our love stronger."

"You're a weird and twisted person," Destiny said cheerfully. "That makes me like you more." She turned to Maya. "Any interest in our newest, most famous resident?"

"Not really," Maya said. "No offense."

"None taken. I know he's amazing."

"He probably knows, as well," Shelby murmured.

Despite the pain inside, Maya joined in the laughter. She hurt everywhere. It was as if she'd been hit by a truck and then thrown off the side of a mountain. Her bones ached, her muscles were sore and her heart, well, it was nothing more than a wound. Odd how her mother had never fallen in love with anyone and yet Maya had turned out to be a one-man woman. Biology was funny that way.

She wanted to tell herself she would get over him, but she knew better. She would always love him.

As if sensing her discomfort, Sophie returned to her side and leaned against her. Maya scratched her ears.

She hoped that with time, she would hurt less. Maybe she would find someone else who made her laugh and love, but even then, there would be Del. She didn't know why she responded so uniquely to him, but she did.

She didn't even have the satisfaction of a breakup, she thought. Because they'd never truly been together. Not in a committed way. They'd worked together, become lovers, but had never talked about their personal relationship. Everything had happened under the umbrella of work. Even his offer for her to go with him had been work related. There hadn't been any intimate words. No confessions. No promises.

She was as guilty as he in that, she thought. She'd never told him how she felt. Not that knowing would change anything for him. He'd made his decision based on what he knew to be true.

Larissa, a pretty blonde in yoga pants and a T-shirt, leaned toward Maya. "Want me to have Jack beat him up?" she offered. "He would. Jack isn't the beat-up kind of guy, but he has a strong sense of fair play."

Patience nodded. "Justice would do it, too," she said. "He knows things."

"We're not going to get into a competition of whose husband or boyfriend could beat up Del the best," Maya said. "Not that I don't appreciate the offer."

"We want to help however we can," Phoebe told her. "Any suggestions?"

Make him love me back. Only that wasn't going to happen, and she had to figure out a way to move on. She wasn't going to be like her mom and blame everything on someone else. So her love life sucked. She could be happy in other ways. And she would find them.

"Be my friend," she told Phoebe.

"Easy enough. I love you and I'll be your friend forever."

"Then I'm going to be fine."

MAYA SAT IN Mayor Marsha's office. She'd already handed over her letter of resignation.

"I'm sorry to be making you find someone else so quickly," she said. "I didn't mean to be irresponsible. I'll stay until you find a suitable replacement, unless you'd like me to leave right away."

Mayor Marsha sat behind her desk, her pleasant expression completely unreadable.

"You're feeling guilty—I can see that. Well, let me be clear. There's no need for any of that nonsense. Maya, you've been a joy to work with. You got Eddie and Gladys to listen, which isn't anything I thought could happen. Now you're ready to go do something else. If you're happy, then the town is happy."

Maya didn't think *happy* was a word she would use to describe herself. She was more than a little hungover, and she had no idea where, exactly, she was going. But when she'd gotten up that morning, she'd known that she wasn't going to be staying in Fool's Gold.

"I appreciate the opportunity you've given me," she said instead. "I've really liked working here."

"I'm glad." The mayor smiled. "May I ask what you're going to do next?"

"I'm going to look for a film partner. I want to make documentaries—more educational than entertainment. Stories that are geared toward children."

"Sounds a little like what Del will be doing," the mayor said.

Maya wasn't surprised she knew about that. From what she could tell, the mayor knew everything happening in her town.

"I would go in a different direction," Maya told the other woman. "The day in the life kind of project is his, of course. But there are a lot of stories to be told. I have some contacts who work with the documentary arm of a major studio. I'll start by talking to them."

"You're very talented, Maya. Anyone would be lucky to have you on their team. What about Ernesto and Robert? Will you be doing the commercials for them?"

"I don't know. I've set up a meeting with them. They were unexpectedly called out of town and won't be back until the weekend."

By then, Maya hoped to have spoken to Del. They might not be friends anymore, but there was still a business deal on the table. Her preference was for them to do it together. If he wasn't interested in that, she would talk to the casino owners about her doing it on her own. As she'd just quit her job, she could sure use the money.

"Do you want me to help with the candidate search?" she asked. "I could ask around, get some names."

Mayor Marsha shook her head. "There's no need for that. The Director of Communications position won't be filled after you leave."

"I don't understand."

"I created the job for you, Maya. You needed us and we certainly needed you. You have the cable access schedule running smoothly. You've created a series of wonderful videos highlighting our town. That's what we needed."

Maya couldn't believe what she was hearing. Tears burned, although she blinked them away.

"You did this," she said quietly. "You made up the job so I could come home."

"I created a position so you could get some work done for me," the older woman corrected with a smile. "Maya, you'll always be one of us, and you'll always have a home here. Having said that, I have to admit that I think you've discovered that Fool's Gold is just a little too small for you right now. It's time to go explore the world. Just don't forget to come back and show us what you've found."

MAYA PULLED THE thumb drive from her computer. She had a stack of DVDs ready to deliver to Del, along with a master set on the drive. She'd finished going through all his footage and editing his videos, just as she'd said she would. What he did with them was up to him, but she thought he had some good material there.

She also went through the B-roll they'd done around town, pulling together a two-minute video of different shots. The last clip was of them kissing.

She'd spent most of the night trying to come up with exactly what to say on the voice-over. She'd paced, written, scratched out, tried to sleep and then had started all over again.

Now she was exhausted, but finished. If there were right words, she couldn't find them. All she was left with was what she felt in her heart. If it wasn't enough, then what she and Del had was never going to work, anyway.

She found the file on her computer and started it. The opening shot was of the town, with a slow pan to the park. Del was doing push-ups on the grass. Even with the emptiness inside of her, she smiled as she watched him.

Her voice came through her speakers.

"I'm sorry about everything that happened, Del. Most especially with your mom. I know you don't agree with what I did. You can't understand how I kept the truth from you. Cancer is a big deal. I get that. I know you're angry. I didn't mean to hurt you."

The scene changed to them on the sidewalk in front of The Man Cave. She was trying to get a light reading and he was crowding next to her. They were both laughing.

"I won't say I should have told you, because I believe that my promise to Elaine was something I couldn't break. I also get that from your perspective I betrayed you and I lied. Both of which are unforgivable."

The shot shifted to one of the mountains, then the field. The two of them came into view. They were standing close, talking. She'd muted the sound of their voices, so there were only the gestures, then intensity. Then the kiss.

"This is the wrong place, the wrong time, but I still wanted you to know. I love you. I've loved you for the past ten years—I just didn't realize it. Whatever happens, you'll always have a place in my heart. I didn't want you to leave without knowing that. Goodbye Del."

Her voice faded and the kiss ended, then the screen went dark.

Maya sat in her chair for a few more minutes, then knew there was nothing left to do. She'd said it all— laid herself bare. Now it was up to him.

She figured her odds were well less than 50 percent. Del didn't believe in second chances and she'd already had hers. He wasn't going to give her a third.

Even so, she could walk away knowing she'd been brave. She'd told the truth.

DEL STAYED UP through the night. There were hours of videos. He didn't know when Maya had found the time to edit it all, but she had. She'd taken raw footage, badly filmed sequences and turned them into something impressive. Somehow she'd discovered the very essence of each scene and highlighted it.

By the time the sun had come up, he knew that he'd been the asshole his brothers had claimed and then some. Maya had done nothing but give since she'd moved back to town. She'd worked hard at her job, she'd helped him, helped his mom and had even taught that class. She'd been a friend, a lover—she'd supported him and his family.

And she'd lied to him. She'd withheld significant information about his mother and her illness. He knew better than to trust her again. How could he—

He put in the last DVD. His computer screen filled with a shot of the town. The camera panned to him doing push-ups in the park. There was plenty of background noise, then Maya's voice as she teased him.

"I'm not impressed by your push-ups," she said, her voice picked up by the microphone he wore.

"Sure you are."

She laughed.

There was a pause in the sound, then he heard her speaking—but not from that day. Instead, it was a voice-over.

He listened to the first couple of sentences, and

then paused the video and leaned back in his chair. He remembered that day in the park and dozens of other days with her. He knew how she liked her coffee and how careful she was when she framed her shots. She would always take time to speak to a kid or pet a dog or make a couple of old ladies feel special. She was loyal and unshakable. She wouldn't betray her friend...not even to her lover.

She'd lied to him, and he would bet anything that if the circumstances happened a second time, she would do it again. Which meant that if he needed to trust her absolutely, he couldn't.

Or could he? Wouldn't she be as loyal to him? Did what she'd been through with Elaine mean she would risk anger and loss to do the right thing?

He was tired and confused, and the truth that would change everything seemed just out of reach. She'd told him, and his mother had told him, and he'd stubbornly refused to believe either of them. Maya hadn't wanted to keep the secret, but she had. She hadn't been acting out of spite but out of love for his mother. For her friend.

That was what it came down to. He didn't have to agree with what she'd done, nor did he have to like it. But if he accepted her reasons, then he had to admit that within that context, she'd done the right thing. Her intent hadn't been to lie—it had been to protect.

He looked at the screen again and pushed the play button. He smiled as he saw Maya trying to read the light meter while he jostled her. She laughed and looked at him. He pushed the pause button again.

She was so beautiful, he thought absently. Her smile, her eyes. He wanted her—what man wouldn't? But it was more than that. He respected her. He needed her. He wanted to work with her and—

The freight train of truth ran right through him then. It whistled and vibrated the house and left him shaken and feeling pretty damned stupid.

He didn't want to just work with Maya. He didn't want a business partner. He wanted to be with her always. Permanently. He wanted to marry her—because he loved her. That was why he was so pissed about his mom and everything else. He didn't want her to be someone he couldn't trust because she was everything to him.

How could he not have seen that before? How could he not have realized she was his world?

He stood and grabbed his truck keys, then ran outside. He hadn't showered or eaten. At least he was dressed and wearing shoes. He drove the short distance to Maya's quiet neighborhood.

It was still early. Kids had yet to leave for school, and most of the adults were getting ready for work. Maya was on her front porch, watering her yellowing plants. She looked up when he pulled into her driveway, but didn't move from the porch. He stepped out of the truck. His chest was tight with nerves and fear. What if he'd waited too long to figure out what mattered?

"Stop watering," he told her. "That's why your plants are dying. They don't need water every single day."

Her eyes widened. "What?"

He pointed to the can she held. "Let them get thirsty once in a while."

"Oh. You think?"

She put down the can and moved to the stairs. He walked closer.

"You look awful," she told him.

"I haven't slept. I watched the videos. You did a great job."

Something flared in her green eyes. An emotion he couldn't read. Hope, maybe? "The last one," she began.

"I didn't finish it."

She bit her lower lip. "That's not why you're here?"

"No. I'm here because I realized the truth." He walked a couple of steps closer. "I don't agree with what you did, Maya, but now I get why you did it. I understand it wasn't about me at all, but about you and my mom."

"It was, and I never wanted to keep the truth from you."

"I know. You're a good person. A loyal friend. You're a lot of things. Beautiful, smart, funny." Damn. He was doing this all wrong. The words all crowded up inside of him, and he didn't know which ones to say first.

"I want us to work together," he told her. "Do the commercials, then start on the other projects we talked about. We're a good team."

He frowned. That wasn't right at all. Why didn't he get to the point?

"But not as a business." He crossed the last few feet separating them, then climbed the two steps to join her on the porch. He took her hands in his. "I love you, Maya. Maybe I never stopped. I was so angry, and I know now it's because I had thought we'd be together always. We belong together. I hope I can make you see that. I want us to be partners in everything. We'll make a home here in Fool's Gold. A home base. Can we do that? Is there a chance, or have I hurt you too much?"

She stared at him. A single tear slipped down her cheek. He brushed it away.

"I love you," he repeated.

"You really didn't watch the end of the video?" she asked.

"No. What does that have to do with anything?"

She smiled, then sniffed, then raised herself on tiptoe and pressed her lips to his.

"I love you, Del. I've loved you for the past ten years. Maybe all my life."

The tightness in his chest eased as he pulled her close. "Yeah?"

She laughed. "Yes. I want all that, too. Us working together and having Fool's Gold as the place we always come back to."

"You're going to marry me?"

She looked up at him. "I'm going to marry you."

"I love it when a plan comes together," he said right before he kissed her.

Later, after they'd made love, they went back to his place. Together, curled up on his sofa, they watched the last video together. Del held her close as he listened to her tell him she loved him.

"You're pretty good on camera," he told her.

She snuggled against him. "Only with you. On my own, I'm a disaster."

"Me, too."

"Then it's good we're a team."

"You know it."

* * * * *

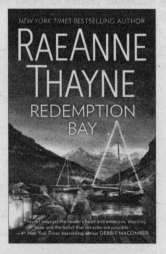

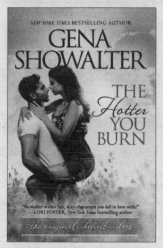

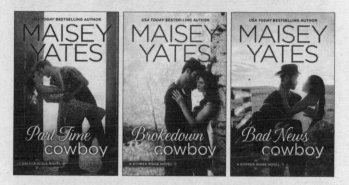

SUSAN MALLERY

78012	KISS ME	___ $8.99 U.S.	___ $9.99 CAN.
77997	HOLD ME	___ $8.99 U.S.	___ $9.99 CAN.
77940	DELICIOUS	___ $7.99 U.S.	___ $8.99 CAN.
77939	TEMPTING	___ $7.99 U.S.	___ $8.99 CAN.
77937	IRRESISTIBLE	___ $7.99 U.S.	___ $8.99 CAN.
77899	CHRISTMAS ON 4TH STREET	___ $7.99 U.S.	___ $8.99 CAN.
77893	UNTIL WE TOUCH	___ $8.99 U.S.	___ $9.99 CAN.
77881	BEFORE WE KISS	___ $8.99 U.S.	___ $9.99 CAN.
77865	WHEN WE MET	___ $8.99 U.S.	___ $9.99 CAN.
77841	DREAM WEDDING	___ $7.99 U.S.	___ $8.99 CAN.
77802	A CHRISTMAS BRIDE	___ $7.99 U.S.	___ $9.99 CAN.
77788	A FOOL'S GOLD CHRISTMAS	___ $7.99 U.S.	___ $8.99 CAN.
77778	THREE LITTLE WORDS	___ $7.99 U.S.	___ $8.99 CAN.
77768	TWO OF A KIND	___ $7.99 U.S.	___ $9.99 CAN.
77760	JUST ONE KISS	___ $7.99 U.S.	___ $9.99 CAN.
77694	ALL SUMMER LONG	___ $7.99 U.S.	___ $9.99 CAN.
77687	SUMMER NIGHTS	___ $7.99 U.S.	___ $9.99 CAN.
77601	ONLY HIS	___ $7.99 U.S.	___ $9.99 CAN.
77594	ONLY YOURS	___ $7.99 U.S.	___ $9.99 CAN.
77588	ONLY MINE	___ $7.99 U.S.	___ $9.99 CAN.
77531	SWEET SPOT	___ $7.99 U.S.	___ $9.99 CAN.
77529	FALLING FOR GRACIE	___ $7.99 U.S.	___ $9.99 CAN.
77527	ACCIDENTALLY YOURS	___ $7.99 U.S.	___ $9.99 CAN.
77490	ALMOST PERFECT	___ $7.99 U.S.	___ $9.99 CAN.
77452	CHASING PERFECT	___ $7.99 U.S.	___ $9.99 CAN.

(limited quantities available)

TOTAL AMOUNT	$ _____
POSTAGE & HANDLING	$ _____
($1.00 FOR 1 BOOK, 50¢ for each additional)	
APPLICABLE TAXES*	$ _____
TOTAL PAYABLE	$ _____

(check or money order—please do not send cash)

To order, complete this form and send it, along with a check or money order for the total above, Payable to HQN Books, to: **In the U.S.:** 3010 Walden Avenue, P.O. Box 9077, Buffalo, NY 14269-9077; **In Canada:** P.O. Box 636, Fort Erie, Ontario, L2A 5X3.

Name: _____
Address: _____ City: _____
State/Prov.: _____ Zip/Postal Code: _____
Account Number (if applicable): _____
075 CSAS

*New York residents remit applicable sales taxes.
*Canadian residents remit applicable GST and provincial taxes.

HQN™

www.HQNBooks.com

PHSM0815BL